Guy de Maupassant

Strong as Death

A novel. Translated by Teofilo E. Comba

Guy de Maupassant

Strong as Death
A novel. Translated by Teofilo E. Comba

ISBN/EAN: 9783337028237

Printed in Europe, USA, Canada, Australia, Japan

Cover: Foto ©Andreas Hilbeck / pixelio.de

More available books at **www.hansebooks.com**

Strong as Death

STRONG AS DEATH

A NOVEL

BY

GUY DE MAUPASSANT

TRANSLATED BY

TEOFILO E. COMBA

TORONTO:
THE MUSSON BOOK COMPANY
1899

𝔖trong as 𝔇eath

PART I

✸✸

CHAPTER I.

DAYLIGHT flooded the vast studio, through the open bay in the ceiling. It was a large square of blue and brilliant light, a luminous breach upon a boundless azure background, across which flocks of birds were swiftly flying.

But the cheerful light of heaven had hardly entered the severe apartment, with its lofty ceiling and hangings, when it declined, falling asleep upon the tapestries, dying in the portières and, with difficulty, penetrating the dark corners where alone the gilded portraits shone like flame. Peace and sleep seemed to be imprisoned there, the peace of the artist's home wherein the human soul had labored. Within those walls, where thought lives, toils, and is exhausted in violent efforts, everything seems to be weary and crushed as soon as it is appeased. All seem dead after these crises of life;

and furniture, hangings, great personages unfinished upon the canvas—everything rests, as
though the whole place had suffered the fatigue
of the master, had labored with him, sharing
daily his renewed struggle. A vague, dull odor
of paints, turpentine and tobacco was floating
about, absorbed and diffused by the carpets and
chairs; and the heavy silence was broken by no
sound save the short, sharp cry of the swallows
as they flew past the open window, and the confused, ceaseless tumult of Paris hardly audible
from over the roofs. Nothing was in motion
but the intermittent rising of a cloudlet of blue
smoke toward the ceiling, with each puff of the
cigarette, which slowly came from the lips of
Olivier Bertin as he lay stretched out upon a
divan.

His gaze was lost in the distant sky; he was
seeking the subject of a new picture. Of what
he should do next he knew nothing. He was
not, however, an absolute artist, certain of himself, but a vacillating dreamer, one whose waver-
ing inspiration was ever hesitating among all
the manifestations of art. He was rich, illustrious, had gained innumerable honors, and yet,
toward the end of his life, continued to be a man
who is not sure what ideal he has been pursuing.
He had obtained the " Prix de Rome," had been
the defender of accepted traditions, conjurer,
after so many others, of the great scenes of his-

tory; then, modernizing his tendencies, he had—still influenced by classic memories—painted living men. Intelligent, enthusiastic, an indefatigable worker, with ever-changing dreams, a nature of fastidious delicacy absorbed in the art which he knew so marvellously well, he had acquired a remarkable degree of executive power and great versatility, born in part of his vacillations and essays in all branches of his work. It is possible also that the sudden infatuation of the world for his productions, elegant, distingué and correct, had somewhat shaped his nature and prevented him from becoming what he naturally would have been. Since the triumph of his first achievement, the constant desire to please embarrassed him without his realizing it, unconsciously influenced his course, weakened his convictions. Moreover, this disposition to court favor manifested itself in various forms, and had contributed not a little to his glory.

The charm of his manners, all the habits of his life, the care he bestowed upon his person, his early reputation for strength and skill as a swordsman and equestrian, had constituted an escort of minor distinctions to his growing renown. After the production of *Cleopatra*, the first painting that made him illustrious, Paris had suddenly lost her heart to him, had adopted him, received him with open arms, and he had immediately become one of those brilliant artists of the world of fashion one meets at the Bois, whom drawing-rooms contend for and the Institute welcomes. He had entered it as a conqueror—approved of all the city.

Fortune had thus led him to the portals of old age, petting and caressing him.

And so, under the spell of the beautiful sunshine into which the day had bloomed, he was seeking a poetical subject. Somewhat drowsy, however, with his cigarette and his breakfast, he was musing, gazing into distance, sketching rapid forms against the blue sky, graceful women in a pathway of the Bois or on the pavement of a street, lovers by the water—all the gallant fancies in which his thought delighted. The changing images stood out against the sky, vague and undulating in the tinted hallucination of his vision, while it seemed as if the swallows which incessantly darted across the space were endeavoring to erase them as with the strokes of a pen.

He found nothing! All these figures, in such glimpses, resembled something he had already done; all the women that appeared to him were either the daughters or the sisters of those which his artistic fancy had brought forth; and still indistinct fear, which for the past year had possessed him, lest imagination had become barren, lest he had finished the round of his subjects and exhausted his inspiration, was taking shape

before this review of his work, before this powerlessness to dream something new or discover
something unfamiliar.

He rose softly, to look among his cartoons,
through his discarded designs, to see whether he
could not find something suggestive of an idea.

Still smoking, he began to turn over the out-
lines, sketches and drawings which he kept shut
up in a large antique cabinet; but he was soon
disgusted with such useless research, and,
bruised in spirit through painful lassitude, he
threw away his cigarette, began to whistle a
popular air, and by accident picked up a heavy
dumb-bell lying under a chair. With the other
hand he raised the drapery covering a mirror
which he used to prove the accuracy of a pose,
to verify perspective, to test truth, and placing
himself before it, commenced his exercise, looking at himself the while.

In the studios he had been famous for his
strength, and later, in the world, for his beauty.
Now, age was weighing on him—made him
heavy. Tall, broad shouldered, full-breasted, he
had grown corpulent, as an ancient wrestler,
though he continued to fence every day and to
ride with assiduity. His head, though formerly
different, was yet beautiful, and continued to
be remarkable. His white hair, thick and short,
heightened the brilliance of his dark eyes beneath
wide grey eyebrows. His heavy moustache—

the moustache of an old soldier—had remained quite brown, and lent his face a rare quality of energy and pride.

Standing before the mirror, with heels on a line and body erect, he was making the two cast-iron balls describe all the appointed motions, at the end of his muscular arm, whose quiet exhibition of strength he followed with complacency.

But suddenly, in the mirror, which reflected the entire studio, he observed the moving of a portière, then a woman's head appeared, nothing but a head, looking in. A voice behind him asked:

" At home ? "

" Oh, yes ! " he answered, turning around. Then, throwing his dumb-bell upon the carpet, he hastened toward the door with a sprightliness that appeared somewhat strained.

A lady entered in a light dress. After they had shaken hands:

" You were practising," said she.

" Yes," he answered, " I was playing peacock, and permitted you to surprise me."

She laughed and continued:

" Your concierge's lodge was empty, and knowing you to be always alone at this hour, I entered without being announced."

He was looking at her.

" Heavens ! how beautiful you are ! What *chic* ! "

" Yes, I have a new dress. Do you think it is pretty ? "

" Charming, and very harmonious. One may certainly say that people understand effects nowadays."

He was walking around her, patting the cloth, deftly re-arranging the drapery, like a man who is as well acquainted with such details as a *modiste*, having during the course of his whole life employed his artistic thought and athletic muscles in recording changing and dainty fashions by means of his slender brush, in revealing feminine grace confined and captive in velvet and silk armor or under the snow of laces.

He finally declared:

" It is exceedingly well done. It is very becoming."

She permitted him to admire her, content in her beauty and the knowledge that she pleased him.

No longer quite young, but still beautiful, not very tall, a little stout, but fresh with that brightness which at forty gives to the flesh a savor of maturity, she looked like one of those roses that go on blooming indefinitely, until finally, they fall in an hour.

Under her blonde hair she preserved the alert and youthful grace which characterizes those

Parisian women who do not grow old, who carry within them a surprising force of life, an inexhaustible power of resistance, and who remain the same for twenty years, indestructible and triumphant, above all things careful of their bodies and economical of their health.

He relieved her of her parasol and light wrap, with swift and sure movements, accustomed to such familiar attentions. Then, as she seated herself upon the divan, he asked with interest:

" Your husband is well ? "

" Very well; indeed, he must be addressing the Chamber at this moment."

" " Ah ! on what subject ? "

" Beets, undoubtedly, or colza oil, as usual."

Her husband, Count de Guilleroy, deputy for the Eure, had during his parliamentary career, made a specialty of all agricultural questions.

But discovering in a corner a sketch which was new to her, she crossed the studio, asking:

" What is that ? "

" A pastel I am beginning, the portrait of Princess de Ponteve."

" Remember," she said gravely, " that if you begin to draw portraits of women again I shall close your studio. I know too well what such work leads to."

" Oh ! " said he, " one does not make twice a portrait of Any."

" Indeed, I hope not."

She was examining the pastel like a person who is familiar with art questions. She drew back, advanced, shaded her eyes with her hand, found the spot from which the sketch was seen in the best light, and finally declared herself satisfied.

" It is very good. You are very successful in pastel."

He murmured, flattered:

" You think so ? "

" Yes, it is a delicate art which demands much skill. It is not intended for the masons of painting."

For the past twelve years she had encouraged his leaning toward conventional art, combated his return toward simple reality, and, influenced by popular standards, had gently urged him toward a somewhat affected and factitious ideal of grace.

" How does the Princess look ? " she asked.

He was obliged to give her a thousand details of all kinds, those minute details in which the jealous and subtle curiosity of women delights, passing from criticisms upon the toilet to speculations upon the mind.

Then suddenly:

" Does she flirt with you ? "

He laughed and swore she did not.

Placing her hands upon the painter's shoulders, she gazed into his eyes intently. The eagerness of the question made the round pupil quiver in the centre of the blue iris, dashed with imperceptible black dots like tiny ink splashes.

Again, she murmured:

" Really, she is not a coquette ? "

" Really."

She added:

" I am quite easy in any case. Henceforth you will love no one but me. It is all over, all over for others. It is too late, my poor friend."

His consciousness seemed to shiver in that faint painful chill which grazes the heart of men of mature age when reminded of advancing years, and he murmured:

" To-day, to-morrow, like yesterday, there has been and there will be none but you in my life, Any."

She then took his arm, and returning toward the divan, made him sit by her side.

" What were you thinking of ? "

" I am looking up a subject for a picture."

" What is it ? "

" I do not know, since I am seeking it."

" What have you been doing lately ? "

He must tell her about all the calls he had received, the dinners and soirées, conversations and gossip. After all, they were both interested in all these trifling and familiar details of a fashionable existence. Petty rivalries, known and suspected attachments, ready-made judgments, heard and repeated a thousand times, upon the same persons, events or opinions, were carrying away and drowning their minds in the troubled and agitated waters of that river called Parisian life. Knowing everybody, in all circles, he as an artist to whom all doors were open, she as the elegant wife of a conservative deputy, they were experienced in that sport of French chat, keen, time-worn, amiably insolent, vainly clever—a distinguished vernacular, which gives a special and much envied reputation to those whose tongues have acquired suppleness in this malicious babble.

"When are you coming to dine?" she asked suddenly.

"When you like; name your day."

"Friday. I shall have the Duchess of Mortemain, the Corbelles, and Musadieu, to celebrate the return of my little girl who arrives this evening. But do not speak of it, my friend; it is a secret."

"Oh! I accept with pleasure. I shall be delighted to see Annette again. I have not seen her these three years."

"'Tis true! Three years!"

Annette had at first been brought up in Paris with her parents, and then became the object of the last and passionate attachment of her grandmother, Mme. Paradin, who, almost blind, lived the whole year round on the estate of her son-in-law, at the castle of Roncières, on the Eure. Little by little, the old lady had kept the child near her more and more, and as the Guilleroys spent about half their lives in this domain to which they were continually called by interests of all sorts, agricultural and electoral, the little girl was finally brought to Paris on rare occasions only, for after all, she preferred the freedom and activity of the country to the cloistered life of the city.

For the past three years she had not come even once, as the Countess preferred to keep her quite remote in order not to awaken her sensibilities until the day appointed for her first appearance in society. Mme. de Guilleroy had bestowed upon her, down in the country, two preceptresses abundantly provided with diplomas, and multiplied her own visits to her mother and daughter. Furthermore, Annette's sojourn in the castle was rendered almost necessary by the presence there of the elderly lady.

Formerly, every summer, Olivier Bertin had spent six weeks or two months at Roncières; but for the past three years rheumatism had driven him to distant watering places, which had so revived and strengthened his love for Paris that he could not leave it after his return.

On principle, the young girl should not have returned until the autumn, but her father had suddenly conceived a marriage scheme for her,

and he summoned her that she might at once
meet the Marquis of Farandal, whom he had
chosen for her betrothed. This arrangement,
however, was kept quite secret, and Olivier
Bertin alone had been told of it, in confidence,
by Madame de Guilleroy.

Therefore, he asked:

" Your husband's idea is quite settled upon ? "

" Yes, I even think it is a very happy one."

Then they spoke of other things.

She returned to painting, and tried to induce
him to paint a Christ. He objected, believing
that the world had already enough of them; but
she obstinately held her ground, and was growing impatient.

" Oh! if I could draw, I would show you my
thought; it would be very novel, very bold. He
is being taken down from the cross, and the man
who has unfastened the hands drops the whole
upper part of the body. It falls and tumbles
down upon the crowd; they raise their arms to
receive it and bear it up. Do you understand ? "

Yes, he understood; he even thought the
conception an original one, but he felt himself
in the vein of the present age, and as his friend
reclined upon the divan, one well shod foot escaping, and giving to the eye the sensation of
flesh through the almost transparent stocking,
he exclaimed:

" There is what should be painted; there is

life; a woman's foot on the edge of a dress! One
may put everything in it, truth, desire, poetry.
Nothing is more graceful or attractive than a
woman's foot, and then what mystery, the hidden limb, lost and yet surmised beneath that
drapery ! "

Sitting on the floor, after the manner of a
Turk, he seized the shoe and took it off; and the
foot, released from its leather sheath, stirred
about like a restless little animal surprised to
find itself free.

Bertin kept repeating:

" Isn't that delicate, distingué and expressive ?
more so than the hand.   Show me your hand,
Any ! "

She wore long gloves, reaching the elbow.
To take one off, she seized it at the top and
slipped it down quickly, turning it, as one would
skin a snake.   The arm appeared, pale, plump,
round, so quickly laid bare that it carried an impression of complete and bold nudity. .

Then she gave him her hand drooping from
the wrist.   The rings glistened on her white
fingers; and the slender pink nails seemed like
amorous claws at the end of that pretty, little
woman's paw.

Olivier Bertin handled it gently, admiring the
while.   He toyed with the fingers like animate
playthings, saying:

" What a curious thing!   What a curious

thing! What a pretty little member, intelligent and dextrous, executing what one wills, books, lace, houses, pyramids, locomotives, pastry and caresses—which are, after all, its best task."

He was removing the rings, one by one; and as in its turn the marriage ring fell, he smilingly murmured:

" The law. Doff hats ! "

" Folly!" she exclaimed, somewhat wounded.

He had always been inclined to raillery, that tendency of the French to mix a touch of irony with the most serious sentiment, and he often unwittingly grieved her, unable to appreciate woman's subtle distinctions and to discern sacred boundaries, as he was wont to say. She was especially displeased whenever he referred with a shade of familiar levity to their intimacy, which had lasted so long that he claimed it was the most beautiful example of love in the nineteenth century. After a silence, she asked:

" Will you take Annette and me to the varnishing day? "

" Why, of course."

Then she questioned him upon the best canvases of the next salon, whose opening was to take place in a fortnight.

But suddenly, recollecting perhaps a forgotten errand:

" Come, give me my shoe; I am going."

He was dreamily playing with the light shoe, turning it over and over abstractedly in his hands.

He bent down, kissed the foot that seemed to float between the dress and the carpet, and, somewhat chilled by the air, was no longer stirring, and replaced the shoe. Madame de Guilleroy, rising, went to the table, strewn with papers, open letters—old and recent—beside a painter's inkstand in which the ink had dried. She looked about curiously, fingered the leaves, raised them to look underneath.

He drew near saying:

" You will disarrange my disorder."

Without answering, she asked:

" Who is the gentleman who wishes to purchase your *Baigneuses ?* "

" An American. I do not know."

" Did you agree about the *Chanteuse des Rues?* "

" Yes, ten thousand."

" You did well. It was fine, but not exceptional. Good-bye, dear."

She presented her cheek then, which he calmly brushed with a kiss, and she disappeared under the portière, after saying in an undertone:

" Friday; eight o'clock. I do not wish you to show me out. You know that. Good-bye."

When she had gone he first lighted a cigarette, then began to walk slowly up and down his studio. All the past of this friendship unrolled itself before him. He recalled its details lost in the distance, sought them out and linked them together, and was interested in this chase after reminiscences, though pursuing it alone.

It was at the moment when he had risen, like a star, upon the horizon of artistic Paris, when painters monopolized public favor and had peopled a quarter with magnificent mansions earned by a few pencil strokes.

Bertin, returning from Rome in 1864, was for a few years without success or renown; then suddenly, in 1868, he exhibited his *Cleopatra*, and in a few days was being lauded to the skies by the critics and the public.

In 1872, after the war, and after the death of Henri Regnault had prepared for all his colleagues a sort of pedestal of glory, Bertin produced a *Jocaste*, a bold subject, which classed him among the daring, though his wisely original execution made him, nevertheless, palatable to the Academicians. In 1873 a first medal placed him *hors concours* with his *Juive d'Alger*, which he exhibited on his return from a visit to Africa; and a portrait of Princess de Salia, in 1874, won for him in fashionable society the reputation of the best portraitist of his time. From that day he became the idolized portrayer

of Parisian ladies and their type, the most skill-
ful and ingenuous interpreter of their grace, their
figures and their souls.   In a few months, all
the prominent women in Paris were suing for artistic favor in the reproduction of their charms
by him.   He was fastidious, and commanded
high prices.

Now, since he had become the fashion, and
was going about like a man of the world, one
day, at the Duchess of Mortemain's he observed
a young woman, in deep mourning, who was
leaving as he was entering, and who in this brief
encounter under a doorway, dazzled him with a
beautiful vision of grace and elegance.

Asking her name, he was told that she was the
Countess of Guilleroy, the wife of a Norman
country squire, agriculturist and deputy; that
she was in mourning for her father-in-law, that
she was clever, very much admired and sought
after.

Still moved by the apparition which had
charmed his artist's eye, he exclaimed:

" Ah!   There is one whose portrait I would
willingly paint."

On the following day this remark was repeated to the young Countess, and that evening
he received a little blue-tinted, vaguely scented
note, written in a small, regular hand, slightly
slanted from left to right, which ran as follows:

" Sir:

" The Duchess of Mortemain, who is just leaving my house, assures me that you would be disposed to use my poor face in the making of one of your master-pieces. I would gladly entrust it to you were I certain that you did not speak in jest and that you see in me something worthy of being reproduced and idealized by you.

" Pray accept, sir, the expression of my sincere regards.

" ANNE DE GUILLEROY."

He replied, asking when he might call upon the Countess, and was very simply invited to breakfast on the following Monday.

It was on the first story of a large and luxurious modern house in the Boulevard Malesherbes. Traversing a vast salon in blue silk hangings framed in white and gold, the painter was ushered into a sort of boudoir done in tapestries of the last century, light colored and coquettish, those Watteau tapestries, with their delicate shades and graceful figures, which seem to have been designed and executed by workmen vaguely dreaming of love.

He had just seated himself when the Countess appeared. She walked so lightly that he had not heard her footstep in the adjoining apartment, and was somewhat surprised when he saw

her.   She extended her hand in a cordial manner.

" It is true, then," she said, " that you will con-
sent to paint my portrait ? "

" I shall be very happy to do so, madam."

Her black tightly-fitting dress made her look
quite slender and gave her a youthful appearance, a grave air, also belied by the smiling face,
brilliantly lighted up by her blonde hair.   The
Count entered, leading by the hand a little girl
six years of age.

Mme. de Guilleroy announced:

" My husband."

He was a man of under stature, without moustache, and with hollow cheeks, shaded under the
skin by his shaven beard.

He looked somewhat like a priest or an actor,
of polished manners, his hair long and tossed
back, and around the mouth two large circular
lines curving from the cheeks to the chin, which
seemed to have been formed by the practice of
public speaking.

He thanked the painter with an exuberance of
expression which betokened the orator.   For a
long time he had desired to have a portrait of
his wife, and certainly he would have selected
none other than Olivier Bertin had he not feared
a refusal, for he was aware that he was overwhelmed with applications.

It was agreed, therefore, with much polite-

ness on both sides, that he should accompany the
Countess to the studio no later than the morrow.
He questioned, however, whether it would not
be best to wait because of her deep mourning,
but the artist declared that he desired to translate his first impression and the striking con-
trast of that sprightly delicate head, luminous
under the golden hair, with the austere black
of her costume.

She came, therefore, the next day, accompanied by her husband, and on the following
days by her daughter, whom the artist placed before a table laden with picture books.

Olivier Bertin, as was his wont, showed himself reserved. Fashionable women made him
uncomfortable, for he knew them but imper-
fectly. He supposed them to be both profligate
and simple, hypocritical and dangerous, trifling
and embarrassing. He had had with women of
the *demi monde* some fleeting adventures, procured him by his reputation, his wit, his elegant
and athletic figure, and his dark spirited face.
And he preferred them, therefore; liked their
free manners and speech, as he was better accustomed to the unrestricted, gay and rollicking atmosphere of the studios and green rooms which
he frequented. He went into society for the
sake of glory, and from no promptings of his
heart; enjoyed it through vanity; received congratulations and orders, attitudinizing before

the great ladies who flattered him, but never paying court to them. As he might not in such presence permit himself an indulgence in audacious pleasantries and pungent raillery, he considered them oppressive—and had acquired a reputation for good taste. Whenever one of them had come to pose to him, notwithstanding her advances in the attempt to please him, he had felt conscious of that generic difference which separates artists from the world of fashion, however they may commingle. Behind the smiles and adulation, which with women are always a little artificial, he defined the impenetrable mental reserve of the being who judged itself of superior essence. In recognizing this his pride engendered a manner so cold as to be almost haughty, and well concealed the vanity of the *parvenu* whose genius has scaled social heights open only to the most exalted rank. People said of him with a little air of surprise: " He is extremely well-bred." This surprise, while it flattered, also wounded him, for it indicated certain boundaries.

The much-to-be-desired, ceremonious gravity of the painter somewhat disconcerted Madame de Guilleroy, who could find nothing to say to this frigid man, with a reputation for cleverness.

After having installed her little daughter, she would come and sit in an armchair near the sketch lately commenced, and endeavor to fol-

low the artist's recommendation in giving some
expression to her countenance.

In the midst of the fourth sitting he stopped
abruptly, and asked:

" What amuses you most in life ? "

She was embarrassed:

" I hardly know. Why do you ask ? "

" I need a happy thought in those eyes, and I
have not yet seen it."

" Well, try to make me talk; I am very fond of
chatting."

" Are you gay ? "

" Very gay."

" Let us chat, then, madam."

He had said " Let us chat, madam," in a very
grave tone; then, resuming his painting, he had
talked of different things, seeking a subject on
which their minds should meet. At first they
exchanged views upon the people whom they
knew; then they spoke of themselves, whch is
always the most agreeable and engaging topic
for a chat.

When they met on the following day they felt
more at ease, and Bertin, perceiving that he was
both pleasing and amusing, began to relate some
details of his artist life, and gave the rein to his
recollections, with that fanciful turn which was
peculiar to him.

Accustomed, as she was, to the formal air of
fashionable literary people, this unwonted ani-

mation surprised her in its frank utterances
sparkling with irony, and she replied, with keen
and fearless grace, in a responsive spirit.

Eight days only had thus passed when she had
charmed and won him by her good humor, her
frankness and simplicity.   He had quite forgotten his prejudices against women of fashion; and
would willingly have affirmed that they alone
are charming and spirited.   While painting,
standing before his canvas, advancing and re-
treating like a man who is fighting, he let his
familiar thoughts flow on, as if he had long
known this lovely woman, blonde and black,
made of sunshine and mourning, seated before
him, who laughed as she listened, and answered
him merrily with so much vivacity that she lost
her pose every moment.

Then he would draw away from her, close one
eye, lean over for a thoroughly comprehensive
glance at his model; now he would come quite
near to note the slightest shades upon her face,
the most fleeting expressions, to seize and reproduce what there is in a woman's face beyond its
visible exterior, that emanation of ideal beauty,
that reflection of we know not what, that elusive
and inexplicable grace peculiar to each which
causes a woman to be adored by one and not by
another.

One afternoon the little girl came and planted

herself before the canvas, with childish gravity, and asked:

" That's mamma, isn't it ? "

He caught her in his arms to kiss her, flattered by this simple homage to the likeness of his work.

Another day, as she appeared very quiet, she was suddenly heard to say, in a low, plaintive voice:

" Mamma, I am so tired."

And the painter was so touched by this first complaint that he ordered a shopful of playthings to be brought to the studio the next day.

The little Annette, astonished, contented and always thoughtful, put them in order with very great care, that she might take them up one after the other, according to the desire of the moment. Dating from this gift, she loved the artist as children love, with that caressing, animal affection, which makes them so pleasing and captivating.

Mme. de Guilleroy was beginning to enjoy the sittings. She was almost wholly unoccupied that winter, being in mourning; so that society failing her, the principal concern of her life lay within the walls of that studio.

Daughter of a very wealthy and hospitable Parisian merchant, who had died several years before, and of a woman confined to her bed six months out of the twelve by chronic ill health, she had acquired while quite young the arts of a perfect hostess, knowing how to receive, to smile, to talk, exercising a keen discernment in her estimates of people and a ready adaptability to each; intuitive and pliant, she at once found her element in the gay world. When the Count de Guilleroy was presented to her for betrothal she immediately comprehended the advantages which such a marriage offered, admitted them without constraint, like the wise girl she was, who quite understood that one cannot have everything, and that in every situation we must strike a balance.

Launched in the world, sought after because of her beauty and cleverness, she had permitted herself to be courted by many men, without disturbing the serenity of a heart that was as reasonable as her mind.

An alluring coquetry distinguished her manner, though guarded by a caution which never relaxed. Compliments pleased her, awakened desires flattered her, so long as she might seem to ignore them, and after an evening spent in this incense of homage, she slept peacefully, like a woman who has accomplished her mission upon earth. Without wearying her or growing monotonous—for she adored this ceaseless agitation of society—that existence which had now lasted seven years, left her, now and then, something to be desired. The men about her, politi-

cal advocates, financiers or idle club men amused
her, as did the drama; she did not take them too
seriously, although she valued their functions,
their places and their titles.

The painter pleased her, at first, in the revelation of a nature which was new to her. She enjoyed the studio, laughed joyously and felt a
sense of exhilaration and grâtitude to him for
the diversion the sittings afforded her. She
liked him also because he was handsome, strong
and famous; no woman, however she may protest, being indifferent to physical beauty and
glory. She was flattered to have been noticed
by an expert, disposed, in turn, favorably toward
him, and had discovered in him a charming intelligence, an alert and cultivated mind, delicacy,
imagination, and a gift of lending to his words
a color that seemed to illumine all he sought to
express.

A rapid friendship sprang up between them,
and more and more each day, their hand-clasp
as she entered seemed also to entwine some emanation of their hearts.

Then, without premeditation, with no definite
purpose, she experienced a growing desire to
charm him, an ambition to which she yielded.
She had foreshadowed nothing, outlined no plan;
she was simply coquetting, with added grace—
an attitude which a woman instinctively assumes
toward the man whom she prefers, and her air,

her glances, her smiles took on that seductive charm with which a woman may invest herself under an awakened thirst for love.

She said graceful things to him, which seemed to imply that she found him agreeable, and she led him on to talk at length, to show him, as she listened, how deeply he might engage her attention. He would lay aside his brush and seat himself beside her, and in that intellectual enthusiasm aroused by an intense desire to please, crises of poetry, wit or philosophy would follow each other according to his mood.

She was amused when he was gay; when he was profound she endeavored to follow, not always successfully, and though her thoughts would sometimes wander, she seemed to listen so intelligently and to enjoy so keenly this initiation that he was lifted up as he looked upon her listening, moved by his discovery of a delicate soul, gentle and receptive, in which thought fell like a seed.

The portrait was progressing, and promised well, for the painter had reached that emotional stage necessary to discover all the attributes of his model and to translate them with that ardent conviction which is the inspiration of all true artists.

Bending toward her, detecting every movement of her features, every tint of her flesh, every shade of the skin, every expression and translucent gleam of the eyes, every secret of the countenance, he had become absorbed in his subject, as a sponge imbibes water; and transferring upon his canvas that emanation of disquieting charm which was gathered by his glance, and flowed like a wave from his thought to his pencil, he was confounded by it, intoxicated, as if he had drank of woman's grace.

She felt that she had touched his heart, and was amused by this game, this victory growing more and more certain, and which stimulated herself.

A new emotion gave her existence a novel charm, awakened a mysterious joy within her. When she heard him discussed her heart beat faster, and she would have liked to say—a desire that never reached the lips—" He is in love with *me*." She was pleased when people praised his talent, and perhaps still more so when he was pronounced handsome. When she thought of him, alone, and with no inconsiderate presence to annoy, she actually imagined that she had acquired a friend in him—one who would always be content with a cordial hand-clasp.

Often, in the midst of a sitting, he would suddenly lay down his palette upon the stool, take the little Annette in his arms and kiss her tenderly upon the eyes or hair, looking at the mother as if to say, " 'Tis you, not the child that I thus caress."

Sometimes, too, Madame de Guilleroy would not bring her daughter, but came alone. On these days there was less work done.

One cold afternoon, toward the end of February, she was late. Olivier had returned early, as had become his custom whenever she was expected, for he always hoped she would come before the hour. While waiting, he paced up and down, smoking, and repeated the question which he was surprised to have asked himself for the hundredth time during the past week:—"Am I in love ?" He did not know, since he was without such experience. Some violent fancies he had had, of some duration also, but he had never mistaken them for love. To-day he was astonished at the feeling within him.

Did he love her? He certainly hardly desired her, the possibility of possession not having presented itself. Heretofore in his caprices, desire had at once possessed him, and he had stretched out his hands toward its object as if to gather fruit, but carelessly, without his soul being ever stirred through her presence or by her absence.

Desire for this woman had hardly touched him, and it seemed to be crouching, hidden behind another feeling, more powerful, vague as yet, and scarcely awakened. Olivier had believed that love began with reveries, with poetical exaltations, while his feeling, on the contrary, seemed to spring from an indefinable

source, far more physical than spiritual. He
was restless, his nerves tense and vibrant, as
when an illness is impending. But there was no
painful element in this fever of the blood which
also, by contagion, agitated his mind. He was
not blind to the fact that this disturbance was
caused by Mme. de Guilleroy, to the memories
she left behind and the expectation of her return.
He did not feel impelled toward her by an over-
mastering impulse, but he felt her ever present,
as though she had not left his side; she sur-
rendered to him something of herself when she
went away, something subtle and ineffable.
What was it? Was it love? He sounded the
depths of his heart in his effort to see, to understand. Though he thought her charming, she
was not the realization of that ideal woman which
his blind hope had created. Whoever invokes
love has forecast the gifts and graces of her who
will charm him, and while Madame de Guilleroy
was infinitely pleasing, she seemed not to be that
woman.

But why did she thus engross his thoughts,
above all others, so differently, so ceaselessly?

Had he simply fallen into the open snare of her
coquetry, which he had long ago detected and
understood and outflanked by his own evolu-
tions? Was he experiencing the influence of
that special fascination which a desire to please
imparts to women?

He walked about, sat down, started up again, lighted cigarettes only to toss them away; and at every instant his eyes sought the hands of the clock moving on toward the usual hour at slow and changeless pace.

Several times already he had been tempted to raise the convex glass over the two revolving golden arrows, and with a touch of his finger to place the longer one upon the figure it was reaching so lazily.

It seemed as if that would suffice to open the door and cause the expected one to appear, deceived and summoned by this trick. Then he smiled at this obstinate, unreasonable and childish desire.

Finally, he asked himself this question: " Could I become her lover ? " This idea seemed strange, hardly to be realized or yet pursued, by reason of the complications with which it might encumber his life.

Yet she pleased him greatly, this woman, and he concluded: " Decidedly, I am in a queer condition."

The clock struck, and the sound startled him, striking upon his nerves rather than his soul. He waited for her with that impatience which is increased by delay from second to second. She was always prompt; therefore, in less than ten minutes he would see her enter. When the ten minutes had elapsed he felt distressed as at the approach of sorrow, then irritated that she should cause him loss of time, and then, suddenly, he comprehended that if she did not come he would suffer. What should he do? Wait for her? No. He would go out, so that if perchance she came late she should find the studio empty.

He would go out, but when? How much grace should he give her? Would it not be wiser to remain and make her understand by a few cold, courteous words that he was not one who might be kept waiting? And if she did not come? Then he would have a telegram, a card, a servant or a messenger. If she did not come, what should he do? The day would be lost; he would no longer be able to work. And then? He would go and inquire about her, for he must see her.

Truly, he felt the need of seeing her, a profound, oppressing, tormenting need. What was it? Love? Yet he felt neither exaltation of mind, nor passion of the senses, nor delirium of the soul in the conviction that if she came not that day he would suffer much.

The street bell sounded in the stairway of the little mansion, and Olivier Bertin suddenly felt himself almost gasping for breath; then, with a gesture of delight, he flung away his cigarette.

She entered; she was alone.

He was at once seized with an impulse of audacity.

" Do you know what I was asking myself while waiting for you ? "

" No indeed."

" I was asking myself whether I was not in love with you."

" In love with me? Why you are mad ! "

But she smiled, and her smile seemed to say :

" That is pretty ; and it pleases me."

She continued :

" Come, you are not serious ; why do you jest in that manner ? "

He answered :

" On the contrary, I am very serious. I do not declare that I am in love with you, but I am questioning whether I am not in danger of becoming so."

" What makes you think that ? "

" My emotion when you are not here, my happiness when you come."

She sat down.

" Oh, don't be so easily disturbed. So long as you sleep well and dine with an appetite, there is no danger."

He laughed.

" And if I lose both sleep and appetite ? "

" Let me know."

" And then ? "

" I will leave you to recover in peace."

" Many thanks."

And with the theme of that love they dallied through the afternoon. On the days following it was the same. Assuming it to be a jest and without importance, she questioned him merrily, on entering:

" How fares your love to-day ? "

And he recited to her seriously and banteringly, all the progress of that malady, all the interior, continuous, profound labor of tenderness in its birth and development. He analyzed himself minutely before her, hour by hour from their separation of yesterday, with the playful manner of a professor who is lecturing; and she listened with interest, somewhat moved, troubled also by this story, which seemed a tale of which she was the heroine. When with courteous and graceful air he had enumerated all the cares to which he had fallen a prey, his voice at times grew tremulous, as he expressed by a word or even an inflection the aching of his heart.

And she continued to question him, vibrating with curiosity, her eyes fixed upon him, her ear eager for those things that are so disquieting to know but so charming to listen to.

Sometimes when he came near her to change a pose, he would seize her hand and try to kiss it. She would impetuously take her fingers from his lips, and with a little frown:

"Come, to work."

He would resume his task, but the lapse of a few moments would find her adroitly leading him back to the one subject which occupied them.

And now her heart began to have some misgivings. She wished indeed to be loved, but not too much. Sure herself of not being borne away, she feared to let him venture too far, and thus lose him, compelled to drive him to despair after she had seemed to encourage him. Yet if it became necessary to give up this tender, sentimental friendship, this converse which flowed on, bearing nuggets of love like a stream whose sand is full of gold, it would bring her great sorrow— a heartrending sorrow.

When she left her home for the painter's studio a warm bright joy filled her soul, making her light and gay. As she put her hand upon the bell of Olivier's door her heart throbbed with impatience, and the carpet of the stairway seemed the softest her feet had ever pressed.

Meantime, Bertin became gloomy, a little nervous, often irritable.

He had fits of impatience which he soon checked, but which frequently returned.

One day, when she had just entered, instead of beginning to paint, he sat down beside her, saying:

" Madame, you can no longer ignore the truth —that it is not a jest and that I love you madly."

Troubled by this opening, and seeing the approach of the dreaded crisis, she endeavored to stop him, but he was no longer listening. Emotion overflowed his heart, and pale, trembling and fearful—she must hear him. He spoke a long time, asking nothing; tenderly, sadly, with sorrowful resignation; and she allowed him to take her hands which he held in his. He had knelt without objection from her, and, with a dreamy look upon his face, begged her to do him no harm. What harm? She did not understand, nor try to understand, benumbed by the cruel grief of seeing him suffer, though that grief was almost happiness. Suddenly she saw tears in his eyes, which so moved her that she cried out, ready to embrace him, as one embraces a weeping child. He was repeating in a very soft voice: " There, there, I am suffering too much," and all at once, won by such grief, by the contagion of tears, she sobbed, with nerves unstrung, her arms trembling, ready to open.

When she felt herself suddenly folded in his arms and passionately kissed upon the lips, she wished to cry out, to struggle, to thrust him back, but she judged herself already lost, for while resisting, she consented, while struggling she yielded, and pressed him to her while crying, " No, no, I will not."

Then she was overwhelmed, her face in her hands she sprang up, caught her hat which had fallen on the carpet, replaced it and darted away, despite the entreaties of Olivier who was still holding her dress.

When she reached the street she would have liked to sit down on the curbstone; she felt so crushed, her limbs powerless. She hailed a passing cab, and told the coachman to drive slowly and go anywhere. She threw herself in the carriage, closed the door, crouched down in the corner, realizing that she was alone—alone to think.

For some minutes she was conscious only of the noise of the wheels and the jostling of the vehicle. She looked at the houses, the omnibuses, the people walking, others in cabs, with eyes that were vacant and saw nothing; nor did she think of anything, as though she were giving herself time, granting herself a respite before daring to reflect upon what had passed.

Then, as she was frank and courageous, she said to herself, " Well, I am a lost woman." For a few moments longer she remained under that sense of certainty, of irreparable misfortune, horrified, as a man who has fallen from a roof, and does not stir, guessing that his legs are broken, and hesitating to confirm the fact.

But, following this catastrophe, so far from being overwhelmed in the suffering she apprehended and the weight of which she dreaded, her heart remained calm and peaceful; it beat slowly, quietly, after the plunge at which her soul was cast down, and seemed to have no share in the bewilderment of her mind.

She repeated aloud, as though to emphasize and convince herself, "Well, I am a lost woman." No echo of suffering responded from her heart to this wail of her conscience.

She permitted herself to be lulled awhile by the motion of the carriage, postponing yet a little longer the reckoning she must have with herself in her cruel situation. No, she was not suffering. She was afraid to think; that is all, afraid to know, to reflect and to comprehend; she seemed, on the contrary, to experience an incredible calm within that mysterious and impenetrable being created in us by the incessant conflict of our inclinations and our will.

After, perhaps, half an hour of this strange repose, understanding finally that the despair she had summoned would not respond, she shook off this torpor, murmuring, " It is strange; I am scarcely sorry at all."

Then, she began to reproach herself. Anger was rising within her against her blindness, her weakness. How had she not foreseen this; understood that the hour for that struggle must come; that she cared enough for this man to be cowardly, and that through the most righteous hearts desire sometimes sends a blast that sweeps away the will?

But when she had taken herself to task, reviled herself, she wondered what would happen now.

Her first thought was to break with the painter, and never see him again.

Scarcely had she formed this resolution when she was assailed with a thousand reasons in opposition.

How would she explain this falling out? What would she say to her husband? Would not the suspected truth be whispered, then scattered everywhere?

Would it not be better to preserve appearances, to enact with Olivier himself the hypocritical comedy of indifference and forgetfulness, and show him that she had erased that moment from her memory and her life?

But could she do it? Would she dare to seem to remember nothing, to look with indignant astonishment upon the man whose swift and passionate emotion she had herself shared, and say to him, " What would you have of me ? "

She reflected long, and decided that no other solution was possible.

She would go to him to-morrow, courageously, and at once make him understand what she wished, what she expected. No word, allusion or glance must ever recall this shame.

Loyal and lofty, he also would suffer, and that suffering would teach him that he must remain in the future only that which he had been in the past.

Settled in this new resolve, she gave her address to the coachman, and returned home, utterly weary and prostrate, longing to lie down, to see no one, to sleep, to forget. Shutting herself up in her room, she remained till dinner time, stretched upon a lounge, benumbed, unwilling to trouble her soul longer with that thought so full of danger.

She appeared punctually at the hour for dining, astonished at finding herself so calm and to be awaiting her husband with her usual air. He came, bearing their little girl in his arms; she took his hand and kissed the child, and yet no anguish disturbed her.

M. de Guilleroy inquired what she had been doing. She answered indifferently that she had been posing, as usual.

" And the portrait—how is it coming on ? "

" Very well."

Then he talked of his affairs, as he liked to do while dining, of the sitting of the Chamber, and the discussion of the proposed law on the adulteration of food.

This babble, which ordinarily she endured with patience, irritated her, aroused a keener observation of the vulgar, verbose man whose interests lay in these things; but she smiled as she listened, more gracious even than usual, more tolerant of these common-places. She was thinking, as she looked at him, " I have deceived him. He is my husband, and I have deceived him. Is it not strange? Nothing can alter that now, nothing can erase it! I closed my eyes. I submitted for a few seconds, a few seconds only to the kisses of a man, and I am no longer an honest woman. A few seconds in my life, a few seconds that cannot be blotted out, have brought to pass for me that little irreparable deed, so grave, so short—a crime, the most shameful one for a woman—and I feel no despair. If some one had told me yesterday I should not have believed it. Had they insisted I should have at once imagined the frightful remorse that would tear my heart to-day. And I feel none—almost none."

M. de Guilleroy went out after dinner, as was his almost daily custom.

Then she took her little girl upon her knee, and the tears fell as she held her in her embrace; they were sincere tears, tears shed by her conscience, not by her heart.

But she slept little.

In the darkness of her room the dangers which confronted her in this new attitude of the artist seemed graver, and she began to fear the morrow's interview and that which she must say to him, looking into his eyes.

Rising early, she spent the morning on her

lounge, endeavoring to foresee what she had to fear, what she would have to answer, and to prepare herself for any surprise.

She started out early, that she might yet reflect as she walked.

He scarcely expected her, and had been asking himself, since the evening before, what he was to do, concerning her.

After her departure—that flight he had not dared to oppose—he had remained alone, and though she was already far away, still listening to the sound of her footsteps, of her dress, of the closing of the door, touched by a bewildered hand.

He remained standing, filled with an ardent joy, profound, fiery. He had clasped her. There was that between them. Was it possible? After the surprise of this triumph he realized it, and more fully to taste its sweetness, he sat down, nay, almost reclined upon the divan where she had been.

He remained there a long while, full of the thought that she was his, and that between them, between the woman he had so greatly desired and himself, had in a few moments been tied that mysterious knot which secretly binds two beings together. He preserved in his still quivering body the keen memory of the fleet moment when their lips had met, when their bodies had mingled and entwined, together thrilled with the supreme emotion of life.

He did not go out that evening, in order still to feed on that thought; he retired early, yet vibrating with happiness.

As soon as he awoke next morning he asked himself what he should do. A " Cocotte " or an actress would have presented no difficulty beyond a gift of flowers or even a jewel, but he was perplexed and tormented before this new situation.

Assuredly he must write, but what? . . . He scribbled, erased, tore up, commenced twenty letters, all of which seemed to him to be offensive, odious and ridiculous.

He wanted to express in delicate and charming language the gratitude of his soul, his transport of mad tenderness, his protestations of never-ending devotion; but for utterance of this passion and fine feeling he could find only set phrases, trite expressions, either abrupt or puerile.

He gave up, therefore, the idea of writing, and decided to see her, as soon as the hour for the sitting had elapsed, for he felt quite confident that she would not come.

Then shutting himself up in his studio, he stood in exultation before the portrait, his lips aching with a desire to touch the canvas where something of herself was fixed; and now and

then he looked out of the window. Every dress
he saw in the distance made his heart beat faster.
Twenty times he thought he recognized her,
then when the figure had passed he sat down a
moment, despondent, as one is who has deceived
himself.

Suddenly he saw her, paused in doubt, caught
up his opera glass, recognized her, and overcome by violent emotion, sat down to await
her.

When she entered he flung himself upon his
knees, and tried to take her hands, but she withdrew them quickly, and as he remained at her
feet, filled with anguish, and looking up at her,
she said, haughtily:

" What are you doing? I do not understand
that attitude ? "

" Oh, madame, I beg of you— "

She interrupted him harshly:

"Rise; you are ridiculous."

He rose, bewildered, murmuring:

" What is the matter? Do not treat me so.
I love you ! "

Then, in a few quick, cold words she signified
her wishes, and defined the situation.

" I do not understand you. Never speak to
me of your love, or I shall leave your studio,
never to return. If you forget for an instant
this condition of my presence here you will never
see me again."

He gazed at her, crushed by a harshness he had not foreseen; but he understood, and murmured:

" Madame, I shall obey."

She answered:

" Very well. It is what I expected of you. Now, to work, for you are long in finishing that portrait."

So he took up his palette and began to paint; but his hand trembled; his troubled eyes looked without seeing; he felt inclined to weep, so crushed was his heart.

He tried to speak; she hardly answered. As he ventured a compliment on her color she stopped him so peremptorily that he suddenly felt that lover's fury which changes tenderness to hatred. His nerves tingled with a shock so violent that it seemed to pierce his soul, and at once he detested her. Ah yes! That was woman! She was like them all! She, too! Why not? She was false, fickle and feeble like the rest. She had lured, seduced him with wanton tricks, kindling a maddening flame only to extinguish it with ice, provoking him to meet but denial, calling to her aid all the arts of that cowardly coquetry which seems ever at the point of revealing its charms so long as its victims, turned to spaniels, cringing, dare not to desire.

The worst, after all, was hers. He had

clasped her; she had been his. She might try to wash that away, and answer him insolently; she could efface nothing, and he would forget nothing. Truly, what folly it would have been to thus entangle himself; she would have eaten into his artist life with the capricious teeth of a pretty woman.

He wanted to whistle as he did in the presence of his models, but he felt that he was losing self-control, and feared to commit some folly. Under pretext of an engagement, he shortened the sitting, and when they bowed at parting, it was in the conviction that they were wider apart than the day when they first met at the Duchess de Mortemain's.

As soon as she had gone, he took his hat and coat and went out. A cold sun in a misty blue sky threw a pale, somewhat artificial and melancholy light upon the city.

When he had walked awhile, with quick and angry steps, jostling the passers by, as he would not himself deviate from a straight line, his great fury against her began to crumble into vexation and regret. After he had reviewed all the reproaches he had heaped upon her, he remembered, as he saw other women passing, how pretty and winning she was. Like so many who do not confess it, he had been awaiting always the meeting with that impossible person, that rare, unique, poetic and passionate affection, the dream of which hovers over our hearts. Had he not almost grasped it? Might not she have given him that well-nigh impossible happiness? Wherefore is it, then, that nothing is realized? Why can we seize nothing of that which we pursue, or only snatches which render still more grievous this chase after illusions?

His resentment toward her had already faded; it was against life itself he rebelled. Now, as he reasoned with himself, he questioned what cause of rancor he had against her. After all, with what could he reproach her? With being amiable, kindly and gracious, while he himself merited the reproach of dishonor!

He returned full of sadness. He would have liked to ask her forgiveness, to dedicate himself to her, to make her forget, and he queried in what manner he should enable her to understand that henceforth, even unto death, she would find him obedient to her wishes.

The next day she came, accompanied by her daughter, with such a sad smile, such a sorrowful face, that the painter imagined he saw in those poor blue eyes, so gay hitherto, all the pain, all the remorse, all the desolation of that womanly heart. His own was touched with compassion, and in order that she might forget, he offered with delicate reserve the most scrupulous attentions. She accepted them with gentleness, with kindness, with the weary and crushed air of a woman who is suffering.

And he, looking at her, again seized with a wild desire of loving and being loved, asked himself why she felt no greater indignation, how she could still come back, listen to him and answer him with that memory between them.

Since she could see him again, hear his voice, and endure before him the one thought which must ever be uppermost, he needed no other proof that this thought had not become intolerable to her. When the woman hates the man who has so transgressed she cannot in his presence restrain her hatred from bursting forth. But neither can that man remain indifferent to her. She must detest him or pardon him, and when she can pardon such an offense love is not far away.

While painting slowly, he resolved this small problem with precision, clearness and certainty; he felt confident, strong and master of events now.

He had only to be prudent, patient, devoted, and one day or another she would again be his.

He knew how to wait. To reassure her and regain her he in his turn resorted to wiles, feigned tenderness under seeming remorse, hesitating attentions and indifferent attitudes. Tranquil in the assurance of happiness to come, he cared not whether it be a little sooner or a little later. He even experienced a peculiar, subtle pleasure in making no haste, in watching her and thinking, " she is afraid," as he saw her coming always accompanied by her child.

He felt that between them a slow process of reconciliation was going on, and that something strange was seeking expression in the glances of the Countess—something constrained, pain-fully sweet, that appeal of a struggling soul, of a will that is fainting and which seems to say, " But—compel me, then."

By and by, she came again alone, reassured by his reserve. Then he treated her as a friend, a companion, talked to her of his life, of his plans, of his art, as to a brother.

Misled by this frankness, she assumed with joy the *rôle* of adviser, flattered at being so distinguished by him from other women, and convinced that his talent would gain in delicacy through this intellectual intimacy. Thus, by means of due deference in seeking her counsel, he made it easy for her to glide naturally from the functions of adviser to the sacred office of inspirer. She was happy in thus spreading her influence around the great man, and almost consented to accept the love—of the artist, whose inspiration she had become.

It was one evening, after a long talk about the loves of illustrious painters, that she let herself slip into his arms. This time she rested there, nor tried to flee, and returned his kisses.

Henceforth she felt no remorse, only the vague sense of a fall, and to satisfy the reproaches of her reason she found it necessary to believe in fatality.

Drawn toward him by her virgin heart and her empty soul, the flesh vanquished by the slow dominion of caresses, her attachment grew, little by little, as with all tender women who love for the first time.

With him it was a crisis of acute love, passionate and poetic. It sometimes seemed to him that he had one day taken flight, with hands outstretched, and been permitted wholly to embrace that winged and magnificent dream which is ever hovering over our hopes.

The portrait of the Countess was finished, the best certainly that he had ever done, for he had been able to discover and reproduce that inexpressible something which a painter rarely unveils, that reflex, that mystery, that likeness of the soul, which flits, evanescent, across a face.

Months then went by, then years, which scarcely loosened the bond that united the Countess de Guilleroy and the painter, Olivier Bertin. With him it was no longer the exaltation of the early days, but a calm, profound affection, a sort of loving friendship to which he had become accustomed.

With her, on the contrary, that passionate, obstinate attachment of certain women who resign themselves completely and forever was ever growing. Honest and straight-forward in unlawful love as they might have been in marriage, they devote themselves to a single affection, from which nothing will turn them aside. Not only do they love their lover, but they desire to love him, and with eyes only for him, they so fill their heart and thought that nothing of a strange nature can enter more. They have bound their lives resolutely, as one who knows how to swim ties his hands before leaping from the height of the bridge into the water, wishing to die.

But from the moment that the Countess had so yielded she was assailed by fears for the constancy of Olivier Bertin. There was nothing to hold him but his will, his caprice, his fleeting fancy for a woman he had met one day as he had already met so many others. She felt him to be so free, so open to temptation, he who lived without duties, habits or scruples—like all men! He was handsome, celebrated, popular, having within reach of his desires, so easily stirred, women of fashion whose modesty is so fragile, women of less severity, and actresses, prodigal of favors to men such as he. One of these, some evening, after supper, might follow him and please him, take him and keep him.

She lived, therefore, in terror of losing him, watching his manner, his attitudes, discomposed by a word, full of anguish when he admired another woman, praised the charm of a face, or the grace of a figure. All that she ignored of his life made her tremble, and all that she knew alarmed her. At each of their meetings she grew ingenuous in questioning him, without his perceiving it, in obtaining his opinion of the people he had seen, the houses at which he had dined, the lightest impressions of his mind. So soon as she fancied that she detected another's possible influence she combated it with prodigious cunning and innumerable resources.

Often did she guess those brief intrigues, taking no root, to be counted only by days, now and then encountered in the life of every conspicuous artist.

She had, as it were, an intuition of danger, even before she perceived the awakening of a new desire in Olivier, in the air of exhilaration which the eyes and the face assume under the influence of a gallant fancy.

Then she would begin to suffer; her sleep disturbed by torturing doubt. To effect a surprise she came to him unexpectedly, threw out questions which seemed simple, probed his heart, listened to his thought, as one tests and listens to detect the illness which the body conceals.

And she would weep when she found herself

alone, confident that this time they would take
him from her, steal that love to which she clung
so tenaciously because she had staked upon it,
without reserve, all her power of affection, all
her hopes and all her dreams.

And when she perceived him coming back
after these brief estrangements, she experienced,
as she held him again, took possession of him
once more, as of something lost and found, a
mute, profound happiness which sometimes, as
she passed a church, constrained her to enter
and thank God.

This occupation of constant effort to please
him above all others, and to hold him against
all rivalry, had made of her life an uninterrupted
battle of coquetry. The struggle to retain him
had been ceaseless, in which she had employed
her grace, her beauty, her elegance, and she
wanted to feel that whenever he heard her name
it should be coupled with praise of her manner,
her taste, her wit and her dress. She sought to
capture the admiration of others in order to stimulate his pride in her and awaken his jealousy,
and when she had succeeded in stirring that emotion to a sufficiently painful degree she permitted him a triumph which revived his affection
and soothed his vanity.

Then, understanding that the world always
holds for a man new possibilities of greater
physical attraction, strong in the power of nov-

elty, she resorted to other means; she flattered and spoiled him.

She sagaciously threw over him a mist of praise; she lulled him with admiration and enveloped him in flattery, in order that he might find all other friendship, all other affection somewhat cold and incomplete, and that if others also loved him, he would finally perceive that she alone understood him.

She made of her house, those two salons which he entered so often, a place as attractive to the pride of the artist as to the heart of the man, the place of all Paris where he liked best to come—where all the cravings of his nature found satisfaction.

Not only did she learn to discover all his tastes, in order that while ministering to them in her own home she might impart a sense of well-being that nothing could replace, but she learned to bring new ones into his life, to create appetites of all kinds, of the senses and of the soul, an habitual atmosphere of small services, of affection, of adoration, of flattery. She strove to enslave his eyes with elegance, his scent with perfumes, his ear with eulogy, and his palate with viands.

But when she had planted in his soul and in the selfish, pampered senses of a bachelor a multitude of little tyrannical wants, when she had assured herself that no mistress would exercise

her care in fostering and maintaining them in
order to entwine him with all the small enjoy-
ments of life, she suddenly feared, as she saw
him weary of his own home, ever complaining
of his lonely life, and unable to come to her except under all the restraints imposed by society,
seeking everywhere for means to temper his isolation—she feared lest he thought of marriage.

Some days she suffered so keenly in this fret
of anxiety that she longed for old age, to have
done with this anguish, and find rest in a cooler
and calmer affection.

Years passed, however, without disuniting
them. The chain with which she had bound
him was a weighty one, and she renewed the
links as fast as they wore away. But ever anxious, she kept a watchful eye upon the artist's
heart, as one watches a child crossing a crowded
street, and still, from day to day, she dreaded
the unforeseen possibility which constantly
menaced her.

The Count, without suspicion or jealousy, regarded as quite natural this intimacy of his wife
with an artist, courted and famous, and by dint
of constant meeting, these two men, growing
used to each other, finally settled into a mutual
affection.

CHAPTER II.

On Friday evening, when Bertin entered the house of his friend, where he was to dine in celebration of the return of Annette de Guilleroy, he found in the little Louis XV. salon only M. de Musadieu, who had just arrived.

He was a clever old man, who might have become perhaps a valuable one, and who could not be consoled for what he had not achieved.

A former commissioner of the Imperial Museums, he had found means to get himself reappointed "Inspector des Beaux-Arts" under the Republic, which did not prevent his being above all else the friend of Princes, of all the Princes, Princesses and Duchesses of European aristocracy and the sworn protector of artists of every description. Gifted with a quick intelligence and the keenest perceptions, with great readiness of speech which enabled him to put attractively the merest common-places, with a mental suppleness that made him at ease in all circles, and a subtle diplomatic scent which enabled him to judge men at first sight, he wandered with his enlightened, useless and babbling activity from salon to salon, by day and by night.

Apt at everything, it seemed, he discussed any

subject with an appearance of engaging competence and an empirical clearness which won
for him the appreciation of fashionable women,
whom he served in the capacity of an ambulant
bazar of erudition. He knew, indeed, many
things without ever having read any but indispensable books; he was on the best possible
terms with the five Academies, with all the
savans, all writers, all the erudite specialists, to
whom he listened with discrimination. He
knew how to forget at once explanations that
were too technical or useless for his require-
ments, remembered the others sufficiently well,
and to the information thus gleaned he lent an
easy, clear and good-natured turn which made
them as little difficult of comprehension as scien-
tific *fabliaux*. He gave one the impression of
a storehouse of ideas, of one of those vast ware-
houses wherein rare articles are never to be
found, but abounding in ordinary productions,
cheap, of every kind, from every source, from
household utensils to the popular apparatus of
parlor physics or domestic chemistry.

Painters, with whom his duties brought him
in daily contact, hoaxed him and feared him.
He rendered them, however, some services,
aided them to sell pictures, liked to introduce
them and patronize them; he seemed to devote
himself to a mysterious office in the fusion of the
fashionable and the artistic worlds, boasted of

his intimate acquaintance with these, of his familiar reception by those, of breakfasting with
the Prince of Wales, on his way through Paris,
and of dining on the same evening with Paul
Adelmans, Olivier Bertin and Amaury Maldant.

Bertin, who rather liked him, finding him
droll, used to say of him, " It is the Encyclo-
paedia of Jules Verne, bound in ass's skin."

The two men shook hands, and began to talk
about the political situation, of the rumors of
war, which Musadieu thought alarming, for ob-
vious reasons which he explained very clearly,
Germany having every interest in crushing us
and in hastening the moment to which Bismarck had looked forward these eighteen years,
while Olivier proved with irrefutable arguments
that these were chimerical fears, since Germany
could not be foolish enough to hazard her conquest in an always doubtful adventure, and the
Chancellor imprudent enough to risk, at the
close of his life, the work he had accomplished
and the glory he had won—at a blow.

M. de Musadieu, however, seemed to be acquainted with facts which he did not care to
state. Besides he had seen a minister during
the day and met the Grand-Duke Vladimir on
his return from Cannes the evening before.

The artist held his ground, and with quiet
irony, questioned the competence of the best
informed. Behind all the rumors were the

manipulations of the Stock Exchange! Bismarck alone might have a fixed opinion on that matter, perhaps.

M. de Guilleroy entered, shook hands cordially, apologizing in unctuous phrase, for having left them alone.

"And you, my dear Deputy," asked the painter, "what do you think of these war clouds?"

M. de Guilleroy launched into a discourse. As a member of the Chamber, he knew more than anybody else on the subject, though differing with the majority of his colleagues. No, he did not believe in the probability of an approaching conflict, unless it were precipitated by French turbulence and the bluster of the so-called patriots of the league. And he laid Bismarck's portrait with bold strokes—a portrait a la Saint-Simon. That man people refused to understand, because one always invests others with his own views, and assumes the probability of a course similar to his own in a like situation. Bismarck was not a false and lying diplomatist, but frank, brutal; one who always hurled the truth, always proclaimed his intentions. "I want peace," said he. It was true; he did want peace, nothing but peace, and everything had proved it in a blinding fashion for the last eighteen years; everything, even his armaments, his alliances, that group of peoples united against our impetuosity. M. de Guilleroy concluded in a tone of deep conviction: "He is a great man, a very great man, who desires peace, but who believes only in menace and violence as the means of obtaining it. In a word, gentlemen, a great barbarian."

"If you want the end you must not stick at the means," M. de Musadieu replied. "I will grant you willingly that he adores peace, if you will concede that he is always determined to fight in order to secure it. That is, however, an indisputable and phenomenal truth: War is waged in this world only to obtain peace!"

A servant here announced: "Madame la Duchesse de Mortemain."

In the open doorway appeared a tall, massive woman, who entered with an air of authority.

Guilleroy hastened forward, kissed the tips of her fingers, saying:

"Ah! how do you do, Duchess?"

The other two men greeted her with a certain distinguished familiarity, for the Duchess had cordial and brusque ways with her.

She was the widow of a General, the Duke of Mortemain, mother of an only daughter married to the Prince of Salia, daughter of Marquis de Farandal, of noble extraction and royally rich, and received at her palace in the Rue de Varenne the notable characters of the whole world, who met and interchanged compliments at her house. No Highness passed through Paris without dining at her table, and no man could arouse public attention without creating in her an immediate desire to meet him; she must see him, talk with him, judge him. All this amused her greatly, furnished an object in life, and fed that flame of imperious and benevolent curiosity which was burning within her.

She was scarcely seated when the servant again announced: " Monsieur le Baron and Madame la Baronne de Corbelle."

They were young; the baron was bald and big; the baroness was slender, elegant and very dark.

This couple occupied a unique position in the French aristocracy, owing solely to a scrupulous choice of connections. Belonging to the gentry, having no value, no cleverness, impelled in all their movements by an immoderate love for what is select, high-bred and distinguished, by dint of frequenting only the most princely houses, by dint of exhibiting their royalist feelings, pious and correct to a supreme degree, by dint of respecting all that should be respected, and despising all that should be despised, of never being mistaken upon a point of .conventional dogma, never hesitating upon a detail of etiquette, they had succeeded in passing in the eyes of many for the very essence of high life. Their opinion formed a sort of code of perfect

breeding, and their presence in a house established a true title of exclusiveness.

The Corbelles were related to the Count of
Guilleroy.

" Well," exclaimed the Duchess in astonishment, " and your wife ? "

" One moment, one instant," the Count
begged. " There is a surprise; she will come
directly."

When Mme. de Guilleroy, a month after her
marriage, had made her début in society she
was presented to the Duchess of Mortemain,
who at once loved her, adopted her and patron-
ized her.

For twenty years that friendship had never
waned, and when the Duchess said " ma petite "
one still felt in her voice the ring of that sudden
and persistent fancy. It was at her house that
the painter and the Countess had chanced to
meet.

Musadieu drew near and asked:

" Has the Duchess been to see the exposition
of the intemperates ? "

" No, what is that ? "

" A group of novel artists, impressionists in a
state of intoxication. Two of them are very
good."

The great lady murmured, disdainfully,

" I do not like these gentlemen's jests."

Authoritative, blunt, scarcely tolerating other

opinion than her own, and founding hers solely upon the consciousness of her social position, considering, without clearly accounting for it, artists and learned men as intelligent mercenaries charged by God to amuse society, or render it services, she based her judgments solely on the degree of astonishment and unreasoning pleasure which the sight of a thing, the reading of a book or the refusal of a discovery afforded her.

Tall, stout, heavy, red, talking in a loud voice, she had a reputation for lofty airs because nothing disconcerted her; she dared to say everything and to patronize the whole world, dethroned Princes with her receptions in their honor, and the Almighty Himself by her liberality to the clergy and her gifts to the churches.

Musadieu continued:

" Does the Duchess know that the assassin of Marie Lambourg is said to have been arrested ? "

Her interest was at once aroused, and she answered:

" No, tell me about that."

And he related the details. He was tall, very thin, wore a white vest, little diamond shirt buttons, spoke without gesture, with a correct air which permitted him to indulge his tendency to say daring things. He was extremely nearsighted, and, notwithstanding his eye-glass, appeared never to see any one, and when he sat down one would have said that his entire frame accommodated itself to the curves of the chair. His figure seemed to fold into plaits, sinking away as if the spinal column were made of rubber; his legs crossed over each other looked like two rolled ribbons, and from his long arms, upheld by those of the chair, depended his pale hands with interminable fingers. His hair and moustache, artistically dyed, with white locks skillfully forgotten, were the subject of a standing jest.

As he was explaining to the Duchess that the jewels of the murdered courtesan had been a gift from the suspected murderer to another of her class, the door of the large drawing-room opened once more quite wide, and two women in white lace, in a cream of mechlin, fair, resembling each other like two sisters of a different age, one a little too mature, the other a little too young, one a little too rotund, the other a little too thin, came forward, smiling, with their arms encircling each other's waists.

There were exclamations and applause. Nobody, except Olivier Bertin, was aware of Annette de Guilleroy's return, and the appearance of the young girl beside her mother, who at a little distance, looked almost as fresh and even more beautiful,—for, like a flower at full bloom, she had not yet lost her brilliancy, while the child, just blossoming, was only beginning to be pretty—made them both look charming.

The Duchess was delighted, and clapping her hands, exclaimed:

" Heavens! how lovely and interesting they are beside each other! Do look, Monsieur de Musadieu, how they resemble each other."

People were comparing; two opinions were at once formulated. According to Musadieu, the Corbelles and Count de Guilleroy, the Countess and her daughter resembled each other only in the complexion, the hair and especially the eyes, which were precisely alike, in both marked with black spots, like infinitesimal drops of ink that had fallen on the blue iris. But shortly, when the young girl should have become a woman, the great resemblance would almost disappear.

According to the Duchess, on the contrary, and Olivier Bertin, they were alike in everything, the disparity in age alone constituting the difference.

The painter was saying:

" Hasn't she changed in the last three years? I would not have recognized her; I shall no longer dare to say ' tu ' to her."

The Countess laughed.

" Ah, indeed, I should like to hear you say ' you ' to Annette."

The young girl, whose future sparkling au-

dacity was now perceptible under timidly arch
airs, replied:

" It is I who will no longer dare to say ' tu ' to
M. Bertin."

The mother smiled.

" You may retain that bad habit. I will permit it. You will soon become acquainted
again."

But Annette shook her head.

" No, no, it would embarrass me."

The Duchess embraced her, and examined her
after the manner of an interested expert.

" Come, little one, look me well in the face.
Yes, you have quite your mother's glance; you
will not look badly in a little while, when you
have acquired some brilliancy. You must gain
roundness, not much, but a little; you are a
little bit thin."

The Countess exclaimed:

" Oh, do not tell her that."

" Why not ? "

" It is so pleasant to be thin; I am going to
diet."

But Madame de Mortemain was angry, for-
getting in the heat of her passion, the presence
of a little girl.

" Ah, yes, always. You are always in the
fashion with bones, because they may be better
dressed than flesh. I belong to the generation
of fat women. To-day it is the generation of

lean women.   That reminds me of the cows of
Egypt.   I do not understand men, for instance,
who seem to admire skeletons.   In my time they
demanded something better."

She paused, amid the smiles, then continued:
" Look at your mamma, little one; she looks
very well; just right; imitate her."

They passed into the dining-room.   When
everybody was seated, Musadieu resumed the
discussion:

"I say that men should be thin, because they
are made for exercises which demand skill and
agility incompatible with portliness.   With
women, it is a little different.   Do you not think
so, Corbelle?"

Corbelle was perplexed, the Duchess being
stout and his own wife more than thin.   But the
Baroness came to her husband's assistance, and
resolutely declared in favor of slenderness.   The
year before she had been obliged to struggle
against an opposite tendency which she very
soon brought under control.

" Tell us what you did," asked Madame de
Guilleroy.

And the Baroness explained the method used
by all elegant women of the day.   One must
not drink while eating.   One hour after meals
only, a cup of tea, very hot, burning, may be
taken.   That succeeds with everybody.   She
cited astonishing examples of large women who

had become in three months thinner than knife
blades. The Duchess, exasperated, exclaimed:

"Heavens! How foolish to torture one's self
so! You may have nothing, absolutely nothing,
not even champagne. Come, Bertin, you who
are an artist, what do you think?"

"My dear Madame, I am a painter. I drape.
It is all the same to me. Were I a sculptor, I
would complain."

"But you are a man; what do you prefer?"

"I?—an—elegance, rather well-fed; what my
cook calls a good little corn-fed chicken. It is
not fat; it is full and fine."

The comparison provoked laughter; but the
Countess, incredulous, looked at her daughter,
and murmured:

"No, it is very fine to be thin; women who
remain thin do not grow old."

That point also was discussed, and opinions
divided. Everybody, however, almost agreed
upon this: that a person who was very fat must
not grow thin too soon.

This remark gave rise to a review of women
known in society, and to new debates upon their
grace, their "chic" and their beauty. Musadieu
thought the fair Marquise de Lochrist incom-
parably charming, but Bertin esteemed without
rival Mme. Mandeliere, with her dark skin and
sombre eyes, her low forehead and rather large
mouth, in which her white teeth seemed to shine.

He was seated beside the young girl, and suddenly turning toward her said:

"Listen attentively, Nanette. You will hear all that we are saying at least once a week until you are old. In eight days you will know by heart all that society thinks about politics, women, the play, and all the rest. There will be needed only an occasional change of names, of persons and of titles of works. When you shall have heard us all disclose and defend our opinions you will quietly choose your own from among those which one must have, and then you will have no more need to think of anything, never; you will have only to rest."

The little one, without replying, looked up at him with a mischievous glance, wherein shone a young, active intelligence, held in check and ready to escape.

But the Duchess and Musadieu, who played with ideas as one plays ball, without perceiving that they kept the same ones rebounding constantly, protested—in the name of human thought and activity.

Then Bertin endeavored to demonstrate how valueless, ill-fed and without range is the intelligence of the fashionable, how shallow are their beliefs, how feeble and indifferent their attention to intellectual interests, how fluttering and questionable their tastes.

Carried away by one of those outbursts of in-

dignation, half sincere, half assumed, induced
first by a desire to be eloquent, and partly
aroused by the sudden stirring of a clear judg-
ment ordinarily obscured by benevolence, he
showed how people whose only occupation in
life is to pay visits and dine in town, find themselves becoming, through irresistible fatality,
light and graceful, but common-place beings,
vaguely agitated by superficial cares, beliefs and
appetites.

He showed that they have no depth, earnestness, or sincerity, that their intellectual culture
is but a name and their erudition a simple varnish; that they remain, in short, manikins who
carry the illusion and imitate the gestures of the
superior beings—whom they are not. He
proved that the frail roots of their instincts having fed upon conventionalities instead of truth,
they really love nothing, that the very luxury of
their existence is the satisfaction of vanity, and
not the indulgence of an exquisite need of their
bodies, for their kitchen is poor, their wines are
bad and very dear.

They live, he said, by the side of everything,
seeing nothing, penetrating nothing; by the side
of science of which they are ignorant; by the side
of nature at which they know not how to look;
by the side of happiness, for they are incapable
of grasping enjoyment; by the side of the beauty
of the world and the beauty of art, of which

they talk without having discovered it, and even without believing in it, for they are ignorant of the intoxication that comes from tasting the joys of life and intelligence. They are incapable of a supreme love for anything or of an interest in any pursuit deep enough to be finally illumined by the happiness of comprehending.

Baron Corbelle thought it devolved upon him to undertake the defense of good company.

He did so with inconsistent and unanswerable arguments that melt before reason as snow before the fire, and which cannot be laid hold of— the absurd and triumphant arguments of a rural curate who would prove God. Finally, he compared fashionable society to race-horses which, to speak the truth, have no use, but are nevertheless the glory of horse-flesh.

Bertin, restive before this adversary, was scornfully and politely silent. But finally, the Baron's inanity irritated him, and skillfully interrupting him, he recounted the life of a society man from his rising to his retiring, without omitting anything.

All the details shrewdly incorporated, made up an irresistibly absurd silhouette. You saw the gentleman dressed by his valet, first expressing a few general ideas to the hair-dresser who came to shave him; then when taking his morning walk, inquiring of the grooms about the health of the horses, then trotting along in the

avenues of the Bois, oppressed with the single
care of exchanging salutations, then breakfasting opposite his wife, who had gone out in a
coupé, and breaking the silence only to enumer-
ate the names of the persons whom he had met
during the morning; going on till evening from
drawing-room to drawing-room, refreshing his
intelligence by contact with his fellows, and dining at last with a Prince where the attitude of
the whole of Europe was discussed, to finish the
evening in the green-room, at the Opera, where
his timid pretensions of excesses were innocently
satisfied by an appearance of questionable surroundings.

The picture was so accurate, while the shaft
wounded no one, that laughter ran round the
board.

The Duchess, shaken by the suppressed mirth
of corpulence, dissipated her amusement in sun-
dry little tremors.

She finally said:

" No, really, you are too ridiculous; you will
make me die of laughter."

Bertin, thoroughly aroused, replied:

" Oh, Madame, in society one does not die of
laughter. One barely laughs. One condescends,
in good taste, to appear amused and to make
believe to laugh. The appearance is imitated
well enough, but the thing is never done. Go
to the people's theatres; there you will see laugh-

ter.   Go to the *bourgeois*, who enjoy themselves;
you will see them laugh to suffocation.   Go to
the soldiers' dormitories; you will see men
choking, their eyes full of tears, rolling on their
beds and splitting their sides at the jokes of a
wag.   But in our drawing-rooms no one laughs.
I tell you that we simulate everything, even
laughter."

Musadieu stopped him:

" Pardon me; you are severe; after all, you
yourself, my dear fellow, do not seem to me to
despise this society that you scoff at so readily."

Bertin smiled:

" Why, I love it."

" How then ?"

" I despise myself a little, like a mongrel of
doubtful pedigree."

" All that is posing," said the Duchess.

And as he disclaimed posing, she brought the
discussion to an end by declaring that all artists
want to make people believe the moon is made
of green cheese.

The conversation soon became general,
touched upon everything, common-place and
common, friendly and discriminating, and as the
dinner was nearly at an end, the Countess exclaimed as she pointed to the glasses, still filled,
before her:

" There!   I have drank nothing, absolutely

nothing, not a drop; we'll see whether I shall grow thin."

The Duchess, furious, tried to make her taste some mineral water; in vain, and she exclaimed:

" What nonsense. Her daughter will turn her head. I beg of you, Guilleroy, preserve your wife from such folly."

The Count, who was explaining to Musadieu the system of a threshing machine invented in America, had not heard :

" What folly, Duchess ?"

" The folly of wanting to grow thin."

He threw upon his wife a glance of benevolent indifference:

" Well, but I have not contracted the habit of thwarting her."

The Countess had risen, taking the arm of her neighbor; the Count offered his to the Duchess, and they passed into the " grand salon," the " boudoir " at the end being reserved for daily use.

It was a vast and brilliantly lighted apartment. Upon the four walls the large and beautiful pale blue silk panels in antique designs, enclosed in frames of white and gold, took on a soft bright, lunar tint under the light of the lamps and the chandelier. In the centre of the principal one the portrait of the Countess by Olivier Bertin seemed to inhabit, to animate the apartment. It was at home there, mingling with the very air of the room its youthful smile, the grace of its glance, the airy charm of the fair hair. It had become almost a custom, a sort of ceremonial of courtesy, like the sign of the cross on entering a church, to compliment the model upon the work of the painter whenever any one paused before it.

Musadieu never failed. The opinion of a connoisseur commissioned by the State, having the value of official sanction, he made it his duty to affirm with frequency and emphasis the superiority of that painting.

" Really," he said, " that is the most beautiful modern portrait I know. It contains prodigious life."

The Count of Guilleroy who had through habitual praise of the portrait, become convinced that he was the possessor of a master-piece, approached to supplement him, and for a few moments they concentrated all the current art technicalities sacred to description in the attempt to analyze its visible merits.

All eyes were lifted to the wall in an apparently enraptured gaze, and Olivier Bertin, accustomed to these praises, to which he hardly paid more attention than to inquiries concerning one's health at a chance meeting in the street, nevertheless adjusted the reflector lamp placed before the portrait to throw the light upon it, as it had been negligently set down a little askew.

Then they sat down, and as the Count approached the Duchess she said to him:

" I believe that my nephew is coming for me, and also to ask you for a cup of tea."

Their wishes had been, for some time past, mutually understood, without any exchange of confidence or even an insinuation.

The brother of the Duchess of Mortemain, the Marquis of Farandal, after having nearly ruined himself gambling, had died in consequence of a fall from a horse, leaving a widow and a son. This young man was now nearly twenty-eight years of age; was one of the most coveted leaders of the cotillon in Europe, for he was sometimes summoned to Vienna and London to crown with a waltz some princely ball. Although with scarcely any fortune, he remained by his position, his family, his name and his almost royal connections, one of the most popular and envied men in Paris.

It was necessary to conclude this revelling stage of youthful glory, and after accomplishing a rich, a very rich marriage, to let political supersede social successes. As soon as he should be a deputy the Marquis would become, *ipso facto*, one of the pillars of the future throne, one of the counsellors of the King, one of the leaders of the party.

The Duchess, who was well informed, knew the extent of Count de Guilleroy's enormous for-

tune, as he had been prudently hoarding, living
in a simple apartment when he might have lived
like a great lord in one of the finest mansions of
Paris. She knew about his always successful
speculations, his keen scent as a financier, his
share in the most fruitful operations of the past
ten years, and she had long thought of effecting
the union of her nephew with the daughter of
the Norman deputy, to whom this marriage
would give an overwhelming influence with
the princely contingent of the aristocratic
class. Guilleroy, who had made a rich marriage and greatly increased a large personal fortune by his skill, was now nursing other ambi-
tions.

He believed in the return of the King, and
wanted on that day to be in a position to derive
the highest possible personal advantages from
that event.

As a simple deputy he counted for but little.
As father-in-law of the Marquis of Farandal,
whose ancestors had been the faithful and chosen
familiars of the royal house of France, he rose to
first rank.

Furthermore, the Duchess' friendship for his
wife lent to this union a very precious element
of intimacy, and lest another young girl be found
who would suddenly please the Marquis, he had
summoned his daughter in order to hasten
events.

Mme. de Mortemain foreseeing and guessing his plans, lent them a silent sanction, and on that very day, although she had not been informed of the expected return of Annette, she had asked her nephew to meet her at the Guilleroys in order that he might become accustomed gradually to often cross that threshold.

For the first time the Count and the Duchess referred to their wishes in ambiguous words, and when they separated a treaty had been concluded.

They were laughing at the other end of the room ; M. de Musadieu was telling the Baroness about the presentation of a negro embassy to the President of the Republic, when the Marquis of Farandal was announced.

He appeared in the doorway and stopped. With a quick and familiar motion of the arm he placed a monocle on his right eye, as if to reconnoitre the room which he was about to enter, but possibly to give the people who were already there an opportunity to see him and note his entrance. Then, with an imperceptible motion of the cheek and eyebrow, he dropped the little circle of glass at the end of a black silk hair, and advanced quickly toward Madame de Guilleroy, whose outstretched hand he kissed, bowing very low. He greeted his aunt in the same manner, and shook hands with the others, going from one to another with an air of elegant ease.

He was a tall fellow, with a red moustache, already a little bald, with the figure of an officer and the gait of an English sportsman. It was evident in looking at him that his limbs were better trained than his head, and that his tastes lay entirely in the field of athletic development. He had some knowledge, however, for he had learned, and was still learning every day with great assiduity, much that would be very useful later—history, dwelling with emphasis upon the dates and mistaking the lesson of events and the elementary notions of political economy necessary for a deputy, the A, B, C of sociology for the use of the ruling classes.

Musadieu esteemed him, saying: " He will be a valuable man." Bertin appreciated his skill and vigor. They frequented the same fencing hall, often hunted together, and met riding in the avenues of the Bois. Between them there had therefore sprung up that sympathy of tastes in common, that instinctive freemasonry which creates between two men a subject of conversation, already established, agreeable to one as to the other.

When the Marquis was presented to Annette de Guilleroy a suspicion of his aunt's coalition instantly entered his mind, and after saluting her, he looked her over with the glance of a connoisseur.

He thought her pleasing, and especially full

of promise, for he had led so many cotillons that he knew young girls well, and, like an expert who is testing wine a little too new, he could predict almost unfailingly the flower of their beauty.

He exchanged only a few insignificant words with her, and then sat down near the Baroness de Corbelle, chatting in an undertone.

All retired early, and when every one was gone, the child in bed, the lamps put out, the servants departed, Count de Guilleroy, walking across the salon, lighted only by two candles, detained yet a little longer the Countess, who was getting very drowsy in an armchair, to unfold his hopes, to detail the attitude they would assume, to forecast all combinations, the chances and precautions to be taken.

It was late when he retired, charmed, however, with his evening, and murmuring:

" I believe that business is settled."

CHAPTER III.

"When will you come, my friend? I have seen nothing of you for three days, and that seems a long while to me. I am much occupied with my daughter, but you know that I can no longer do without you."

The painter, who was making sketches, always looking for a new subject, read the Countess's note twice over, then opening the drawer of a desk, laid it upon a pile of other letters that had accumulated there since the beginning of their intimacy.

Thanks to the opportunities afforded in fashionable society, they had become accustomed to see each other almost every day. Now and then she came to him, and without interrupting his work, would sit for an hour or two in the easy chair which she had formerly occupied for her portrait. But as she was somewhat apprehensive of the criticism of his household, she preferred to receive him at her home, or meet him in some salon, for that daily intercourse, that small change of love.

These meetings would be previously arranged, and they seemed always quite natural to M. de Guilleroy.

Twice a week at least, the painter dined at the Countess's with a few friends; on Mondays he regularly paid his respects to her at her box in the Opera; then they would agree to meet at such-and-such a house where chance brought them at the same hour. He knew on what evenings she remained at home, and he went in to have a cup of tea with her, feeling at home even near her dress, so tenderly and so surely lodged in that ripe affection, so established in the habit of finding her somewhere, of spending a few moments by her side, of interchanging a few words, mingling a few thoughts, that, although the vivid flame of his love had long ago been quenched, he felt an incessant need of seeing her.

The longing for family ties, for an animated, tenanted household, for meals in common, for the evenings when one chats without fatigue with old and familiar acquaintances, that desire for contact, for elbowing each other, for that intimacy which lies dormant in every human heart, and which every old bachelor carries from door to door to his friends, where he installs a part of himself, all this added an element of selfishness to his affection. In this house where he was loved, spoiled, where he found everything, he might still rest and indulge his solitude.

For three days he had seen nothing of his friends, who must be quite disorganized by the return of their daughter, and he was already feeling lonesome, a little affronted even, that they should not have summoned him sooner, but reluctant to call their attention to himself.

The Countess's letter roused him like the stroke of a whip. It was three o'clock in the afternoon, and he immediately decided to see her before she went out.

His valet answered the ring of his bell.

" What is the weather, Joseph ? "

"Very fine, sir."

" Warm ? "

"Yes, sir."

"White waistcoat, blue jacket, grey hat."

He dressed always with great elegance, and although his tailor was unexceptionable, the very way he wore his clothes, the way he walked, with a white waistcoat buttoned tightly over his portly form, a soft, grey hat, high crowned, tipped slightly back, seemed at once to reveal the artist and the bachelor.

When he reached the Countess's he was told that she was preparing for a drive in the Bois. This annoyed him, and he waited.

According to his habit, he began to pace the floor, going from one seat to another, or from the windows to the opposite wall, in the large apartment darkened by the drawn shades. The light tables, resting on gilded feet, held trifles of all sorts, useless, pretty and costly, strewn in studied disorder. There were little antique boxes of chisélled gold, miniature snuff boxes, ivory statuettes, articles made of dead silver, quite modern, severely absurd, in which English taste was apparent; a diminutive kitchen stove, and on top of it a cat drinking from a pan, a cigarette case in the shape of a loaf of bread, a coffee-pot for matches, and in a casket a complete doll's set of jewelry, necklace, bracelets, rings, brooches, ear-rings with diamonds, sapphires, rubies, emeralds—a microscopic fancy which seemed to have been executed by Liliputian jewellers.

Here and there he touched an object given by himself on some anniversary, took it up, handled it, examined it with a dreamy indifference, then put it back in its place.

In a corner, a few works rarely opened, luxuriously bound, were at hand, upon a round stand with a single support, placed before a little round sofa. There was also the *Revue des Deux Mondes*, somewhat rumpled, showing use, the edges dog-eared, as though it had been read over and over again; other publications with leaves uncut, the *Arts Modernes*, costing four hundred francs a year, and the price of which alone ensured subscription, and the *Feuille libre*, a thin blue-bound book, in which are launched the most recent poets, called "*les Enervés.*"

Between the windows stood the Countess's

writing desk, a coquettish bit of furniture of the last century, at which she wrote her answers to the hurried questions handed to her during calls. A few works were on that desk, familiar books, the sign-board of woman's mind and heart— *Musset, Manon Lescaut, Werther;* and, to show that one was not altogether unacquainted with the complex sensations and mysteries of psychology, *les Fleurs du Mal, le Rouge et le Noir, la Femme au XVIIIe Siècle, Adolphe.*

Beside the books, a charming hand mirror, a masterpiece of the goldsmith's art, the glass of which was turned over upon a square of embroidered velvet, exposing to admiring eyes a curious design of gold and silver on the back.

Bertin took it up and looked at himself. In the last few years he had aged greatly, and although he considered his face more original than formerly, he was beginning to be saddened by his wrinkles and the weight of his cheek.

A door opened behind him.

" Good morning, Monsieur Bertin," said Annette.

" Good morning, little one; you are quite well ? "

" Quite well; and you ? "

" What really, you do not say 'tu' to me ? "

" No, really; it embarrasses me."

" Nonsense."

" Yes, it does; you make me timid."

" Why ? "

" Because—because you are neither young enough nor old enough."

The painter laughed.

"Against that reason I do not insist."

A sudden blush deluged that white skin to the roots of her hair, and she replied, confused:

"Mamma requested me to tell you that she would come down directly, and to ask you if you would not accompany us to the Bois de Boulogne."

" Yes, certainly.   Are you alone ? "

" No; with the Duchess of Mortemain."

" Very well, I'll join you."

" Then you will permit me to go and put on my hat ? "

"Go, my child."

As she left the room the Countess entered, veiled, ready to go out.   She held out her hands.

" We do not see you any more.   What are you doing ? "

" I did not wish to trouble you these days."

The tone in which she said " Olivier " expressed all her reproaches and all her attachment.

"You are the best woman in the world," he said, moved by the sound of his name.

That little lover's quarrel settled, she continued in her ordinary tone:

" We are to call for the Duchess at her house,

and then we will take a turn in the Bois; we shall
have to show Nanette all that."

The landau was waiting at the carriage entrance.

Bertin seated himself opposite the two ladies,
and the carriage started amidst the noise of the
horses' hoofs, pawing under the echoing arch-
way.

Along the Boulevards, down toward the
Madeleine, all the gaiety of the new springtime
seemed to have descended from the sky upon
human life.

The sunshine and the balmy air gave to men
a holiday appearance and to women new fasci-
nations, caused the urchins to caper about with
the white-liveried scullions, who had left their
baskets on the benches for a frolic with their
brothers, the young *voyous*.   The dogs seemed
in a hurry, the concierges' canaries were singing
loud; the sorry old cab horses alone continued
at their exhausted gait, their moribund trot.

The Countess murmured:

"Oh, what a beautiful day; how good it seems
to live."

The painter was contemplating, under the
strong light both mother and daughter, one
after the other.   Surely they were different, but
at the same time so alike that the latter was indeed a perpetuation of the former, of the same
blood, the same flesh, animated by the same life.

Their eyes, especially those blue eyes, splashed with tiny black drops, of such a fresh blue in the daughter, a little faded in the mother, looked at him with such a similarity of expression that he expected to hear them give the same answers. And he was a little surprised to find, as he made them laugh and chat, that there were before him two very distinct women, one who had lived and one who was beginning to live. No, he did not see what would become of that child when its young mind, influenced by tastes and instincts that were yet dormant, should have grown and expanded amid the adventures of the world. It was a pretty little new person, ready for chances and for love, ignored and ignorant, who was sailing out of port like a vessel, while her mother was returning, having traversed life and loved!

He was moved at the thought that it was he whom she had chosen, and still preferred, this still pretty woman, rocked in that landau, in the balmy air of springtime.

His gratitude sought expression in a glance, which she understood, and he thought he felt her thanks in the rustle of her dress.

In his turn, he murmured:

"Oh, yes, what a beautiful day!"

When they had taken up the Duchess, in Rue de Varenne, they spun along towards the Invalides, crossed the Seine and reached the Avenue des Champs-Elyseés, going up toward the Arc

de Triomphe de l'Etoile, amid a sea of carriages.

The young girl had seated herself beside Olivier, riding backwards, and her eyes opened in
eager wonder upon this river of equipages.
Now and then, when the Duchess acknowledged
a salutation with a short motion of the head, she
would ask, " Who is that ? " He would answer,
" les Pontaiglin " or " les Puicelci " or " the
Countess de Lochrist " or " the beautiful Mme.
Mandeliere."

They were following the Avenue of the Bois
de Boulogne now, amidst the noise and the rumbling of wheels. The carriages, a little less
crowded than below the Arc de Triomphe,
seemed to struggle in an endless race. The
cabs, the heavy landaus, the solemn eight-spring
wagons, passed each other again and again, suddenly distanced by a rapid victoria drawn by a
single trotter, carrying along at a thundering
pace, through all that rolling crowd, plebeian and
aristocratic, through all societies, all classes, all
hierarchies, a young woman with an indolent air,
whose light and striking costume threw into the
carriages it grazed a strange perfume of some
unknown flower.

" Who is that lady ? " asked Annette.

" I don't know," Bertin answered, while the
Duchess and the Countess exchanged a smile.

The leaves were unfolding, the familiar night-

ingales of that Parisian garden were already singing in the young verdure, and when, as they
neared the lake they fell into line at a walk, it was
from carriage to carriage an incessant exchange
of greetings, smiles and pleasant words, as the
wheels touched. It seemed now like the gliding
of a fleet of boats in which were seated extremely
well-behaved ladies and gentlemen. The Duchess, who was bowing every instant before the
raised hats or lowered heads, seemed to sit in review and to refresh her memory with what she
knew, thought or supposed of people, as they de-
filed before her.

"Here, little one, look again at Mme. de Mandeliere, the beauty of the Republic."

In a light, coquettish carriage, the beauty of
the Republic, with apparent indifference to this
indisputable glory, permitted people to admire
her dark eyes, her low forehead under a helmet
of black hair, and her wilful mouth, a trifle too
large.

"Very beautiful, all the same," said Bertin.

The Countess did not enjoy hearing him praise
other women. She shrugged her shoulders
gently and answered nothing.

But the young girl, in whom the instinct of
rivalry was instantly aroused, ventured to say :

" I don't think so."

The painter turned round :

" What, you do not think her beautiful ? "

" No, she looks as if she had been dipped in ink."

The Duchess was laughing, delighted.

"Bravo, little one; here for six years half the men in Paris have been prostrating themselves before that negress. I believe they are making fools of us. Here, look rather at the Countess of Lochrist."

Alone in a landau, with a white poodle, the Countess, fine as a miniature, fair, with brown eyes, whose delicate lines for the last five or six years also had served as a theme for the pane-gyrics of her admirers, was bowing, a set smile upon her lips.

But Nanette still showed no enthusiasm.

" Oh," said she, " she is no longer quite fresh."

Bertin, who did not, ordinarily, in the daily discussions on these two rivals, agree with the Countess, was at once stung by this intolerance of a little girl.

"Bigre," said he, "be she loved little or much, she is charming, and I only wish you may be-come as pretty as she."

"Never mind," the Duchess replied, "you do not notice women until after they are thirty. The child is right. You only praise them when they have lost their freshness."

"Permit me, a woman is really beautiful only late, when all her expression is developed."

And enlarging upon this idea, that the first

bloom is but the varnish of the beauty which
ripens, he argued that men of the world are not
mistaken in paying small heed to young women
in all their brightness, and that they are right in
not considering them "beautiful" except in the
last period of their bloom.

The Countess, flattered, murmured:

"He is right; he judges like an artist. A
young face is very pretty, but always a little commonplace."

And the painter insisted, indicating at what
moment a face, losing by degrees the unsettled
grace of youth, takes its definite shape, its character, its physiognomy.

With a little motion of the head, indicating
conviction, the Countess assented to every word;
and the more he affirmed with the earnestness of
a pleasing advocate, the animation of an accused defending his cause, the more emphatic
became her approval with glance and gesture, as
though they were allied to resist a common danger, to defend themselves against a false and
threatening opinion. Annette was engrossed,
looking around her, and was hardly listening.
Her face, so often smiling, had grown grave, and
she was silent, giddy with joy in this commotion.
This sunshine, this verdure, these carriages, this
beautiful, rich and gay life, all this was hers.

Day after day she might thus come, in her turn
known, greeted, envied, and certain men point-

ing her out, would possibly say that she was beautiful. She looked for the men and women who appeared the most elegant, and always asked their names, troubling herself with no more than this collection of syllables, which at times awakened within her an echo of respect and admiration when she happened to have seen them often in the newspapers, or learned of them in history. She could not accustom herself to this procession of celebrities, and could not even quite believe that they were actual, as if she had been witnessing a theatrical performance. The cabs inspired her with scorn tinged with disgust; they annoyed and irritated her, and she suddenly exclaimed:

"It seems to me they should permit none but liveried carriages here."

Bertin answered:

"Well, young lady, and what about equality, liberty and fraternity ? "

She pouted as though to say, "Talk of that to somebody else," and continued:

"There might be a Bois for cabs, that of Vincennes, for instance."

"You are behind the age, little one, and you do not yet know that we are on a flood tide of democracy. However, if you wish to see the Bois free from all mixture, come in the morning; you will then see only the flower, the cream of society."

And he drew a picture, one of those he painted so well, of the Bois in the early morning, with its horsemen and amazons, of that choicest of all circles, where every one knows every one else, by his names, surnames, relations, titles, virtues and vices, as if all lived in the same "quartier" or the same little town.

" Do you come often ? " said she.

"Very often; it is really the most charming spot in Paris."

" Do you ride mornings ? "

"I do"

"And then afternoons, you make calls ? "

"Yes."

" Then when do you work ? "

" Why, I work—sometimes, and then as I have chosen a specialty after my tastes, as I am a painter of fine ladies, I am obliged to see them and follow them everywhere, a little."

She murmured, always gravely:

" On foot or horseback ? "

He glanced at her sideways, with a satisfied air that seemed to say: "Ha! ha! spirit already; you will do."

A breath of cold air swept by, come from afar, from the country which was hardly awake yet, and the whole Bois shivered, that coquettish, chilly and wordly park.

For a few seconds this chill caused the sprouting leaves to tremble on the trees, and garments

on the shoulders.   All the women with an almost
simultaneous motion brought upon their arms
and bosoms the wraps fallen behind them, and
the horses, from one end of the avenue to the
other, began to trot, as though the sharp breeze
that was coming had lashed them with a whip.

They returned quickly, to the silvery accom-
paniment of jingling curb chains, under an
oblique shower of red setting sunbeams.

"Are you returning home ? " asked the
Countess of the painter, whose every habit she
knew.

"No, I am going to the Club."

" Then, shall we drop you on the way ? "

"That will just suit me, thanks."

"And when do you invite us to breakfast with
the Duchess ? "

" Name your day."

This painter in ordinary to the "Parisiennes,"
whom his admirers had named a "realist Watteau" and his detractors a "photographer of
gowns and cloaks," often received at breakfast or
at dinner the beautiful persons whose features
he had reproduced, and also all the celebrated
and the well known, who were greatly amused
by these little fêtes in bachelor quarters.

"Day after to-morrow?   Does day after to-
morrow suit you, my dear Duchess ? " asked
Mme. de Guilleroy."

"Yes, indeed.   How charming of you. .. M.

Bertin never thinks of me for these affairs. It is very clear that I am no longer young."

The Countess accustomed to consider the artist's house almost as her own, replied:

"Only we four, the four of the landau, the Duchess, Annette, you and I, shall it be, great artist?"

"No one but ourselves," said he, alighting, "and I shall order you some crabs à *l'Alsacienne.*"

"Oh. You will give the little one ideas."

He bowed, standing at the carriage door, then quickly entered the vestibule of the main entrance to the Club, threw his overcoat and cane to the assembled footmen who had risen like soldiers at the passing of an officer, went up the wide staircase, encountered another body of servants in short breeches, pushed open a door, feeling suddenly alert as a young man, as he heard at the end of the lobby, the continuous click of clashing foils, the stamping of signals and exclamations in strong tones: "*Touche!*" "*A moi!*" "*Passe!*" "*J'en ai!*" "*Touche!*" "*A vous!*"

In the fencing hall the masters, dressed in gray linen, with leather vest, trousers tight around their ankles, a sort of apron falling in front of the body, one arm in the air, one hand falling back, while the other hand encased in the huge glove held the thin flexible foil, extended and recov-

ered with the abrupt agility of mechanical jump-
ing-jacks.

Others rested, chatted, still out of breath,
flushed, perspiring, handkerchief in hand to
sponge their faces and necks; others again seated
upon the square divan which lined the entire hall,
were looking at the fencing. Liverdy against
Landa, and the Club master, Taillade, against
the tall Rocdiane.

Bertin, smiling, feeling at home, was shaking
hands.

" I speak for you," cried the Baron de
Bavrie.

" I am with you, my dear fellow."

And he passed into the dressing room.

It was a long time since he had felt so nimble
and vigorous, and, conscious that he should do
well, he was hurrying with the impatience of a
schoolboy for his play. As soon as his adversary was before him he attacked him with great
energy, and in ten minutes he had struck him
eleven times, and so tired him out that the Baron
begged off. Then he fenced with Punisimont
and with his colleague Amaury Maldant.

The cold shower bath which followed, freez-
ing his palpitating flesh, reminded him of his
baths at twenty, when he used to dive into the
Seine from the bridges on the outskirts, late in
the Autumn, in order to confound his plebeian
audience.

"Are you going to dine here ?" Maldant asked.

" Yes."

" We have a table with Liverdy, Rocdiane and Landa ; hurry up ; it is a quarter past seven."

The dining-room was filled with men and the hum of their voices.

There were all the nocturnal vagabonds of Paris, idlers and workers, all those who from seven o'clock at night are at a loss to know what to do with themselves, and dine at the Club to catch at anything or anybody chance may offer them.

When the five friends were seated, the banker Liverdy, a vigorous and thick-set man of forty, said to Bertin :

" You were rampant this evening."

The painter answered :

" Yes, I could have done surprising things to-day."

The others smiled, and the landscape painter, Amaury Maldant, a thin, bald, grey-bearded little man, said shrewdly :

" I also feel always a return of the sap in April that makes me sprout a few leaves, half a dozen at the most ; then it runs into sentiment ; there is never any fruit."

The Marquis of Rocdiane and Count Landa felt sorry for him. Both of them older than he, though no expert eye could guess their age,

clubmen, horsemen, swordsmen, whose incessant exercise had given them bodies of steel, it
was their boast to be younger in everything than
the enervated scapegraces of the new generation.

Rocdiane was of good family, to be seen in all
salons, though suspected of financial involutions
of all sorts, which was not surprising, Bertin
would say, after having lived so long in the
" *tripots ;*" he was married, separated from his
wife, who paid him alimony, a director of Belgian
and Portuguese banks, and carried high upon
his energetic Don Quixotic face the somewhat
tarnished honor of an aristocratic factotum,
which was burnished now and then by the blood
which followed a sword thrust in a duel.

The Count of Landa, an amiable colossus,
proud of his size and shoulders, although married and the father of two children, dined at
home three times a week, with great difficulty,
and on other days remained at the Club, with
his friends, after the hour in the fencing hall.

The Club is a family, he would say, the family
of those who yet have none, of those who will
never have any, and of those who find their own
a bore.

The conversation, which started on the subject of women, passed from anecdote to reminiscence, from reminiscence to boasts, and thence
as far as incautious confidences.

The Marquis of Rocdiane permitted the names of his conquests to be surmised by unmistakable insinuations, fashionable women whose names he did not designate, that they might more easily be guessed. The banker Liverdy indicated his by their first names. He would say :—" I was at that time on the best of terms with the wife of a diplomat. Now, one evening upon leaving her, I said to her : ' My little Margaret ' "—he stopped amid the smiles, then proceeding : " Humph, something has escaped me. One should adopt the habit of calling all women ' Sophie. ' "

Olivier Bertin, very reserved, was in the habit of declaring, when he was questioned :

" As for me, I am content with my models."

They professed to believe him, and Landa who was simply a great rover, grew enthusiastic at the thought of all the pretty women who ran the streets and all the young persons who posed before the painter at ten francs an hour.

Gradually, as the bottles became empty, these grey-beards, as they were called by the young men of the Club, all these " grisons " whose faces were growing crimson, kindled, stirred by re-vived emotions and fermented fancies.

After coffee, Rocdiane was in the habit of fall-ing into more veracious deviations and of for-getting society women to celebrate the simple " cocottes."

"Paris," said he, a glass of kummel in his hand, "the only city where a man does not grow old, the only one where at fifty, so he be firm and well preserved, he will always find a young girl of twenty, as pretty as an angel, to love him."

Landa, finding again his Rocdiane of the cordials, encouraged him enthusiastically and enumerated the young girls who still adored him every day.

But Liverdy, more sceptical, and assuming a knowledge of the exact value of women, murmured:

"Yes, they tell you so—that they adore you."

Landa replied:

"They assure me, my dear fellow."

"Such assurances do not count."

"They suffice me."

Rocdiane was exclaiming:

"But they think it, sacrebleu! Do you think that a pretty little jade of twenty, who has been amusing herself for the past five or six years already, in Paris, where all moustaches have taught her to like kisses, and spoiled her taste for them, is still capable of distinguishing a man of thirty from one of sixty? What arrant nonsense! She has seen and known too many of them. Here, I'll wager that she prefers, way down in her heart, really prefers, an old banker to a young 'gommeux.' Does she know, does she reflect upon that ? Do men have an age here ? Eh ! my dear fellow, we grow young as we grow grey, and the greyer we grow, the more they tell us they love us, the more they show it, and the more they believe it."

They rose from the table, their blood stimulated and lashed by alcohol, ready for any conquest, and began to consider a way for disposing of the evening, Bertin naming the Cirque, and Rocdiane the Hippodrome, Maldant the Eden and Landa the Folies Bergère, when the light, faraway sound of violins being tuned reached them.

" Hallo ! " said Rocdiane, " there is music at the Club to-day."

" Yes," answered Bertin ; " suppose we listen for ten minutes before going out ? "

" Say we do."

They crossed a drawing-room, a billiard-room, a card-room, and then reached a sort of box above the musicians' gallery. Four gentlemen, buried in easy chairs, were already waiting, in a contemplative attitude, while below, in the midst of rows of empty seats, half a score more were chatting, seated or standing.

The orchestral conductor rapped on his desk with his bow ; they began.

Olivier Bertin worshiped music as some men worship opium. It evoked dreams.

As soon as the sonorous wave from the instruments had reached him he felt himself carried away in a sort of nervous intoxication, his mind and body vibrating indescribably. His imagination ran like mad, made drunk by melody, through soft reveries and happy dreams. With his eyes closed, legs crossed, arms inert, he listened to the sounds, and visions passing before his eyes sank into his mind.

The orchestra was playing a symphony of Haydn, and when his eyelids had fallen the painter saw again the Bois, the crowd of carriages about him, and before him in the landau, the Countess and her daughter. He heard their voices, followed their words, felt the motion of the carriage, breathed the air filled with the scent of leaves.

Thrice his neighbor speaking to him, interrupted this vision, which three times he began over again, as the motion of a vessel is revived when, after crossing the sea, one lies motionless in bed.

Then it extended, stretched out to a distant voyage, with the two women always seated before him, now on the railway, now at strange "tables d'hôte." During the whole time the music lasted they thus accompanied him, as if during that drive in the sunshine they had left the image of their two faces imprinted upon his retina.

There was silence, then a noise of voices and

of seats being removed which dispelled this vapor of a dream, and he perceived, dozing around him, his four friends, their simple listening attitudes changed to the careless ones of sleep.

After awaking them :

" Well, what shall we do now ? " he said.

" I feel like sleeping here a little longer," answered Rocdiane, candidly.

" So do I," added Landa.

Bertin rose :

" Well, I am going home, I feel a little weary."

He felt, on the contrary, very animated, but he wanted to go, fearing that end of the evening which he knew so well around the Club baccarat table.

He returned home, therefore, and the next day, after a restless night, one of those nights which puts artists in that condition of cerebral activity which is called inspiration, he decided not to go out, and to work until evening.

It was an excellent day, one of those days of facile production when conception seems to descend into the hands and fix itself upon the canvas.

With doors shut, aloof from the world, in the quiet of his home, closed to every one, in the friendly peace of his studio, his eye clear, his mind lucid, exalted, alert, he tasted that happiness granted to artists alone, that of bringing

forth their work in gladness. There was nothing
for him in the world during such working hours
but the piece of canvas upon which, under the
caresses of his brush, an image was born, and
he felt during these crises of fertility a strange,
beneficent sensation of abundant life which diffused itself intoxicatingly. At night he was exhausted as by a healthy fatigue, and he went
to sleep with an agreeable reflection upon his
breakfast on the morrow.

The table was covered with flowers, the
" menu " very choice, for Mme. de Guilleroy's
sake, who was a refined epicure, and, notwithstanding an emphatic but brief resistance, the
painter forced his guests to drink champagne.

" We shall have the child intoxicated," said
the Countess.

The indulgent Duchess answered :

" Mon Dieu ! there must be a first time."

Everybody, as they returned to the studio,
felt a little exhilarated under the influence of
that light gaiety which raises one up as though
wings were growing on the feet.

The Duchess and the Countess, being obliged
to meet with the " Committee of French Mothers," were to take the young girl back before
going to the Society, but Bertin offered to take
her for a walk, then to the Boulevard Malesherbes ; and they both departed.

" Let us take the longest way home," she said.

"Would you like to wander about the Monceau Park? It is a very pretty place, and we will look at the little children and the nurses."

"Yes, I should like that."

Passing through the Avenue Velasquez, they entered the gilded and monumental gate which serves for sign and entrance to that beautiful jewel of parks, displaying in the middle of Paris its artificial and flowery grace surrounded by a belt of princely mansions.

Along the wide walks which unroll their masterly curves through lawns and groves, crowds of people, seated upon iron chairs, gaze at the passersby, while in the little paths deep under the shade, winding along like streams, swarms of children crawl in the sand, run, jump the rope under the indolent eyes of the nurses or the uneasy watchfulness of mothers. The enormous trees, rounded into domes, like leafy monuments, the gigantic horse chestnuts, whose heavy foliage is splashed with white or red clusters, the conspicuous sycamores, the ornamental plane-trees with their highly polished trunks, set off the tall, waving grass into enticing perspectives.

The weather is warm, turtle doves are cooing in the foliage, and exchanging visits from the top of one tree to another, while sparrows bathe in the rainbow formed by the sunshine and the spray which is sprinkled over the fine grass. White statues upon their pedestals look happy in this green freshness. A young boy in marble extracts from his foot an introuvable thorn, as though he had just pricked himself while running after the Diana who is leaping yonder toward the little lake, imprisoned by the thickets that shelter the ruins of a temple.

Other statues, amorous and cold, embrace on the edge of the groves, or sit dreaming, with one knee in hand. A cascade rolls and foams over pretty rocks. A tree, broken like a column, supports an ivy vine ; a grave bears an inscription. The shafts of stone erected upon the sward hardly represent better the Acropolis than this elegant little park recalls wild forests.

It is the place, charming and artificial, where city dwellers go to scrutinize flowers grown in hot houses, and to admire, as one admires the spectacle of life at the theatre, that pleasing representation which gives in the very heart of Paris a beautiful bit of nature.

Olivier Bertin for years past had come almost every day to this choice spot to look at the " Parisiennes " moving about in their real frame. " It is a park made for dresses," he would say ; " ill-dressed people are shocking in it." And he roamed about for hours, knowing every plant and every habitual visitor.

He was walking by the side of Annette, along the avenues, his eye distracted by the motley, stirring life of the garden.

" Oh ! the lovely thing," she cried.

She was gazing at a little boy with fair hair who looked at her with his blue eyes, surprised and delighted.

Then she passed all the children in review, and the pleasure she felt in seeing those living, be-ribboned dolls made her chatty and communicative.

She walked slowly, giving Bertin the benefit of her remarks, her reflections on the little ones, the nurses and the mothers. She cried out for joy at the big children, while the puny ones moved her to pity.

He listened, amused by her more than by the children, and without forgetting his work, murmured : " It is delicious," thinking that he must do an exquisite picture, with a corner of the park, and a bouquet of nurses, mothers and children. Why had he never thought of it?

" You like those urchins ? " he asked.

" I adore them."

From the way she looked at them, he felt that she was aching to take them up, embrace them, caress them, the natural and tender desire of a future mother ; and he was surprised at this latent instinct hidden in this feminine nature.

As she was inclined to talk, he questioned her on her tastes. She confessed, with gentle simplicity, to hopes of worldly success and glory, wished for fine horses, which she knew with almost the accuracy of a jockey, for a portion of the Roncières farms were devoted to breeding ; and she took no more thought of a betrothed than of the apartment which one could always find in the multitude of houses to rent.

They approached the lake, where a pair of swans and half a dozen ducks were gently floating, as clean and calm as porcelain birds, and they passed before a young woman seated on a chair, a book open in her lap, her eyes looking upward before her, whose soul had taken flight in a dream.

She was as motionless as a wax figure. Homely, humble, dressed as a modest girl who is not thinking of pleasing, a teacher perhaps, she had gone to Dreamland, carried away by a phrase or word that had bewitched her heart. She was continuing, undoubtedly, according to the tendency of her hopes, the adventure commenced in the book.

Bertin stopped, surprised.

" How beautiful," said he, " to wander like that."

They had passed in front of her ; they turned back and passed again, without her perceiving them, so attentively did she follow the distant flight of her thought.

The painter said to Annette :

" I say, little one, would it bore you to pose in one or two figures for me ? "

" Not at all ; on the contrary."

" Look carefully at that young lady who is wandering in the realm of the ideal."

" Yonder in that chair ? "

" Yes. Well, you also will sit down in a chair, you will open a book on your knee and try to do what she does. Did you ever dream while awake ? "

" Yes, indeed."

" Of what ? "

And he tried to confess her concerning her ex-cursions in the blue ether ; but she would not answer, avoided his questions, looked at the ducks swimming out after the bread thrown them by a lady, and seemed embarrassed, as if he had touched a sensitive chord within her.

Then, to change the subject, she related her life at Roncières, spoke of her grandmother to whom she read aloud for a long while every day, and who must feel very lonely and sad now.

The painter as he listened felt as gay as a bird, gay as he had never been. All that she said to him, all the little, trifling and common-place details of that simple life of a young girl, amused and interested him.

" Let us sit down," said he.

They sat down near the water ; and the two swans came floating toward them, expecting to be fed.

Bertin felt recollections awakening within

him, recollections that had faded, drowned in
forgetfulness, and which suddenly revive, we
know not why. They rose rapidly, of varying
nature, so numerous at the same moment that
he experienced the sensation of a hand stirring
the mire of his memory.

He sought to know what caused this surging
up of his old life which several times already,
less powerfully than to-day, however, he had
felt and noticed. There was always a cause for
these sudden evocations, material and simple ;
a scent, often a perfume. How many times a
woman's dress had flung to him in passing, with
the evaporated breath of an essence, a full recollection of forgotten incidents. At the bottom of
old scent bottles he had also often found again
portions of his existence; and all the wandering
odors, of the streets, of the fields, of the houses,
of the furniture, the sweet and unwelcome, the
warm odors of summer evenings, the cold odors
of winter evenings, ever revived within him faraway memories, as if scents, like the aromatics
which preserve mummies, retained and em-
balmed these extinct events.

Was it the damp grass or the chestnut bloom
that so recalled the past ? No. What then ?
Was he indebted to his eye for this awakening ?
What had he seen ? Nothing. Among the people he had met, one of them perhaps resembled a face formerly known, and although he

failed to recognize it, rung within his heart all the changes of the past.

Was it not rather a sound? Very often he had by chance heard a piano, an unknown voice, even a hand organ on the square playing an old tune, had sometimes made him feel twenty years younger, filling his bosom with forgotten sensations.

But that continuous, incessant, intangible, almost irritating appeal! What was there around him, near him, so to revive his extinguished emotions ?

" It is a little cool," he said; " let us go home."

They rose and resumed their walk.

He was looking at the poor seated on the benches, for whom a chair was too expensive a luxury.

And Annette also was observing them, and felt uncomfortable at the thought of their existence, their callings, surprised that, looking so pitiable, they should come to lounge in this beautiful public garden.

And yet, more than he had a little while before, Olivier was threading the past years. It seemed to him that a fly was humming in his ears, filling them with the confused buzzing of spent days.

The young girl, noticing his dreamy mood, asked :

" What is the matter ? You look sad."

And he was stirred to his heart. Who had
said that ? She or her mother ? Not her mother
with her present voice, but with her former
voice, so changed that he had only just recognized it.

He replied with a smile :

" Nothing ; I am enjoying myself very much ;
you are very pleasant ; you remind me of your
mother."

How was it that he had not recognized sooner
this strange echo of the once so familiar voice,
now coming from fresh lips ?

" Talk on," said he.

" Of what ?"

" Tell me what your governesses have taught
you. Did you like them ? "

And she began to chat again.

And he listened, seized by a growing anxiety ;
he watched, waited, among the phrases of this
little girl, almost a stranger to his heart, for a
word, a sound, a laugh, which seemed to have
lingered in her throat since her mother's youth.
An intonation sometimes made him tremble with
astonishment. Assuredly, there were differences
in their speech, the similarity of which he had
not at first noticed, so great that often he even
no longer confounded them at all, but these differences rendered all the more striking this sudden echo of the maternal speech. Thus far he
had observed the likeness of their faces with a

friendly and curious eye, but lo! the mystery of this resurrected voice mingled them in such a fashion that turning his head in order not to see the young girl, he questioned sometimes if it were not the Countess who was speaking to him thus—twelve years ago.

Then, when deluded by this conjuration, he turned towards her, he still found, as their glances met, a little of that faltering with which in the early days of their love the eye of the mother had rested upon him.

They had already gone three times around the park, always passing before the same persons, the same nurses, the same children.

Annette was now inspecting the mansions which surround the garden, inquiring the names of their inmates.

She wished to know everything about all these people, questioned with a voracious curiosity, seemed to store her feminine memory with this information, and, her face lighted up with interest, listened with the eyes as much as with the ears.

But when they arrived at the pavilion which separates the two gates on the outward boulevard, Bertin noticed that it was nearly four o'clock.

" Oh ! " he said, " we must go home."

And they quietly reached the Boulevard Malesherbes.

After he had left the young girl the painter went down towards the " Place de la Concorde," to make a call on the other bank of the Seine.

He was humming, wanted to run, and would willingly have leaped over the benches, so agile did he feel. Paris looked radiant to him, prettier than ever. " Undoubtedly," he said, " Spring revarnishes everybody."

He was in one of those moods of exaltation when the mind comprehends everything with keener pleasure, when the eye sees more perfectly, seems more receptive and clear, when one finds a livelier joy in seeing and feeling, as if an all-powerful hand had revivified all the colors of the earth, reanimated all conscious life, and wound up again in us, like a watch that has stopped, the activity of sensation.

He thought, as he gathered in his vision a thousand amusing incidents, " To think that there are moments when I find no subject for painting!"

And he experienced such a sense of freedom and clear sightedness that all his artistic work seemed trivial to him, and he conceived a new method of expressing life, the truest and most original. And suddenly he was seized with a desire to return home and work, which led him to retrace his steps and shut himself up in his studio.

But no sooner was he alone before the picture already begun than the ardor which but just now had fired his blood cooled. He felt weary, sat down on the divan, and again relapsed into dreams.

The sort of happy indifference in which he was living, that unconcern of the satisfied man whose almost every want is gratified, was gradually leaving his heart, as though something were wanting. He felt that his house was empty and his studio deserted. Then, looking about him, he seemed to see the shadow of a woman whose presence was sweet to him pass by. For a long time he had forgotten the impatience of the lover awaiting his mistress's return, and lo! all at once he felt that she was afar, and he wished her near, with the restlessness of youth.

It moved him to think how much they had loved each other, and in that vast apartment, where she had come so often, he found again innumerable memories of herself, her gestures, her words, her kisses. He recalled certain days, certain hours, certain moments; and he felt around him the soft touch of her former caresses.

He rose, unable any longer to keep still, and began to walk, thinking once more that notwithstanding this affection which had so filled his life, he yet remained alone—always alone. After the long hours of work, when he looked around him, dazed by the awakening of the man who returns to life, he saw and felt only walls within

reach of his hand and voice. Since no woman
presided over his home, and he had been unable
to meet her whom he loved except with the
stealth of a thief, he had been compelled to drag
his leisure into public places, where one finds,
or purchases, various means of killing time. He
had adopted the habit of going to the Club, to
the Cirque and the Hippodrome, on fixed days,
to the Opera, here, there and everywhere, in
order not to return to his home, where he would
doubtless have rested joyfully had he dwelt there
beside her.

In the earlier days, in certain moments of passionate fondness, he had suffered cruelly in his
inability to take and keep her with him; then,
with diminished ardor, he had accepted unresistingly their separation and his own liberty ;
now he regretted them again as if he were beginning anew to love her.

And this recourse of tenderness absorbed him
so unexpectedly, almost unreasonably, because
the weather was fine, and perhaps because he
had just now recognized the rejuvenated voice
of that woman. How little it takes to move a
man's heart, a man who is growing old, for
whom recollection turns into regret!

As formerly, the need of seeing her again returned and took possession of his mind and body
like a fever; and he began to think of her somewhat as young lovers do, exalting her in his

heart, and growing elate in his renewed longing for her; then he resolved, though he had seen her that morning, to go and ask for a cup of tea that very evening.

The hours seemed long, and, as he went out and down the Boulevard Malesherbes, he was seized with a fear of not finding her, which would compel him to still spend the evening alone, as, after all, he had spent so many others.

To his question: " Is the Countess at home ? " the servant answering, " Yes, sir," filled him with joy.

With a radiant air he said: " It is I again," as he appeared at the threshold of the little salon where the two ladies were working under the pink shades of a double lamp of English metal, upon a high thin standard.

The Countess exclaimed:

" What, is it you?   How delightful ! "

" Why, yes.   I felt very lonely, so I came."

" How kind of you."

" You are expecting some one ?"

" No—perhaps—I can never tell."

He had seated himself, gazing scornfully at the piece of grey knitting of heavy wool which they were rapidly executing by means of long wooden needles.

" What is that ? " he asked.

" Coverlets."

" For the poor ? "

" Yes, of course."

" It is very ugly."

" It is very warm."

" Possibly, but it is very ugly, especially in a
Louis XV. apartment where everything is pleasing to the eye.   If not for the sake of your poor,
you should, for the sake of your friends, let your
alms be more elegant."

" Dear me, these men ! " she said, shrugging
her shoulders. " Why, they are making blankets
of this kind everywhere just now."

" I know it well; I know it too well.   One
may no longer make a call of an evening without
seeing that frightful grey rag dragging over the
prettiest gowns and the daintiest pieces of furniture.   This Spring it is a benefaction in poor
taste which is the fashion."

The Countess, to test the truth of his opinion,
spread out the knitting she held upon an unoccupied silk chair at her side, then assented with
indifference:

" Yes, indeed, it is ugly."

And she resumed her work.   A flood of light
fell upon the two bended heads, a pink glimmer
from the two shaded lamps, over the hair and
the flesh of the faces, extending to the dresses
and the busy hands ; and they watched their
work with that light, continuous attention of
women accustomed to this labor of the fingers
which the eye follows without a thought.

At the four corners of the room four more lamps of Chinese porcelain, supported by ancient columns of gilded wood, shed upon the tapestry a mellow, even light softened by transparencies of lace thrown over the globes.

Bertin took a very low seat, a dwarf armchair, into which he could just get, but which he had always preferred while chatting with the Countess, placing him almost at her feet.

She said to him:

"You took a long walk with Nané a little while ago in the park."

"Yes; we gossiped like old friends. I like her very much, your daughter. She resembles you altogether. When she utters certain phrases, one would believe that you had forgotten your voice in your mouth."

"My husband has already told me that very often."

He watched them work, bathed in the light of the lamps, and the thought which had made him suffer so often, from which he had suffered again that very day, the anxiety concerning his desolate home, still, silent, cold, whatever the weather might be, whatever fire there be kindled in the chimney or the furnace, grieved him as if for the first time he quite understood his isolation.

Oh! how truly he would that he were the husband of that woman and not her lover. Formerly he had wished to carry her off, to take her

from this man, to steal her from him completely.
To-day he envied that deceived husband who
was installed by her side forever, in the habits
of her house and the caressing influence of her
presence. Looking at her he felt his heart full
of old things revived that he desired to say to
her. Truly, he loved her much yet, even a little
more, much more to-day than he had for a long
time, and this need of expressing to her this return of youth, which would please her so much,
made him wish they would send the little girl
to bed as soon as possible.

Beset by this desire to be alone with her, to
get close to her knees, on which he might rest
his head, to take her hands, from which she
would let fall the coverlet of the poor, the
wooden needles, and the ball of worsted which
would go rolling under a chair at the end of a
string, he looked at the clock, scarcely spoke,
and thought it really reprehensible to accustom
young girls to spend their evenings with their
elders.

Steps broke the silence in the adjoining room,
and the servant, whose head appeared, announced:

" M. de Musadieu."

Olivier Bertin restrained a rising rage, and
when he shook hands with the " Inspector des
Beaux-Arts " he felt much inclined to take him
by the shoulders and throw him out.

Musadieu was full of news; the ministry was about to fall, and there was a scandal whispered about concerning the Marquis of Rocdiane. He added, glancing at the young girl, " I will tell you that a little later."

The Countess looked up at the clock and discovered that it was about to strike ten.

" It is time for you to retire, my child;" she said, addressing her daughter.

Annette, without replying, folded her work, wound up her worsted, kissed her mother's cheeks, held out her hand to the two men and left the room swiftly, as if she had glided away without disturbing the air as she passed.

When she had gone:

" Well, your scandal?" asked the Countess.

" They say that the Marquis of Rocdiane, who had separated from his wife, under an amicable arrangement, she paying him an income considered by him insufficient, had found a certain and unusual means to get it doubled. The Marchioness, shadowed by his order, had been surprised and had been obliged to purchase with a new pension the official report drawn up by the commissary of police."

The Countess listened, with curiosity in her glance, hands motionless, holding her interrupted work in her lap.

Bertin, who was already exasperated by Musadieu's presence since the withdrawal of the

young daughter, was annoyed, and asserted with
the indignant manner of a man who knows, and
who has not chosen to discuss the calumny with
any one, that it was an odious lie, one of those
shameless slanders that society should never listen to or repeat.   He was growing angry, standing now against the chimney, with the nervous
manner of a man disposed to make a personal
question of a common report.

Rocdiane was his friend, and if on certain
occasions he might have been accused of levity,
he could not be accused, or even suspected, of
any really questionable act. Musadieu, surprised
and embarrassed, was defending himself, reced-
ing, finding excuses.

" Permit me," said he, " I heard that state-
ment just now at the house of the Duchess of
Mortemain."

Bertin asked:

" Who told you that?   A woman, without
doubt."

" No, not at all; it was the Marquis of Farandal."

And the painter, in a fidget, answered:

" That does not surprise me, from him.".

There was silence.   The Countess resumed her
work.   Then Olivier continued in a calmed voice:

" I know to some purpose that it is false."

He knew nothing of the kind, having just
heard the story for the first time.

Musadieu was preparing to retreat, finding the position dangerous, and he was already suggesting his departure, to pay a call on the Corbelles, when the Count de Guilleroy, who had dined in town, appeared.

Bertin sat down again, overwhelmed, despairing now of being able to get rid of the husband.

"You do not know the great scandal of the evening?" said the Count.

As no one answered, he continued:

"It seems that Rocdiane has surprised his wife under compromising circumstances, and is making her pay for the indiscretion very dearly."

Then Bertin, looking distressed, with grief in his voice and gestures, laying his hand upon De Guilleroy's knee, repeated in gentle, friendly terms, what he had just seemed to fling into Musadieu's face.

And the Count, half convinced, sorry to have lightly repeated a doubtful and possibly compromising tale, pleaded his ignorance and innocence. Indeed, people repeated so many false and wicked things.

In a moment all were agreed upon this: that people accuse, suspect and slander with deplorable facility, and for five minutes the entire party seemed convinced that all whispered gossip is false, that women never have the lovers they are supposed to have, that men never do the

9

infamous things of which they are accused; in
brief, that the surface is much worse than the
depths.

Bertin, who was no longer incensed at Musadieu since Guilleroy's arrival, said some compli-
mentary things to him, started him on his favorite topics, opened the floodgate of his eloquence,
and the Count seemed pleased, like a man who
carries with him everywhere conciliation and
cordiality.

Two servants whose steps were muffled in the
carpet, entered, bearing the tea table on which
the boiling water was steaming in a pretty shining service over the bluish flame of an alcohol
lamp.

The Countess arose, poured the warm bever-
age with all the care and precaution introduced
by the Russians, then offered Musadieu a cup,
another to Bertin, and returned with plates containing sandwiches " aux foie gras " and delicate
Austrian and English pastry.

The Count approaching the movable table,
on which there was also a row of syrups, cordials
and glasses, concocted a grog, then consider-
ately slipped into the adjoining room and disappeared.

Again Bertin found himself face to face with
Musadieu, and again he was violently possessed
with the desire of throwing out this bore, who,
full of vivacity, was now, by way of peroration,

relating anecdotes, repeating witticisms, was even witty himself. And the painter continuously looked at the clock whose long hand was approaching midnight. The Countess saw his glance, understood that he wished to speak to her, and with the tact of skilful society women in changing, by imperceptible stages, the tone of a conversation or the atmosphere of a drawing-room, in making one understand, without a word, that he is to remain or to leave, she threw around her by her attitude, the expression of her face and the weariness of her eyes, a sort of chill, as though she had just opened the window.

Musadieu felt this draught congealing his thoughts, and, without asking himself why, he felt a disposition to rise and withdraw.

Bertin courteously followed his example. The two men withdrew together, crossing the two drawing-rooms, accompanied by the Countess, who kept chatting with the painter. She detained him on the threshold of the antechamber for a casual explanation, while Musadieu, assisted by a footman, was putting on his overcoat. As Mme. de Guilleroy continued talking with Bertin, the Commissioner of Fine Arts waiting a few seconds before the door of the stairway, held open by the other servant, finally decided to go out alone, in order not to remain standing before the valet.

The door was quietly closed upon him, and the Countess carelessly asked the artist:

"Why, after all, do you leave so early? It is not midnight. Do stay a little while longer."

And they re-entered together the little salon.

As soon as they were seated:

"Heavens! how exasperating that dunce was," said he.

"And why?"

"He was taking from me a little of yourself."

"Oh! not much."

"It is possible, but he annoyed me."

"Are you jealous?"

"To find a man an incumbrance is not an exhibition of jealousy."

He had resumed his little arm-chair, and, quite near her now, he fingered the cloth of her dress, as he told her of the warm breath that had blown in his heart that day.

She listened, surprised, delighted, and laid a hand on his white hair, gently stroking it as if to thank him.

"I wish so much that I might live near you!" he said.

He kept thinking of that husband, reposing, asleep probably, in a neighboring room, and continued:

"There is really only marriage to unite two lives."

She murmured:

"My poor friend"—full of compassion for him, and also for herself.

He had laid his cheek upon the Countess's knees, and was looking at her fondly, a fondness mingled with a little melancholy, a little pain—less burning than a few moments before, when he was separated from her by her daughter, her husband and Musadieu.

She said, smiling, as she continued to draw her light fingers through his hair:

"Dear me! how white you are. Your last black hair has disappeared."

"Alas! I know it; time flies."

She feared to have saddened him:

"Oh! but you were grey quite young. I have always known you pepper and salt."

"Yes, that is true."

To efface completely the shade of regret she had summoned she leaned over and, raising his head between her hands, kissed his forehead slowly and tenderly, with those lingering kisses which it seemed should never end.

Then they looked at each other, seeking in the depths of their eyes the reflection of their love.

"I should very much like," said he, "to spend a whole day by your side."

He felt vaguely tormented by an inexpressible need of intimate companionship.

He had thought a moment ago that the de-

parture of the people who were there would
suffice to realize that desire, aroused since morning, and, now that he was alone with his love,
he felt the warmth of her hands upon his forehead and against his cheek, through her dress
the warmth of her body; he found in himself
again the same restlessness, the same incomprehensible and fleeting desire for affection.

And he imagined now that outside of that
house, in the woods, perhaps, where they would
be quite alone, with nobody near them, this dis-
quietude of his heart would be satisfied and
calmed.

She murmured:

"What a child you are! But we see each
other almost every day."

He begged her to find means to come and
breakfast with him somewhere in the suburbs of
Paris, as they had formerly done occasionally.

This caprice astonished her, it was so difficult
to realize it, now that her daughter had returned.

She would try, however, as soon as her husband should go to Ronces, but that would not
be until after "varnishing" day, which was the
following Saturday.

"And between now and then," said he, "when
shall I see you?"

"To-morrow night at the Corbelles. Besides, come here Thursday, at three o'clock, if

you are disengaged, and I believe we are to dine together at the Duchess's on Friday."

" Yes; very well."

He arose.

" Good-bye."

" Good-bye, my friend."

He remained standing, hesitating to leave, for he had found almost nothing of all he had come to say to her, and his mind remained full of unexpressed thoughts, full of vague effusions which were still suppressed.

He repeated " Good-bye " as he took her hands.

" Good-bye, my friend."

" I love you."

She gave him one of those smiles in which a woman reveals to a man in an instant all that she has given him.

With palpitating heart he repeated for the third time: " Good bye."

Then he went out.

CHAPTER IV.

On that day one would have thought that all the carriages of Paris were making a pilgrimage to the Palais de l'Industrie. Since nine o'clock in the morning they had been gathering from all the streets, avenues and bridges, toward the hall of Fine Arts, where artistic " Tout Paris " had invited fashionable " Tout Paris " to be present at the simulated varnishing of three thousand and four hundred pictures.

A long line was crowding against the doors, and, disdaining sculpture, ascended at once to the picture galleries. Already, in mounting the steps, were to be seen canvases exhibited upon the walls of the stairway where are hung the special category of vestibule painters who have either sent works of uncommon proportions or works the refusal of which might scarcely be ventured. In the square salon there was a surging crowd, clamorous and confused. The painters, on exhibition themselves till evening, were to be recognized by their activity, their sonorous voices and authoritative gestures. They were beginning to drag their friends by the sleeve toward pictures which they indicated with a wave of the arm, with exclamations and the

136

energetic assumption of connoisseurs. They
were of all sorts, tall, long-haired, wearing grey
or black soft hats of shapes indescribable, broad
and round like roofs, with sloping brims, shading
a man's entire bust. Others were small, active,
slender or stout, with silken ties, arrayed in short
jackets, or encased in the hybrid costumes char-
acteristic of young art students.

There were the clique of the " elegant," of the
" gommeux," of the artist of the boulevard; the
clique unexceptionable, of academicians, decorated with red rosettes, huge or microscopic,
according to their various conceptions of elegance and " bon-ton," the clique of the plebeian
painters, supported by their families, surround-
ing the father like a triumphal choir.

Upon the four gigantic panels hung those
paintings admitted to the honor of the " Salon
carré," dazzling even at the entrance by the
brightness of the tones, the flashing of the frames
and the crudeness of new colors heightened by
the varnish, blinding under the merciless light
falling from above.

The portrait of the President of the Republic
faced the door, while upon another wall a general attired in scarlet breeches, gold lace and
ostrich plumes, consorted with woodland
nymphs, attired in nothing, beneath some wil-
lows, and a laboring ship almost engulfed in the
waves; a mediæval bishop excommunicating a

barbarian king, a street of the Orient reeking
with pestiferous dead, the shade of Dante on an
excursion to Hades, attracted and captured
one's glance by the irresistible violence of expression.

The immense room afforded also a charge of
cavalry, some forest skirmishers, some grazing
cows, two lords of the last century engaged in
mortal combat on a street corner, a mad-woman
resting upon a curbstone, a priest ministering
at a death-bed, a sunset, a moonlight, reapers,
rivers, and finally, examples of all that has been.
is now, and ever will be done by painters until
the day of doom.

Olivier, in the midst of a group of famous colleagues, members of the Institute and of the
Jury, was exchanging views with them. He
felt uneasiness, oppressive concern about his own
picture, regarding the success of which he did
not feel assured, notwithstanding eager congratulations. He rushed forward. The Duchess of
Mortemain had appeared at the entrance.

She asked:

" Has not the Countess arrived ? "

" I have not seen her."

" And M. Musadieu ? "

" Nor him."

" He had promised me to be at the head of
the staircase at ten o'clock to show me through
the rooms."

"Will you permit me to take his place, Duchess ?"

"No, no; your friends need you. We shall meet again presently, for I expect that we shall breakfast together."

Musadieu was arriving in haste; he had been detained a few moments in the Department of Sculpture, and was making his excuses, already out of breath, saying:

"This way, Duchess, this way; we begin at the right."

They had just disappeared in an eddy of heads, when the Countess of Guilleroy, on the arm of her daughter, entered, looking around for Olivier Bertin.

He saw and joined his friends, saying, as he greeted them:

"Heavens! how pretty they are! Really, Nannette grows pretty by the hour. In a week she has changed."

He watched her with his keen glance, adding:

"The lines are softer, more blended, the complexion more brilliant. She is already much less of a young girl and much more of a 'Parisienne.'"

But suddenly he returned to the great absorbing business of the day.

"Let us begin at the right; we shall soon overtake the Duchess."

The Countess, familiar with everything per-taining to painting and as preoccupied as an exhibitor, asked:

" What do they say ? "

" Fine salon: The Bonnat is remarkable, two excellent Carolus Durans, an admirable Puvis de Chaovannnes, an astounding Roll, entirely new; an exquisite Gervex and a great many others, some Berauds, some Cazins, some Duez—in short, a heap of good things."

" And you ? " she asked.

" They compliment me, but I am not content."

" You never are content."

" Yes, sometimes. But to-day, really, I think I am right."

" Why ? "

" I do not know."

" Let us go and see."

When they reached the picture—two little peasant girls bathing in a brook—they found an admiring group before it. She was pleased, and speaking low:

" Why, it is delightful; it is a gem; you have done nothing better."

He pressed close to her lovingly, grateful for every word that soothed a pain or assuaged a wound. Various arguments flashed through his mind in the attempt to convince himself that she was right; that she must see correctly, with

the intelligent eyes of a " Parisienne." He forgot, in his effort to reassure himself, that for
twelve years past he had justly reproached her
with undue admiration for elfish pranks, dainty
elegance, the expression of sentiment and fashion's illegitimate vagaries, and never art, art
alone, art untrammeled by ideas, by fashionable
tendencies and prejudices.

Still guiding them, " Let us keep on," he said.

And he walked with them for a long time, from
room to room, showing them the pictures, explaining the subjects, happy between them,
made happy by them.

Suddenly the Countess asked:

" What time is it ? "

" Half-past twelve."

" Oh! Let us hurry to breakfast. The
Duchess is to wait for us at Ledoyen's, where
she requested me to bring you, if we did not
find her again in the galleries."

The restaurant, in the centre of an islet of trees
and shrubbery, seemed like a humming, overflowing bee-hive. Around it and from all the
windows and wide-open doors came the confused murmur of voices, of calls, and the clink-
ing of glass and china. The crowded tables,
surrounded by people breakfasting, were scattered in long lines down the neighboring walks,
to the right and left of the narrow passage
through which the waiters were darting, deaf-

ened, excited, holding at arm's length trays,
loaded with meats, fish and fruit.

There was such a multitude of men and women
under the circular gallery that they looked like
animated dough. They laughed, shouted, ate
and drank, made merry by the wine and inun-
dated with that cheer which, with the sunlight,
falls upon Paris on certain days.

A waiter conducted the Countess, Annette
and Bertin to the private room where the Duchess was waiting.

As he entered, the painter perceived, near his
aunt, the Marquis of Farandal, attentive and
smiling, holding out his arms to receive the para-
sols and wraps of the Countess and her daughter.
He felt such a rush of annoyance that he was
almost overcome by the temptation to be disagreeable.

The Duchess explained the meeting with her
nephew and M. Musadieu's departure, who had
been carried away by the Minister of Fine Arts;
and Bertin, at the thought that this beauish
Marquis was to marry Annette, that he was
there on her account, that he already looked
upon her as destined for his arms, was growing
nervous and rebellious, as though his mysterious
and sacred rights were violated and unrecog-
nized.

As soon as they were seated at the table the
Marquis—by the young girl's side—devoted

himself to her with that assured air of a man authorized to pay his court.

His glances were full of a curiosity that seemed impertinent and inquisitive to the painter, self-satisfied smiles that were almost tender, and a familiar and officious gallantry. There appeared already something decided in his manner and words, like the announcement of a not distant investiture title.

The Duchess and the Countess seemed to favor and approve this air of a suitor, and exchanged confederate glances.

Immediately after breakfast they returned to the Exhibition. The rooms were so crowded that it was almost impossible to enter. The atmosphere was sickening and heavy with living heat and a dull personal odor of dresses and coats which had long since lost their freshness. People were no longer gazing at the pictures, but rather at the faces and the toilettes, looking for well known characters; and there was sometimes a crush in that thick mass momentarily half opened to permit the passing of the tall double ladder of the varnishers crying: " Attention, messieurs; attention, mesdames."

Within five minutes, the Countess and Olivier found themselves separated from the others. He wanted to find them, but she said, as she leaned upon him:

" Isn't this all right? Let them go, since it

is arranged that if we lose each other we are to meet at four at the 'buffet.' "

" True," he said.

But he was absorbed in the thought that the Marquis was accompanying Annette and was besieging her with his affected and conceited gallantry.

The Countess murmured:

" You still love me, then ? "

He answered, absent-mindedly:

" Why, certainly."

And he endeavored to discover M. de Farandal's grey hat over the people's heads.

Conscious that he was abstracted, and anxious to recall his thoughts to herself, she continued:

" If you knew how delighted I am with your picture of this year! It is your masterpiece."

He smiled, at once forgetting the young people, remembering only her solicitude of the morning.

" Really? You think so ? "

" Yes; I prefer it to any of them."

" It has cost me much trouble."

With insinuating words she entwined him anew, having long since learned that nothing is more potent with an artist than loving and unceasing flattery. Captivated, reanimated, cheered by those sweet phrases, he began to chat again, seeing no one but her, listening to her only in that great floating, tumultuous crowd.

To thank her, he murmured in her ear:

" I have a wild desire to embrace you ! "

A wave of emotion swept over her, and lifting her shining eyes to his, she repeated the question:

" You still love me, then ? "

And he answered this time with the intonation she desired, and which she had not heard a moment ago.

" Yes, I love you, my dear Any."

" You will come to see me often, evenings ? " she said. " Since my daughter is with me I seldom go out."

Now that she observed in him that unexpected revival of tenderness, a great happiness filled her heart. Since Olivier's hair had grown white and years had brought tranquillity, she feared far less that he should be charmed by another woman than that in his horror of solitude he should marry. This fear, already old, was ceaselessly growing, and gave birth in her mind to impossible projects for having him near her as much as practicable, in order to prevent his spending long evenings in the cold silence of his empty house. Unable to always attract and retain him, she suggested distractions, sent him to the theatre, urged him to go into society, preferring rather to know him in the society of women than in the sadness of his home.

She continued, following her secret thought:

" Ah ! if I could keep you always, how I should spoil you ! Promise to come very often, since I shall no longer go out much."

" I promise you."

A voice murmured near her ear:

" Mamma."

The Countess, startled, turned and found Annette, the Duchess and the Marquis joining them.

" It is four o'clock," said the Duchess. " I am very tired and would like to go."

The Countess answered:

"I am going also, I am completely tired out."

They reached the inner staircase which starts from the galleries, where drawings and water colors are hung in line, and overlooks the immense glass-covered garden where the statuary is exhibited.

From the landing of this stairway one could see from one end to the other of this gigantic hot-house filled with statues disposed about the walks, around clumps of green shrubbery, and overtopping the black, billowy mass of humanity that covered the grounds. It seemed a dark damask of hats and shoulders from which the white, gleaming marbles seemed to spring, rending it in a thousand places.

As Bertin bowed to the ladies at the exit, Mme. de Guilleroy whispered to him:

" Then, are you coming this evening ? "

" Yes, indeed."

He re-entered the Exhibition to have a chat with the artists about the impressions of the day.

The painters and sculptors were standing in knots around the statues, before the buffet, and there they engaged in discussion, as they did every year, supporting and attacking the same ideas, with the same arguments, upon very much the same kind of work. Olivier, who ordinarily became excited in these discussions, being specially endowed with a gift of repartee and disconcerting onslaughts, and having the reputation of a clever theorist, of which he was proud, exerted himself to become impassioned; but his perfunctory answers interested him no more than what he heard, and he was tempted to go away, to listen no longer, to understand no further, knowing beforehand all that would be said upon these questions of art, every phase of which he knew.

Yet he liked those things, and had liked them hitherto almost exclusively; but on this day his mind was diverted from them by one of those small, though tenacious preoccupations, one of those little cares, which it would seem ought not to disturb, but which is there, despite everything, whatever we may say or do, fixed in the mind like an invisible thorn in the flesh.

He had even forgotten his concern for his " Bathers," only to remember the unpleasant bearing of the Marquis toward Annette. What mattered it to him, after all? Had he any right? Why should he have desired to prevent this precious marriage, settled in advance, and suitable from every point of view? But no argument would efface that impression of discomfort and discontent which had taken possession of him when he saw Farandal talking and smiling as if he were betrothed, caressing with his glances the face of the young girl.

When he entered the house of the Countess that evening and found her alone with her daughter, continuing by the light of the lamps their knitting for the poor, he had great difficulty in refraining from words of scorn and disparagement of the Marquis, and revealing to Annette's eyes all the veiled vulgarity of his " chic."

For a long while past, in these after-dinner calls, he often fell into a rather sleepy silence and the easy attitudes of an old friend who no longer stands upon ceremony. Buried in his easy chair, with his legs crossed and head thrown back, he would talk dreamily, resting his body and his mind in this tranquil intimacy. But lo! suddenly, he was aroused again, and felt that activ-

ity of a man who exerts himself to please, who
is interested in what he is about to say, and who
in the presence of certain people seeks the most
rare and brilliant expressions of his ideas in order
to render them more captivating. He no longer let the conversation drag, but sustained and
enlivened it, lashing it with his fervor; and when
he had provoked a joyous peal of laughter from
the Countess and her daughter, or when he felt
that they were moved, or lifted their eyes to him
in surprise, or discontinued their work to listen
to him, he experienced a sensation of pleasure,
a little shiver of success which rewarded him for
his trouble.

He came whenever he knew them to be alone,
and never, perhaps, had he spent such happy
evenings.

Mme. de Guilleroy, whose constant fears were
allayed by this assiduity, exerted every means
to attract and hold him. She declined invitations to dine in town, to balls and theatres, that
she might have the pleasure of going out at
three o'clock and throwing into the telegraph
box the little blue message that said: "We
shall see you presently." At first, desiring to
afford him sooner the tête-à-tête he sought, she
sent her daughter to bed when the clock struck
ten. Then, noticing one day that he evinced
surprise at it, and asked laughingly that Annette be no longer treated like a naughty little

child, she granted a quarter of an hour's grace, then half an hour, then an hour. He did not remain long, however, after the young girl had retired, as if half the charm which held him there had gone out with her. Immediately drawing near the Countess' feet, he would sit quite close to her, and with a coaxing gesture, rest his cheek now and then against her knees. She would give him one of her hands, which he held in his, and this feverish mental excitement suddenly subsiding, he would stop talking, and seem to rest in loving silence from the efforts he had made.

Little by little, she grew to understand, with woman's keen intuition, that Annette attracted him almost as much as herself. This did not trouble her, but she was happy that he might find with them something of the home life of which she had deprived him; and she enchained him as much as she could between them, playing mother that he might almost believe himself the father of this little girl, and that a new element of tenderness might be added to all that charmed him in that house.

Her coquetry, always on the alert, but accentuated since she felt on all sides certain hints, as yet almost imperceptible, the innumerable attacks of age, took a more active form. To become as slender as Annette, she continued to drink nothing, and the real slenderness of her

waist restored to her indeed the figure of a
young girl so far, that from behind, they could
scarcely be distinguished from one another, but
her face, grown thin, suffered under this treat-
ment. The skin, once distended, formed
wrinkles and assumed a yellowish tint which rendered the superb freshness of the child the more
striking. Then she protected her face by the
processes of the stage, and although she thus
created for herself a rather suspicious fairness
in the strong light of day, she obtained under
the gaslight that artificial and charming brilliancy which gives an incomparable complexion
to well-painted women.

The realization of this decadence and the employment of these artifices modified her habits.
She avoided as much as possible comparisons
in broad daylight, and sought them by the light
of the lamps, which gave her an advantage.
When she felt fatigued, pale, older than usual,
she had accommodating headaches, which
caused her to forego balls or theatres; but on
those days when she felt at her best she tri-
umphed, and played the elder sister with the
grave modesty of the young mother. In order
that her appearance should be always similar to
her daughter's she gave her dresses suitable for
a young matron, somewhat grave for her; and
Annette, whose playful and vivacious character
became more and more conspicuous, wore them

with a sparkling sprightliness which rendered her still more pleasing. She lent herself unreservedly to the coquettish manœuvres of her mother, instinctively enacted with her graceful little scenes, knew how to kiss her at the proper time and put her arm lovingly about her waist, showing by a motion, a caress, some ingenious invention, how pretty they both were, and how they resembled each other.

Olivier Bertin, by dint of seeing them together and ceaselessly comparing them, at times almost confounded them. Occasionally, if the young girl spoke to him while he was looking in another direction, he was obliged to ask: " Which one said that ? " Often, even, he amused himself in playing this confusing game when the three were alone in the little Louis XV. salon. Then he would close his eyes and request them to address him the same question, one after the other at first, then changing the order of interrogations, to see if he could recognize the voices. They endeavored, so skillfully, to find the same intonations, to utter the same phrases, with the same expression, that often he could not guess. Indeed, they had come to pronounce so much alike that the servants answered the young girl with a " Oui, madame," and her mother with a " Oui, mademoiselle."

By dint of imitating each other for amusement and copying each other's motions, they had acquired so great a similarity of carriage and gestures that M. de Guilleroy himself, when he saw either of them traversing the dark background of the drawing-room confounded them at every turn, and would ask: " Is that you, Annette, or is it your mother ? "

From this natural and acquired resemblance, both real and artificial, was born in the mind and heart of the painter the whimsical impression of a double being, old and new, intimately known and almost unknown, of two bodies created successively, of the same flesh, of the same woman perpetuated, rejuvenated, having become once more what she had been. And he lived near them, divided between the two, uneasy, troubled, feeling his passion for the mother revived and covering the daughter with a mysterious tenderness.

PART II

❧❧

CHAPTER I.

" Paris, July 20, Eleven o'clock at night.
" My Friend :
" My mother has just died at Roncières. We
leave at midnight. Do not come, for we advise
no one. But pity and think of me. Your
"Any."

" July 21, Noon.
" My Poor Friend:
" I would have set out in spite of you,
had I not become accustomed to regard all
your wishes as commands. Since yesterday I
have been thinking of you with poignant grief.
I think of that speechless journey you made last
night, opposite your daughter and husband, in
that dimly-lighted carriage, which was dragging
you toward your dead. I could see you all
three under the oil lamp, you weeping and Annette sobbing. I saw your arrival at the station,
the horrible drive, your entering the castle in
the midst of the servants, your rushing up the
stairway toward that room, toward that bed on

which she lies, your first glance upon her, and
your kiss upon her motionless, thin face. And I
thought of your heart, your poor heart, that poor
heart one-half of which belongs to me and which
is breaking, which suffers so, which stifles you
and which makes me suffer so, too, at this time.
" I kiss your tearful eyes with profound pity.
                                        " OLIVIER."

"RONCIÈRES, July 24.
" Your letter would have done me good, my
friend, if anything could do me good in the terri-
ble misfortune that has befallen me. We buried
her yesterday, and since her poor lifeless body
has gone out of this house I feel alone in the
world. We love our mothers almost unknow-
ingly, unconsciously, for it is as natural as it is to
live; and we fully realize how deep-rooted that
love is only when we come to the last separation.
No other affection can be compared to that, for
all others are fortuitous; this is from birth. All
the others are brought to us later by the chances
of life; this has lived in our very blood since we
first saw the light of day. And then, and then,
we have not only lost a mother, but all our own
childhood, which half disappears, for our little life
of young girlhood belonged to her as much as
to us. She alone knew it as we do; she knew a
host of things, remote, insignificant and dear
which are, which were, the first sweet emotions

of our hearts. To her alone could I still say:
' Do you remember, mother, the day when——?
Do you remember, mother, the porcelain doll
which grandmother had given me ? ' We both
mumbled over a long, sweet chapter of small
and childish reminiscences which no one on
earth knows now but me. It is therefore a part
of myself that died, the oldest, the best. I have
lost the poor heart wherein the little girl I once
was still lived complete. Now, no one knows
her any more; no one remembers the little
Anne, her short skirts, her laughter and her
faces.

"And a day will come, which may not be far
distant, when I in my turn shall so depart, leaving my dear Annette alone in the world, as my
mother leaves me to-day. How sad all this is,
how harsh, how cruel. Yet, we never think of
it; we do not look about us to see death taking
some one at every instant, as it will take us soon.
If we looked at it, if we thought of it, if we were
not distracted, gladdened and blinded by all that
goes on before us, we could no longer live, for the
sight of this endless massacre would drive us
mad.

"I am so crushed, so hopeless, that I have no
longer strength to do anything. Night and
day I think of my poor mother, nailed in that
box, buried in that earth, in that field, under the
rain, and whose old face, which I used to caress

with so much happiness, is now but frightful decay. Oh! how horrible! My friend, how horrible!

" When I lost my father I was just married, and did not feel all these things as I do to-day. Yes, pity me, think of me, write to me. I have so much need of you, now.

"ANY."

" PARIS, July 25.

" MY POOR FRIEND :

" Your grief causes me horrible pain. Nor does life seem in any way bright to me. Since your departure I am lost, forsaken, without bond or refuge. Everything fatigues me, bores or irritates me. I am continuously thinking of you and Annette; I feel that you are both quite far when I so greatly need you to be near me.

" It is extraordinary how far you seem to me to be, and how I miss you. Never, even when I was young, have you been my *all* as you are at this moment. For some time have I had a premonition of this crisis, which must be a sun-stroke in Indian Summer. So strange even is what I feel, that I wish to tell it you. Imagine that since you are gone I can no longer go walk-ing. Formerly, and even during the last months, I was very fond of starting out alone, and lounging through the streets, diverted by people and things, enjoying the pleasure of see-

ing, of rambling about carelessly. I wandered
about carelessly, without knowing where, to
walk, to breathe, to dream. Now it is impossible. As soon as I descend into the street I
am oppressed by anguish, by the fear of a blind
man who has lost his dog. I become uneasy,
precisely like a traveller who has lost his path
in a wood, and I am compelled to return home.
I ask myself, ' Where shall I go ? ' I answer,
'Nowhere, since I am walking.' Well, I cannot ;
I can no longer walk without an aim. The
mere thought of walking along weighs me down
with fatigue and worries me to death. Then I
drag my melancholy to the Club.

" And do you know why? Simply because
you are no longer here. I am certain of it.
When I know you to be in Paris there are no
more useless walks, since it is possible that I may
meet you in any street. I can go anywhere
because you may be everywhere. If I do not
find you, I may at least find Annette, who is an
emanation of yourself. You two fill the streets
full of hope for me, hope of recognizing you,
whether you come toward me from afar, or I
guess who you are as I follow you. And then
the city becomes charming to me, and the
women whose figures resemble yours stir up
my heart with all the bustle of the streets, engross my attention, occupy my eyes, give me a
sort of longing to see you.

" You will think me very selfish, my poor friend, as I thus speak of the solitude of an old cooing pigeon when you are shedding such painful tears. Pardon me, I am so accustomed to be spoilt by you, that I cry: Help! Help! when I have you no longer.

" I kiss your feet that you may have pity on me.   OLIVIER."

"RONCIÈRES, July 30.
" MY FRIEND:

" Thanks for your letter. I need so much to know that you love me. I have just passed through frightful days. I really believed that grief would kill me, too.

" It felt within me like a block of suffering shut up in my bosom, and was continually growing, choking, strangling me. The physician who was called, in order to relieve the nervous crisis which afflicted me, recurring frequently during the day, gave me morphine, which drove me almost wild, and the great heat of these days aggravated my condition and threw me into a state of over-excitement which was almost delirium. I am a little more quiet since the violent storm of Friday. I must tell you that since the day of the burial I could weep no more, but during the storm, the approach of which had quite upset me, I suddenly felt that the tears were beginning to flow from my eyes, slow, few, small, burning. Oh! how painful those first tears were! They were tearing as if they had claws, and my throat was so contracted as hardly to admit my breath. Then they became more rapid, larger, less hot. They gushed from my eyes as from a spring, and there came so many, oh! so many, that my handkerchief was saturated with them, and I had to get another. The great block of pain seemed to soften and to flow from my eyes.

" From that moment I have been weeping night and day, and that is saving me. We should really go insane, or die, finally, if we could not weep. I am very lonely here. My husband is taking some excursions in the country, and I insisted on his taking away Annette, to distract and console her a little. They drive or ride as far as eight or ten leagues from Roncières, and she comes back to me rosy with youth, notwithstanding her sadness, and her eyes shining with life, quite brightened by the country air and the outing she has had. How beautiful it is to be at that age. I think that we shall remain here a fortnight or three weeks longer; then, the month of August, notwithstanding, we shall return to Paris for the reason you know.

" I send you all that remains to me of my heart.   ANY."

" PARIS, August 4.
" I can stand it no longer, my dear friend; you must return, for something is surely going to

happen to me. I wonder whether I am not ill, so distasteful has everything become to me which I had been doing so long with a certain pleasure or with indifferent resignation. In the first place, the weather is so warm in Paris that every night means a Turkish bath of eight or nine hours' duration. I rise overcome by the fatigue of this sleep in a hot-air bath, and I pace for an hour or two before a white canvas, intending to draw something. But my mind is empty; my head is empty. I am no longer a painter! This useless effort to work is exasperating. I have models come to me; I place them, and they give me poses, motions, expressions which I have painted to satiety. I make them dress again, and put them out. Really, I can no longer see anything new, and I suffer from it as if I were becoming blind. What is it? Fatigue of the eye, or the brain; exhaustion of the artistic faculty or extreme weariness of the optical nerve? Who knows! It seems to me that I have ceased discovering in the unexplored corner which I have been permitted to visit. I no longer perceive but what everybody knows, I do what all poor painters have done; I have no longer but one subject and the observation only of a vulgar pedant. Formerly, not so very long ago, the number of new " motifs " seemed to me unlimited, and I had such a variety of means to express them that I was puzzled how to choose,

and this alone made me hesitate.   And now, all
at once, the world of subjects, of which we have
had but a glimpse, has become depopulated, my
pursuit has become powerless and fruitless.
People who pass by have no more sense for me;
I no longer find in every human being that character and savor which I so liked to discover and
reproduce.   I believe, however, that I could
make a very pretty portrait of your daughter.
Is it because she resembles you so much that
you are confounded in my mind?   Perhaps so.

"So that, after having endeavored to sketch
a man or a woman unlike all the known models,
I decide to go and breakfast somewhere, for I
have no longer the courage necessary to sit down
alone in my dining-room.   The Boulevard Malesherbes seems like a forest avenue imprisoned
in a dead city.   All the houses have an empty
smell.   On the street the sprinklers throw fan-
shaped showers of white rain, splashing the
wooden pavement, from which there ' rises a
vapor of wet tar and stable washings; and from
one end to the other of the long descent from the
Park Monceau to Saint Augustin one perceives
five or six black forms—passers-by, of no importance, tradesmen or servants.   The shade of
the plane trees spreads out at their feet, on the
burning sidewalks, an odd stain, which one
would take to be liquid, like spilled water drying.
The stillness of the leaves in the branches and of

their grey shadows on the asphalt expresses the weariness of the roasted city, sleepy and perspiring like a workman asleep on a bench in the sun. Yes, she sweats, the beggar, and smells horribly through her sewer holes, the cellars and kitchen vent holes, the streams in which the filth of the streets is flowing. Then, I think of those Summer mornings, in your orchard full of little wild flowers which give the air a taste of honey. Then, sickened already, I enter the restaurant to see bald and fat, exhausted-looking men eat, with half opened waistcoats and shining foreheads covered with perspiration. All that food feels the heat, the melon melting under the ice, the soft bread, the flabby chine, the cooked-over vegetables, the purulent cheese, the fruit ripened in the shop front. And I come out nauseated, and return home to take a nap until dinner time, when I go to the Club.

" I always find there Adelmans, Maldant, Rocdiane, Landa and many others, who bore and tire me as much as barrel organs. Every one has his air, or his airs, which I have heard for the last fifteen years, and they play them altogether, every evening, at the Club, which is, it would seem, a place where one goes to be amused. They ought to change my generation for me, for my eyes, ears and mind are satiated with it. They continue to make conquests, they boast of them, and congratulate each other.·

"After yawning as many times as there are
minutes between eight o'clock and midnight, I
return home to retire, and undress, thinking that
it will be the same thing over again on the
morrow.

"Yes, my dear friend, I am at that age when
the life of a bachelor becomes intolerable, because there is nothing new for me under the sun.
A bachelor should be young, curious, greedy.
When one is no longer all that, it becomes dangerous to be free. O God! How much I loved
my liberty once, before I loved you more! How
it weighs on me now. Liberty, for an old bachelor like me! It is emptiness, emptiness everywhere; it is the path of death, with nothing
within to keep him from seeing the end; it is the
ceaseless repetition of this question: What shall
I do? Whom shall I go and see, not to be
alone? And I go from companion to companion; from handshaking to handshaking, begging a little friendship. I gather crumbs which
do not constitute a loaf. You, I have you, my
friend, but you do not belong to me. Perhaps
it is even you who are the cause of the anguish
from which I suffer, for it is the desire for your
contact, your presence, for the same roof over
our heads, the same walls enclosing our existence, the same interests oppressing our hearts,
the need of that community of hopes, of sorrows, of pleasures, of joy, of sadness, and also

of material things which fill me with so much care. You are mine, that is to say, that I steal a little of you now and then. But I would breathe always the same air that you breathe, share everything with you, make use of those things only which belong to us both, feel that all which constitutes my life is yours as much as mine,—the glass from which I drink, the seat on which I rest, the bread I eat and the fire that warms me.

" Good-bye; return soon. I suffer too much away from you.   OLIVIER."

"RONCIÈRES, August 8.

" My friend, I am ill, and so fatigued that I believe you would not recognize me. I believe I have wept too much. I must rest a little before returning, for I cannot show myself to you as I am. My husband leaves for Paris day after to-morrow, and will take you news from us. He expects to take you to dinner somewhere, and requests me to ask you to wait for him at your house at about seven o'clock.

"As for me, as soon as I feel a little better, as soon as I have no more this face of a disinterred body which frightens myself, I shall return near you. I have also only Annette and you in the world, and I wish to offer each of you all I can give without robbing the other.

" I hold out my eyes that have wept so much,
that you may kiss them.   ANY."

When Olivier Bertin received this letter,
which announced the still protracted return, he
had a great mind, an immoderate desire, to take
a carriage for the station, and the train for Roncières; then, thinking that M. de Guilleroy was
to return on the morrow, he was resigned, and
began to wish for the arrival of the husband with
almost as much impatience as if it had been that
of the wife herself.

Never had he loved Guilleroy as he did during
those twenty-four hours of waiting.

When he saw him enter he rushed toward
him, with hands outstretched, exclaiming:

" Ah! dear friend; how happy I am to see
you ! "

The other also seemed much gratified, especially delighted to return to Paris, for he had
not led a very gay life in Normandy the past
three weeks.

The two men sat down on a sofa just large
enough for two, in a corner of the studio, under
a canopy of Oriental stuffs, and again they shook
hands, visibly affected.

" And how is the Countess ? " Bertin asked.

" Not very well. She has been very much
broken up, very much affected, and she recovers

too slowly. I even confess that I am rather uneasy about her."

" But why does she not return ? "

" I do not know; it has been impossible for
me to induce her to come back here."

" What does she do all day ? "

" Well, she weeps, and thinks of her mother.
It is not good for her. I would much like to
have her decide on a change of air, to leave the
spot where it took place, you understand ? "

" And Annette ? "

" Oh! she is a blooming flower."

Olivier smiled with joy. Again he asked:

" Did she feel much grief ? "

" Yes, much, very much; but, you know, grief
at eighteen years of age cannot last."

After a silence, Guilleroy continued:

" Where shall we dine, my dear fellow? I
greatly need to brighten up, hear some noise
and see some life."

" Why, at this season of the year, it seems to
me that the Café des Ambassadeurs is the place."

And they started out, arm-in-arm, toward the
Champs Elyseés. Guilleroy, agitated by the
reawakening of Parisians when they return, and
to whom the city, after every absence, seems
younger and full of possible surprises, questioned the painter upon a thousand details, on
what had been done, on what had been said; and
Olivier, after some indifferent replies, which re-

flected all the weariness of his solitude, spoke
of Roncières, endeavored to catch from this man,
to gather around him that almost material something imparted to us by people whom we meet,
that subtle emanation of being which one carries
away on leaving them and retains in one's self
for a few hours, and which evaporates in the new
atmosphere.

The heavy sky of a Summer evening was
weighing down upon the city and on the great
avenue where, under the foliage, the lively re-
frains of open-air concerts were beginning to
flutter.　The two men, sitting on the balcony of
the Ambassadeurs, looked down beneath them
upon the still empty benches and chairs of the
enclosure up to the little theatre, where the
singers, in the dull, mingled light of the electric
globes and waning day, displayed their brilliant
toilets and their rosy complexions.　Odors of
fried things, of sauces, of warm dishes, floated
in the imperceptible breezes wafted back and
forth by the chestnut trees; and when a woman
passed, looking for her reserved place, followed
by a man in a dress coat, she scattered on her
way the fresh intoxicating perfume of her dress
and herself.

Guilleroy radiantly murmured:

" Oh!　I would rather be here than yonder."

" And I," said Bertin, " would rather be yonder than here."

' Nonsense ! "

" Parbleu! Paris seems tainted to me this Summer."

" Eh! my dear fellow. It is Paris all the same."

The Deputy seemed to be having a happy day, one of those rare days of buoyancy and effervescence in which serious men do foolish things. He was looking at two " cocottes" dining at the next table with three thin young men, superlatively correct, and he slyly questioned Olivier upon the women, whose names were familiar and to be heard every day. Then he murmured in a tone of profound regret:

" You were lucky to have remained a bachelor. You can do and see many things."

But the painter dissented, and like all those who are tormented with a persistent idea, he made Guilleroy the confidante of his dreariness and isolation. When he had said everything, recited the litany of his melancholy to the end, and, urged by the need of relieving his heart, had related with simplicity how much he would have liked the love and contact of a woman installed by his side, the Count, in his turn, granted that marriage had its good points. Then he recovered his parliamentary eloquence to praise the sweetness of his family life and to glorify the Countess. Olivier listened gravely, and frequently nodded his approval.

Glad to hear her spoken of, yet jealous of that

intimate happiness which Guilleroy was duti-
fully extolling, the painter finally murmured,
with an air of conviction:

" Yes, you are the one who was fortunate."

The Deputy, flattered, assented; then continued:

" I would be very glad to see her back; really,
she gives me some concern just now.   Here,
since you are bored in Paris, you should go
down to Roncières, and bring her back.   She
will listen to you, for you are her best friend:
while a husband—you know—"

Olivier, delighted, exclaimed:

" I! but I ask nothing better.   However, do
you think it will not annoy her to see me coming
in this fashion ? "

" Not at all; do go, my dear fellow."

" Then I will.   I shall leave to-morrow by the
one o'clock train.   Must I send her a despatch ? "

" No, I'll take care of that.   I shall advise her,
that you may find a carriage at the station."

As they had finished dinner, they returned up
the Boulevard; but in about half an hour the
Count left the painter suddenly, under pretext
of an urgent matter which he had quite forgotten.

CHAPTER II.

The Countess and her daughter, dressed in black crape, had just seated themselves opposite each other, for breakfast, in the large room at Roncières. Ancestral portraits artlessly presenting one in a cuirass, another in a leathern jerkin, this in the powdered costume of an officer of the French Guards, that as a Colonel of the Restoration, were hung in line upon the walls, forming a collection of the dead and gone Guilleroys, in old frames from which the gilt was falling. Two servants, with muffled steps, were beginning to wait upon the two silent women, and the flies made a little cloud of black dots, whirling and buzzing around the glass chandelier suspended over the centre of the table.

" Open the windows," said the Countess; " it is a little cool here."

The three tall windows, extending from the floor to the ceiling, and as large as bay windows, were opened wide. A breath of balmy air, laden with the perfume of warm grass, and the far-off noises of the country, poured in through these three large gaps, mingling with the somewhat damp air of the room, shut in by the thick walls of the castle.

"Ah! that is good," said Annette, drawing a deep breath.

The eyes of the two women had turned toward the outside, and they were looking, beneath the clear blue sky—somewhat veiled by the midday mist which was reflected upon the fields overflowing with the sunshine—at the long greensward of the park, with its clumps of trees here and there, and its perspective opening afar on the yellow country, illuminated to the distant horizon by the golden glimmer of ripening grain.

"We shall take a long walk after breakfast," said the Countess. "We might walk as far as Berville, following the river, for it would be too warm in the plain."

"Yes, mamma, and we'll take Julio along to get up some partridges."

"You know that your father forbids it."

"Oh! but since papa is in Paris! It is so amusing to see Julio pointing. Here he is, teasing the cows. Dear me, how funny he is."

Pushing back her chair, she rose and ran to the window, whence she cried out: "At them, Julio, at them!"

Upon the lawn, three heavy cows, stuffed with grass, overcome with the heat, were resting, lying on their sides, their bellies protruding from the pressure of the ground. Bounding from one to another, barking, scampering wildly, mad with joy, both furious and feigned, a hunting spaniel, slim, white and red, whose curly ears were flying at every bound, was bent on making the three great beasts get up, which they would not do. That was evidently the dog's favorite trick, in which he indulged whenever he saw the cows lying down. Annoyed, but not frightened, they looked at him with their great moist eyes, turning their heads around to follow him.

Annette, from her window, shouted:

"Fetch them! Julio, fetch them!"

And the spaniel, excited, grew bolder, barked louder, ventured as far as their cruppers, making believe that he would bite. They began to grow uneasy, and the nervous shivering of the skin, to shake the flies off, became more frequent and longer.

Suddenly the dog, carried along by the speed which he was unable to check in time, came bounding so close to a cow that, in order not to tumble against her, he had to clear her with a leap. Grazed by the bound, the heavy animal was frightened, and first raising her head, finally gathered herself slowly upon her four legs, sniffing loudly. Seeing this one up, the other two immediately followed her example, and Julio began to circle around them in a triumphal dance, while Annette congratulated him.

"Bravo, Julio, bravo!"

" Come," said the Countess, " come to breakfast, my child."

But the young girl, shading her eyes with her
hand, exclaimed:

" Look, there comes the telegraph messenger!"

In the invisible path, lost amid the wheat and
oats, a blue blouse seemed to glide along the surface of the grain, and approached the castle with
the uniform ring of a man's step.

" Heavens !" murmured the Countess; " I
only hope he does not bring bad news."

She was still trembling with that fear which
long remains after the death of some beloved
companion announced in a despatch. Now she
could not tear off the gummed band to open the
little blue paper without feeling her fingers tremble and her soul bestirred, believing that from
those folds so long in straightening out was to
come a grief which would again cause her tears
to flow.

Annette, on the contrary, full of youthful curiosity, hailed the advent of the unknown. Her
heart, which life had just bruised for the first
time, could anticipate only joys from that black
and threatening pouch suspended at the side of
the mail carriers who scatter so many emotions
through the streets of the cities and over the by-
ways of the country.

The Countess was no longer eating, following

in her thoughts the man who was coming towards her, the bearer of a few written words
which might wound her as a knife thrust in her
throat. The anguish of experience made her
breathless, and she sought to guess what this
hurried news might be. About what? About
whom? The thought of Olivier shot across her
mind. Was he ill? Dead, perhaps, also!

The few minutes she had to wait seemed interminable; then when she had torn open the
despatch, and recognized her husband's name,
she read:—" I am to tell you that our friend
Bertin leaves for Roncières by the one o'clock
train. Send phaeton, station. Regards."

" Well, mamma ? " said Annette.

" M. Olivier Bertin is coming to see us."

" Ah! how delightful! And when ? "

" Very soon."

" At four o'clock ? "

" Yes."

" Oh! how kind he is."

But the Countess had turned pale, for a new
anxiety was growing of late within her, and the
sudden arrival of the painter seemed to her as
painful a menace as anything she might have
been able to foresee.

" You will go to meet him with the carriage,"
said she to her daughter.

" And you, mamma, will you not come ? "

" No, I shall wait for you here."

"Why? He will be sorry."

"I do not feel very well."

"You wanted to walk as far as Berville a moment ago."

"Yes, but my breakfast has made me ill."

"Before that time you will feel better."

"No; in fact, I shall go up to my room. Let me know as soon as you arrive."

"Yes, mamma."

Then after giving orders that the horses be put to the phaeton at the right time and the apartment prepared, the Countess re-entered and shut herself up in her own room.

Her life thus far had been spent almost without suffering, varied only by Olivier's affection and agitated only by the desire to retain it. She had succeeded, had been always victorious in that struggle. Her heart, lulled by success and flattery, having become the exacting heart of a beautiful worldling to whom is due all the sweets of earth, after consenting to a brilliant marriage with which inclination had nothing to do, after having later accepted love as the complement of a happy existence, after having resigned herself to a guilty affection, mainly from impulse, a little from a worship of sentiment itself, as a compensation for the daily treadmill of existence—her heart had taken up a position, barricaded itself in this happiness which chance had given her, with no other desire than to defend it against the surprises of each day. She had, therefore, accepted, with a pretty woman's complacency, the agreeable conditions that presented themselves, and, venturing but little, tormented but little by new wants and longings for the unknown, though loving, tenacious and cautious, content with the present, apprehensive by nature of the morrow, she had known how to enjoy the elements furnished her by Destiny with sparing and sagacious prudence.

Now, little by little, without her daring even to realize it, the indistinct prepossessions of passing days, of advancing years, had slipped into her soul. It had, in her mind, the effect of a little ceaseless irritation. But well knowing that this descent of life was without interruption, that once begun it could be no longer stayed, yielding to the instinct of danger, she closed her eyes as she let herself slip along, that she might preserve her dream, that she might not be made giddy by the abyss or desperate by her helplessness.

She lived on, therefore, smiling, with a sort of factitious pride in preserving her beauty so long; and when Annette appeared by her side with the freshness of her eighteen years, instead of suffering from this association, she was proud, on the contrary, of the fact that she should be preferred, in the accomplished grace of her maturity, to that blooming young girl in the radiant freshness of her early years.

She even thought herself at the beginning of a happy and tranquil period, when the death of her mother came, an overwhelming blow to her heart. During the first days it was that profound despair which leaves room for no other thought. She remained from morning till night buried in her desolation, endeavoring to recall a thousand incidents connected with the dead, her familiar expressions, her former face, the dresses she once wore, as if she had stowed her memory with relics, and she gathered from the past, now out of sight, all the intimate and trifling recollections with which she might feed her cruel reveries. Then, when she had reached such paroxysms of despair that at every instant they culminated in fainting fits, all that accumulated grief gushed out in tears, and day and night they flowed from her eyes.

One morning, as her maid had just entered and opened the blinds and raised the shades, asking: " How does Madame do to-day ? " she answered, feeling utter exhaustion and lassitude as the result of so much weeping, " Oh, not at all well. Really, I am worn out."

The servant, who was holding the tea-tray, looked at her mistress, and affected by the sight of her pale face, amid the whiteness of the bed, stammered, in a voice of sincere sadness:

" Indeed, Madame looks very badly. Madame would do well to take care of herself."

The tone in which the words were spoken wounded the heart of the Countess like the pricking of a needle, and as soon as the maid had gone she rose to look at her face in the large mirror.

She was stupefied before herself, frightened by her hollow cheeks, her red eyes, the havoc created by these few days of suffering. The face she knew so well, which she had so often gazed upon in many mirrors, whose every expression, every smile she was familiar with, whose paleness she had already corrected many times, repairing the little fatigues, effacing the faint wrinkles at the corner of the eye, perceptible in a too strong light—this face suddenly seemed to her that of another woman, a new face that was distorted, irreparably ill.

To see herself better, to ascertain more accurately this unexpected evil, she approached the glass near enough to touch it with her forehead, so that her breath, covering the mirror with a vapor, obscured, almost blotted out the pallid image she was contemplating. She took a handkerchief to wipe off this mist of her breath, and, trembling with a strange emotion, she examined long and patiently the alterations in her face; with a light finger she stretched the skin of her cheeks, smoothed that of the forehead, pushed back her hair, turned the eyelids to see the white of the eye. Then she opened her mouth, to look at her teeth, which were a little tarnished where

gold points were shining, and was troubled by
the livid gums and the yellowish tint of the flesh
above the cheeks and on the temples.

She was so intent upon this inspection of waning beauty that she did not hear the door open,
and was violently startled when her maid, standing behind her, said:

" Madame has forgotten to take her tea."

The Countess turned around, confused, surprised, ashamed, and the servant, guessing her
thought, continued:

" Madame has wept too much; there is nothing worse to drain the skin. It is the blood that
turns to water."

As the Countess was adding sadly:

" There is age also,"

The maid replied:

" Oh! Oh! Madame has not arrived at that
point. With a few days of rest no trace will be
left. But Madame must go walking, and be very
careful not to weep."

As soon as she was dressed the Countess went
down into the park, and for the first time since
her mother's death she visited the little orchard
where she had once liked to cultivate and gather
flowers; then she reached the river and walked
along the water till breakfast time.

As she sat down at the table opposite her husband, by the side of her daughter, she asked, so
that she might learn their opinion:

" I feel better to-day; I must be less pale."

The Count answered:

" Oh! you look quite ill yet."

Her heart shrivelled up and tears rose to her eyes, for she had contracted the habit of weeping.

Till evening, and the next day, and the following days, whether she thought of her mother or herself, she felt at every instant sobs filling her throat and tears rising to her eyes; but to prevent them from overflowing and furrowing her cheeks she held them back, and by a superhuman effort of the will, shifting her thought to different subjects, ruling it, controlling it, keeping it away from her grief, she endeavored to console, to amuse herself, no longer to think of sad things, in order to regain the healthfulness of her complexion.

Above all, she did not wish to return to Paris and meet Olivier Bertin before she was herself again. Understanding that she had grown too thin, that with women of her age the flesh must be full to keep fresh, she sought for an appetite in the roads and neighboring woods, and though she would return fatigued and with no hunger, would yet try to eat much.

The Count, who wished to be off again, could not at all understand her obstinacy. Finally, finding her resistance implacable, he declared that he would go away alone, leaving the

Countess free to return when she might feel disposed.

The next day she received the despatch announcing Olivier's arrival.

So much did she fear his first glance that she
was seized with a desire to flee. She would have
liked to wait another week or two. In a week,
with good care, one's appearance may change
entirely, since women, even when healthy and
young, under the least stress are unrecognizable
from one day to another. But the idea of appear-
ing before Olivier in the full light of the sun, in
the open fields, in this August weather, beside
Annette, who was so blooming, made her so
uneasy that she decided at once not to go to the
station, but await him in the softened light of the
drawing-room.

She had gone up to her room, and was in a
dream. Breaths of heat now and then stirred the
curtains. The song of the crickets filled the air.
Never yet had she felt so sad. It was no longer
the great overwhelming blow that had crushed
her heart, harrowing and prostrating her before
the soulless body of the old, beloved mother.
That grief which she once believed incurable
had in a few days become so softened as to be
now but a sorrow of the memory; but at this
moment she felt carried away, drowned in a deep
wave of melancholy which she had entered gradually and out of which she would never come.

She had a desire, an irresistible desire, to weep —yet would not. Every time that she felt her eyelids moisten she wiped them quickly, rose, walked, looked into the park, out upon the tall forest trees and the slow, black flight of the crows against the blue sky.

Then she passed before her mirror, judged herself with a glance, effaced the trace of a tear by a brush of the powder puff, and looked at the time, trying to imagine what point of the route he must then have reached.

Like all women who are carried away by a distress of soul, either irrational or real, she clung to him with desperate tenderness. Was he not everything to her—all, everything, more than life, all that a being may be who becomes the sole object of the heart and life of one who feels already in the shadow of advancing years ?

Suddenly she heard afar the crack of a whip, ran to the window and saw the phaeton, drawn by the two horses at a brisk pace, as it wound around the lawn. Seated by Annette's side, in the back of the carriage, Olivier shook his handkerchief as he discovered the Countess, and she answered the signal by waving both hands in salutation. Then she descended, her heart beating, but happy now, quivering with the joy of knowing him so near, of speaking to him and seeing him.

They met in the antechamber, before the drawing-room door.

He opened his arms toward her with an irresistible impulse, and with a voice warmed by sincere emotion, he said:

" Ah, my poor Countess, permit me to embrace you."

She closed her eyes, leaned forward, pressing close to him, lifting her face, and as he touched her cheeks with his lips she whispered in his ear:

" I love thee."

Olivier, without freeing the hands which he pressed, looked at her, saying:

" Let us look at that sad face."

She was ready to faint. He continued:

" Yes, a little bit pale; but that is nothing."

To thank him, she murmured:

" Ah, dear friend, dear friend," finding no other words.

But he had turned round, looking behind him for Annette, who had disappeared, and speaking brusquely:

" Is it not strange, hein! to see your daughter in mourning?"

" Why ? " asked the Countess.

He exclaimed with extraordinary animation:

" How! why? But it is your portrait painted by me; it is my portrait. It is you such as I met you long ago on entering the Duchess's

house, hein! Do you remember that door where
you passed under my glance, like a frigate under
the cannon of a fort? *Sacristi!* When I noticed
the little one just now at the station, standing
on the platform, all in black, with the sunshine
of her hair around her face, my heart gave a
jump. I thought I was going to weep. I tell
you it is enough to drive one mad when he has
known you as I have, looked at you better than
anybody, and reproduced you in painting,
Madam. Ah, indeed, I felt quite sure you had
sent her alone to me at the station to give me
that surprise. God of Heaven! how astonished
I was. I tell you, it is enough to drive one
mad."

He called:

"Annette, Nané."

The young girl, who was feeding the horses
sugar, answered from without:

"Here I am."

"Do come here."

She hastened to obey the summons.

"Here, stand there near your mother."

He placed her there and compared them, but
he was repeating mechanically, without conviction: "Yes, it is astounding, it is astonishing,"
for they resembled each other less side by side
than they did before they left Paris, the young
girl having taken on a new expression of luminous youth in that black dress, while the mother

had long since lost the sheen of hair and complexion which had dazzled and intoxicated the painter when they had met for the first time.

Then the Countess and he entered the drawing-room. He seemed radiant.

" Ah! what a capital idea it was to come," he said. Then continued: "No, it was your husband's idea for me. He recommended that I should bring you back. And I, do you know what I propose? You don't, do you? Well, I propose, on the contrary, to remain here. With this hot weather, Paris is odious, while the country is delicious. Heavens! how pleasant it is here."

Eventide immersed the park in its freshness, caused the trees to tremble, and the earth to exhale imperceptible vapors which threw a transparent veil upon the horizon. The three cows, standing with heads lowered, were feeding with avidity, and four peacocks, with a great flutter of their wings, flew up into a cedar where they were accustomed to roost, under the windows of the castle. Dogs were barking afar in the country, and in the quiet air of the day's close were heard the calls of human voices, phrases thrown across the fields, from one field to another, and those short guttural cries by which beasts are guided.

The painter, bare-headed, with shining eyes,

was breathing deeply, and as he caught the Countess's glance, he said:

" This is happiness."

She came nearer:

" It never lasts."

" Let us take it when it comes."

And she, then, with a smile:

" Until now you did not like the country."

" I like it to-day because I find you in it. I could no longer live where you are not. When one is young, he may be in love from afar, through letters, thoughts, or pure exaltation, perhaps because he feels life before him, perhaps also because passion calls more vehemently than the heart; at my age, on the contrary, love has become the habit of an invalid; it is a binding up of the soul, which, almost done for, takes less frequent flights into the ideal. The heart rises no more in ecstasies, but speaks in selfish exigencies. And then, I feel very keenly that I have no time to lose to enjoy what is left me."

" Oh! old!" said she, taking his hand.

He went on:

" Yes, indeed, I am old. Everything indicates it,—my hair, my changing character, the sadness which is coming. *Sacristi!* There is a thing I had not known thus far, sadness. If I had been told when I was thirty that some day I would become sad without cause, uneasy, dis-

contented with everything, I would not have
believed it. That proves also that my heart has
grown old."

She replied with an air of profound certainty:

" Oh! as for me, my heart feels quite young.
It has never changed. Yes, it has grown
younger, perhaps. It was twenty once; it is
only sixteen now."

They remained a long while thus talking in
the open window, mingled with the soul of evening, very near one another, nearer than they
had ever been, in this hour of tenderness—this
twilight of their love, as of the day.

A servant entered, announcing:

" Madame la Comtesse is served."

She asked:

" You have called my daughter ? "

" Mademoiselle is in the dining-room."

They all three sat down at the table. The
shutters were closed, and two great chandeliers
with half a dozen candles, lighted Annette's
face, and seemed to cover her head with gold-
dust. Bertin, smiling, did not take his eyes
from her.

" Heavens! how pretty she is in black," said
he.

And he turned toward the Countess while
admiring the daughter, as if to thank the mother
for having afforded him that pleasure.

'When they returned to the drawing-room the moon had risen upon the trees of the park. Their sombre mass seemed like a large island, and the country beyond a sea hidden under the light mist which floated on the surface of the plains.

"Oh, mamma, shall we take a walk?"

The Countess assented.

"May I take Julio?"

"Yes, if you like."

They went out, the young girl walking in front, playing with the dog. When they neared the lawn they heard the breathing of the cows which, awake and scenting their enemy, were raising their heads to look. Under the trees, further on, the moon was shedding among the branches a shower of fine beams that reached the ground, that seemed to wet the leaves, spreading out upon the road in little yellowish pools. Annette and Julio were running, and appeared under this clear night to have the same joyful and care-free hearts, their exuberance expressing itself in gambols.

In the openings, where the lunar wave descended as in a well, the young girl passed like a ghost, and the painter called her back, amazed by this dark vision with its radiant face. Then, when she had started off again, he would take and press the Countess' hand, and often sought her lips as they crossed in thicker shadow, as if the sight of Annette revived the impatience of his heart.

They finally reached the edge of the plain where they could barely discern in the distance, here and there, the clumps of trees of the farmhouses. Across the milky mist that covered the fields the horizon looked boundless, and the soft silence, the living silence of that great luminous warm space was full of inexpressible hope, of the indefinable expectancy which make summer nights so very sweet. Away, high up in the sky, a few little long slender clouds seemed made of silver shells. Standing motionless for a few seconds, one might hear in that nocturnal peace a confused and continuous murmur of life, a thousand feeble sounds, the harmony of which at first resembled silence.

A quail in a neighboring meadow was sounding her double cry, and Julio, his ears raised, stole away toward the two flute-like notes of the bird, Annette following him, as light·as he, holding her breath and bending low.

" Ah," said the Countess, who was left alone with the painter, " why do such moments as this pass so quickly? One can hold nothing, one can keep nothing. We do not even have time to taste what is good; it is already over."

Olivier kissed her hand, and replied, smiling:
" Oh ! this evening I cannot philosophize. I belong wholly to the present hour."

"You do not love me as I love you," she murmured.

"Oh! why do you say—"

She interrupted him:

"No, you love in me, as you very well said before dinner, a woman who satisfies the wants of your heart, a woman who has never caused you a pain and who has put a little happiness into your life. That I know, I feel. Yes, I have the consciousness, the deep joy of having been good, useful, helpful to you. You have loved, you still love all that you find in me that is agreeable, my solicitude for you, my admiration, my desire to please you, my passion, the complete gift I made to you of my very self. But it is not I you love, do you understand? Oh! that I feel as one feels a cold draught. You love in me a thousand things—my beauty, which is fading, my devotion, the wit people find in me, the opinion the world has of me, the opinion I have of you in my heart; but it is not I, I, nothing but myself; do you understand ?"

"No, I do not quite understand you. You are reciting an unexpected list of reproaches."

She exclaimed:

"Oh! my God! I would like to make you understand how *I* love you. Let us see. I seek and cannot find. When I think of you, and I am always thinking of you, I feel in the depths of my body and soul an unspeakable longing to be yours, and an irresistible need of giving you more of myself. I would like to sacrifice myself in an absolute fashion, for there is nothing better, when one loves, than to give, to give always, all, everything, one's life, one's thought, one's body, all one has, and absolutely to feel that one is giving, and to be ready to risk everything to give still more. I love you to the extent of loving to suffer for you, loving my fears, my torments, my jealousies, the grief I feel when I am conscious you are no longer tender toward me. I love in you a some one I alone have discovered, a you that is not the you of the world which is admired and known, a you that is my own, which cannot change, which cannot grow old, which cannot outlive my love, for I have, to look at it, eyes that see nothing else besides. But those things cannot be told; there are no words to express them."

He kept repeating softly, many times in succession:

" Dear, dear, dear Any."

Julio came back bounding along, without finding the quail that had kept silent at his approach, and Annette behind him, out of breath with running.

" I am tired to death," said she; " I will cling to you, sir painter."

She leaned on Olivier's disengaged arm, and they returned, walking thus, he between them, under the dark trees. They no longer spoke. He advanced, possessed by them, penetrated by a sort of feminine exhalation with which their contact filled him. He did not try to see them, since he had them close beside him, nay, he closed his eyes the better to feel their presence. They guided him, led him, and he walked straight ahead, charmed with them, with the one on the left as the one on the right, without knowing which was on his left or which on his right, which was the mother or which the daughter. He abandoned himself unresistingly to the enjoyment of that involuntary and exquisite agitation of the senses. He even sought to mingle them in his heart, not to distinguish them in his mind, and lulled desire with the charm of this confusion. Were not that mother and daughter, so alike, one woman alone? And did not the daughter seem to have come upon earth solely to revive his former love for the mother?

When he again opened his eyes upon entering the castle he felt that he had just spent the most delightful moments of his life, that he had just experienced the strangest and most complete emotion a man might feel, an emotion which defied analysis—intoxicated with the same love, by the charm emanating from two women.

"Ah! what a delightful evening!" he said,

as soon as he found himself again between them by the light of the lamps.

Annette exclaimed:

"I am not at all sleepy; I could spend the whole night walking when the weather is fine."

The Countess looked at the clock:

"Oh! it is half-past eleven. It is time to retire, my child."

They separated, proceeded toward their own apartments. The young girl who did not like to go to bed, was the only one who went to sleep directly.

The next day, at the usual hour, when, after she had drawn the curtains and opened the blinds, the maid brought the tea and looked at her mistress, still half asleep, and said to her :

"Madame already looks better, to-day."

"You think so?"

"Oh! yes, Madame's face is more rested."

The Countess, though she had not yet looked at herself, knew very well that it was true. Her heart was light. She did not feel its throb; she felt herself living. The blood that coursed in her veins was no longer rushing as on the day before, warm and feverish, carrying through her whole being nervousness and disquiet, but distributed a soothing comfort and a happy confidence.

When the servant had gone out she went to look at herself in the mirror. She was some-

what surprised, for she felt so well that she expected to find herself grown perceptibly younger,
in a single night. Then she felt the chidishness
of such a hope, and after a second glance, resigned herself to the discovery that her complexion was only clearer, her eyes less fatigued,
her lips more brilliant than on the day before.
Her soul being content, she could not be sad,
and she smiled, thinking: " Yes, in a few days
I shall be quite well. My trial was too severe for
me to recover so soon."

But she remained a long, long time seated
before her toilet table upon which were laid
out in graceful order upon a muslin cover
trimmed with lace, before a fine glass of cut
crystal, all her little ivory-handled implements
of coquetry, stamped with her arms surmounted
by a coronet. There they were, innumerable,
pretty, various, designed for delicate and clan-
destine duties, some of steel, thin and sharp, in
odd shapes, like surgical instruments intended
for petty operations, others round and soft, of
feather, of down, of skin of unknown animals,
made to spread over the tender flesh the caresses of fragrant powders or liquid perfumes.

She handled them a long while with her experienced fingers, carrying them from lips to
temples with touches softer than kisses, correct-
ing the imperfect tints, underlining the eyes,
looking after the lashes. Finally, when she went

down, she was almost sure that the first glance which fell upon her would not be too unfavorable.

"Where is M. Bertin?" she asked of the servant whom she met in the vestibule.

The man answered:

"M. Bertin is in the orchard playing tennis with mademoiselle."

She heard them from afar counting the points.

One after the other, the deep voice of the painter and the thin tones of the young girl, called out: "Fifteen, thirty, forty, vantage, deuce, vantage, game."

The orchard, where a place had been leveled for a tennis court, was a large square grass plot planted with apple trees, enclosed by the park, the vegetable garden and the farms belonging to the castle. Along the slope that constituted its boundaries on three sides, like the fortifications of an intrenched camp, flowers were growing, long borders of flowers of all sorts, wild and rare, roses in quantity, pinks, heliotropes, fuchsias, mignonettes, and many others which, as Bertin would say, gave the air a taste of honey. In addition, the bees, whose straw-domed hives lined the fruit wall of the vegetable garden, covered that blooming field in their golden, humming flight.

In the very centre of this orchard, a few apple trees had been cut down, in order to obtain sufficient room for the court, and a tarred net, stretched across, divided it.

Annette on one side, bare-headed, her black gown caught up, showing her ankles half way to the knee when she rushed to volley a ball, ran hither and thither, with shining eyes and flushed cheeks, tired, out of breath with the sure and unerring play of her antagonist.

He, in visored cap and snug white flannels revealing a somewhat too rounded figure, coolly awaited the ball, judged of its fall with precision, received and returned it without haste, without running, with the easy elegance, the passionate attention and the professional skill with which he indulged in all sports.

Annette was the first to discover her mother. She cried:

" Good morning, mamma; wait a minute till we have finished this."

That second's inattention lost her the game. The ball passed against her, rolling almost, touched the ground and went out of the court.

Then Bertin shouted " Won," and the young girl, surprised, accused him of taking advantage of her momentary diversion. Julio, trained to look for and find the lost balls that were scattered like partridges fallen in the underbrush, sprang after it, rolling before him in the grass, seized it daintily with his mouth, and brought it back, wagging his tail.

The painter was now greeting the Countess, but, urged to continue the game, animated by the struggle, pleased to find himself so nimble, he gave but a short and hasty glance to the face so carefully prepared for his sake, asking:

" Will you permit, dear Countess? I am afraid of catching cold and getting neuralgia."

" Oh, yes," she answered.

She sat down upon a hay-stack, mowed that very morning to give the players a clear field, and with her heart suddenly a little sad, looked on.

Her daughter exasperated by her continual failures, was getting animated, excited, dashing impetuously from one end of the court to the other with cries of vexation or triumph. Her violent motions would often loosen locks of hair which fell upon her shoulders, which she would seize impatiently, and with the racket held between her knees, fasten them up again, sticking hair pins here and there in the soft mass.

And Bertin, from afar, would shout to the Countess:

" Hein! isn't she pretty now, and fresh as day ? "

Yes, she was young, she might run, get warm, red, loosen her hair, defy or dare everything, for everything made her only more beautiful.

Then, when they resumed their vigorous play, the Countess more and more melancholy, felt that Olivier preferred that game of tennis, that childish excitement, that enjoyment of little kittens jumping after paper balls, to the sweetness of sitting by her side that warm morning, and her loving pressure against him.

When the bell, at a distance, sounded the first signal for breakfast, it seemed to her that she was set free, that a weight was taken from her heart. But as she returned, leaning on his arm, he said to her:

" I have been amusing myself like a little boy. It is a capital thing to be, or to feel, young. Yes, indeed! There is nothing like it. When we do not care to run any more we are done for."

After breakfast, the Countess, who for the first time on the day before, had omitted her visit to the cemetery, proposed that they should go together, and they all three started for the village.

They had to cross a piece of woods, traversed by a stream called " La Rainette," doubtless because of the frogs that occupied it; then walk over a bit of plain before arriving at the church, surrounded by a group of houses which sheltered the grocer, the baker, the butcher, the wine merchant and a few other modest dealers who furnished the peasants with their simple supplies.

Their walk was silent and contemplative, the

thought of the dead oppressing their souls. The
two women knelt upon the grave and prayed
for a long time. The Countess, bending low,
was motionless, her handkerchief to her eyes,
for she feared to weep lest the tears flow on her
cheeks. Her prayer was not as it had been
hitherto, a sort of invocation of her mother, a
desperate appeal to that object beneath the marble of the tomb until she seemed to feel by the
weight of her distress that the dead was hearing
her, listening to her, but in simple earnestness,
stammering out the consecrated words of the
Pater Noster and the *Ave Maria*. She would not
have had at this hour the strength and elasticity
requisite for that cruel, responseless communion
with what might remain of the being who had
disappeared in the vault which concealed the
remains of her body. Her woman's heart was
besieged by other cares and fears which stirred
her, wounded her, distracted her; and her fer-
vent prayer ascended toward Heaven, laden with
vague supplications. She implored God, who
has thrown all poor creatures upon the earth,
to be pitiful to herself as well as to the one
He had recalled to Himself.

She could not have told what she asked Him,
so obscure and confused were her apprehensions
still, but she felt she had need of Divine help,
superhuman support against impending dangers
and inevitable grief.

Annette, with eyes closed, having stammered through the formulas, fell into a revery, for she would not rise before her mother.

Olivier Bertin stood looking at them, thinking that he had before him a ravishing picture, and regretting somewhat that he could not be permitted to make a sketch.

On their return they began to speak of human life, softly stirring those bitter and poetic fancies of a tender and hopeless philosophy, a common subject of conversation between men and women whom life has wounded a little, and whose hearts mingle as they blend their sorrows.

Annette, who was not ripe for such reflections, wandered off every instant, to gather flowers growing wild about them.

But Olivier, possessed with the desire of keeping her near him, nervous at seeing her continually darting away, never permitted his eyes to wander from her. He was annoyed that she should be more interested in the colors of the plants than in his words. He experienced an inexpressible sense of discomfort in seeing that he did not fascinate her, could not sway her, as he could her mother, and a desire to stretch out his hand to grasp her, hold her, forbid her to go away. He felt that she was too alert, too young, too indifferent, too free, free as a bird, like a young dog that does not obey, which does not come back, which has independence in its

veins, that pretty instinct of liberty yet uncon-
quered by voice or whip.

In the effort to attract her he spoke of gayer
things, and sometimes he asked her a question,
sought to awaken her woman's curiosity and a
desire to listen; but one would have thought
that the capricious wind of the broad heavens
was blowing in Annette's head that day, as upon
the undulating grain, carrying away and dis-
persing her attention into space, for she had
scarcely flung back even the mechanical answers
expected of her, thrown in between the flights,
with an abstracted air, than she returned to her
flowers. Finally, he was exasperated, bitten by
puerile impatience, and as she came to beg her
mother to carry her first bouquet, so that she
might gather another, he caught her by the
elbow, and pressed her arm to keep her from
running away again. She struggled, laughing,
trying with all her might to free herself; then,
dictated by his masculine instinct, he resorted to
the wiles of weakness, and unable to gain her
attention otherwise, sought to purchase it by
tempting her vanity.

" Tell me," said he, " what flower you prefer.
I will have you a brooch made of it."

She hesitated, surprised.

" A brooch, how ? "

" In stones of the same color," he replied;
" in rubies if it is a wild poppy; in sapphires

if it is a corn-flower, with a little leaf in emeralds."

Annette's face lighted up with that affectionate joy with which promises and presents irradiate a woman's features.

" The corn-flower," she said; " it is so pretty."

" The corn-flower it is. We'll go and order it as soon as we return to Paris."

She no longer wandered off, attracted to him by the thought of the jewel she was already endeavoring to see, to imagine. She asked:

" Does it take very long to do a thing like that ? "

He laughed, feeling that she was caught.

" I do not know; it depends upon the difficulties. We shall make the jeweller hurry up."

A distressing thought suddenly shot through her head.

" But I could not wear it, since I am in mourning."

He had passed his arm under that of the young girl, and pressing it against him, said:

" Well, you will keep the brooch until you put off mourning; that will not prevent you from looking at it."

As on the evening before, he was between them, held a close captive between their shoulders, and in order to see their eyes of a like blue, looking up to him with their tiny black spots, he spoke to them in turn, turning his head

now this way, now that. Under the full light
of the sun he was not so apt to mistake the
Countess for Annette, but he confounded more
and more the daughter with the reviving recollection of what the mother had been. He had a
great desire to embrace both of them; the one
to find once more upon her cheek and neck a
little of that pink and fair freshness which he
had formerly tasted, and which he saw to-day
miraculously reproduced; the other because he
still loved her, and felt that from her came the
potent appeal of habit. He even realized at
this moment, and understood that his affection
for her and his desire for her, somewhat abated
for a long time past, had revived at the sight of
her youth brought to life again.

Annette was off again after flowers. Olivier
no longer recalled her, as if the touch of her
arm and the satisfaction of the pleasure he had
given her had contented him, but he followed
her every motion, with the pleasure we find in
the persons or the objects which charm and intoxicate our vision. When she returned bearing
a large bouquet he breathed deeply, unconsciously seeking something of her, a little of
her breath, or her warmth, in the air stirred by
her running. He gazed at her with rapture, as
one watches the dawn, as one listens to music,
with thrills of pleasure when she bent down, rose
again, lifted both arms at the same time to re-

arrange her hair. And then, more and more, hour by hour, she evoked in him the memory of former days. Her laughter, her pleasing manners, her motions, brought to his mouth the taste of former kisses given and returned; she made of the far-off past, the precise sensation of which he had lost, something like a present dream; she mingled epochs, dates, the ages of his heart, and, kindling anew emotions that had cooled, she mixed without his realizing it, yesterday with to-morrow, recollection with hope.

He was asking himself as he searched his memory, whether the Countess in her fullest bloom had possessed that fawn-like, **supple** charm, that bold, capricious, irresistible fascination like the grace of a bounding animal. No. She had had a fuller bloom, and been less wild. A city girl, then city woman, having never drank the air of the fields and lived in the grass, she had grown pretty under the shade of walls and not in the sunshine of Heaven.

When they had returned to the castle the Countess began to write letters at her little low table in the embrasure of the window; Annette went up to her room, and the painter went out again to walk slowly, a cigar in his mouth, his hands behind his back, through the winding paths of the park. But he did not go far enough to lose sight of the white façade or the sharp pointed roof of the dwelling. As soon as it had

disappeared behind the clumps of trees or clusters of shrubbery there came a shadow over his
heart, as when a cloud hides the sun, and when
it reappeared in the verdant openings he halted
for a few seconds to gaze at the two rows of
high windows. Then he resumed his walk.

He felt agitated but content, content with
what? Everything.

The air seemed pure to him, life good that
day. His body again felt the vivacity of a little
boy, a desire to run, to catch the yellow butter-
flies fluttering on the green turf, as if they had
been suspended on the end of an elastic thread.
He was humming airs from an opera. Several
times in succession he repeated the famous strain
of Gounod: " Laisse-moi contempler ton visage," discovering in it a profoundly tender expression which he had never felt so deeply.

Suddenly he asked himself how it was that
he had so soon become different from himself.
Yesterday, in Paris, dissatisfied with everything,
disgusted, irritated; to-day calm, satisfied with
everything. One would have thought that a
beneficent God had changed his soul. "That same
bountiful God," he thought, " might as well have
changed my body at the same time, and made
me a little younger." Suddenly, he saw Julio
hunting in the thicket. He called him, and when
he had come to place his delicate head, adorned
with its long curly ears, under his hand, he sat

down in the grass, the more easily to pet him,
spoke kindly to him, laid him on his knee, and,
softening as he caressed him, embraced him after
the manner of women whose hearts are moved
by trifles.

After dinner, instead of going out as on the
day before, they spent the evening in the drawing-room *en famille.*

The Countess spoke abruptly:

" We shall have to be going soon."

Olivier exclaimed:

" Oh, do not speak of that yet. You did not
wish to leave Roncières when I was not here. I
come, and you think only of running away."

" But my dear friend," said she, " after all, we
cannot all three of us remain here indefinitely."

" It is not a question of indefinite time, but
of a few days. How many times have I stayed
at your house for whole weeks ? "

" Yes, but under different circumstances,
when the house was open to everybody."

Then Annette, in a coaxing tone:

" Oh ! Mamma, a few days more, two or three.
He teaches me so well how to play tennis. I
am vexed when I lose, and then afterward I am
so glad that I have improved."

That very morning the Countess was purpos-
ing to extend until Sunday this mysterious visit
of her friend, and now she wished to go away,
without knowing why. That day which she had

hoped would be so enoyable had left an inexpressible and penetrating sadness in her soul, an
unreasonable apprehension, tenacious and confused as a presentiment.

When she found herself alone in her room she
even tried to find the source of this new access
of melancholy.

Had she experienced one of those imperceptible emotions whose touch has been so tran-
sient that reason remembers it not, but whose
vibration remains in the most sensitive heart-
strings? Perhaps. Which? She recalled, it is
true, some unspeakable vexations in the thousand shades of sentiment through which she
had passed, every minute bringing its own. They
were really too insignificant to leave her in such
despondency. " I am exacting," she thought.
" I have not the right to torment myself thus."

She opened the window, to breathe the night
air, and rested there on her elbows, looking at
the moon.

A light noise made her look down. Olivier
was walking before the castle. " Why did he
say he was going to his room," she thought;
" why did he not tell me he was going out again;
ask me to go with him? He well knows it
would have made me happy. What can he be
thinking of ? "

This thought that he had not wished her presence for this walk, that he had preferred to go

out alone this beautiful night, alone, a cigar in his mouth, for she could see the red spark of fire—alone, when he might have afforded her the joy of taking her with him, this thought that he did not need her continually, did not care for her ceaselessly, poured into her soul a new leaven of bitterness.

She was about to close the window so that she might see him no longer, to be no longer tempted to call him, when he looked up and saw her. He cried:

" Well, you are star-gazing, Countess ? "

She answered:

" Yes, so are you, it seems."

" Oh! I am simply smoking."

She could not resist the desire to ask:

" How is it that you did not tell me you were going out ? "

" I only wanted to burn a weed. I am coming in, however."

" Then, good night, my friend."

" Good night, Countess."

She stepped back as far as her low chair, sat down in it, and wept, and the maid summoned to assist her to bed, seeing her red eyes, said to her compassionately:

" Ah. Madame is going to make herself a wretched face again for to-morrow."

The Countess slept badly, she was feverish, troubled by nightmare. When she awoke, before ringing she herself opened her window and curtains to see herself in the glass. Her features looked drawn, her eyelids swollen, her complexion yellow, and she felt such violent grief on this account that she was tempted to call herself ill, to keep in bed, and not show herself till evening.

Then she was possessed with a sudden, irresistible desire to go away, to leave at once by the first train, to quit the country, where one perceived too clearly by the strong light of the fields the indelible traces of sorrow and years. In Paris one lives in the half shadow of apartments, where heavy curtains, even at midday, admit only a mellow light. She herself would be beautiful again there, with the pallor one needs in that dim, discriminating glimmer. Then Annette's face passed before her eyes, rosy, her hair a little rumpled, so fresh, when she was playing lawn tennis. She comprehended then the unacknowledged anxiety from which her soul had suffered. She was not jealous of the beauty of her daughter. No! assuredly; but she felt, she confessed for the first time, that she must never more appear by her side in the bright sunlight.

She rang, and before drinking her tea she gave her orders for departure, wrote some despatches, even ordered her dinner for that night by telegraph, settled her accounts in the coun-

try, gave her last instructions, arranged everything in less than an hour, a prey to a feverish
and increasing impatience.

When she went down, Annette and Olivier,
advised of her decision, questioned her with surprise, and, finding that she gave no satisfactory
reason for this hurried departure, they grumbled
a little, and manifested their discontent until
they separated at the station in Paris.

The Countess, holding out her hand to the
painter, said to him:

"Will you come to dine to-morrow?"

He answered, rather sullenly:

"Certainly, I shall come. No matter. It is
too bad, what you have just done. We were so
comfortable down there, we three."

CHAPTER III.

So soon as the Countess was alone with her daughter in the coupé that was bringing her back to her home she at once felt tranquil, appeased, as if she had just passed through a severe crisis. She breathed easier, smiled at the houses, recognized with joy throughout the city those familiar details which real Parisians seem to bear in their eyes and hearts. By every shop she passed she could foresee the ones beyond, on a line along the Boulevard, and imagine the face of the tradesman so often seen behind his showcase. She felt saved. From what? Reassured! Why? Confident! Of what?

When the carriage had passed under the arch of the entrance she descended lightly, and entered, as though flying, into the shadow of the stairway, then into the shadow of her drawing-room, then into the shadow of her apartment. She remained standing a few moments, glad to be there, in security, in this dim, misty day of Paris, which, scarcely brightening, compels one to guess as well as to see, where one may choose what he will permit to be seen and what concealed; and the unreasoning memory of the resplendent light which bathed the country remained within her like the impression of past suffering.

When she went down to dinner, her husband, who had just come in, embraced her affectionately, and said smiling:

"Ha! Ha! I knew well enough that friend Bertin would bring you back. It was not a bad idea to send him for you."

Annette gravely interposed, in that peculiar tone she affected when she jested without a smile:

"Oh! He had much trouble; mamma could not decide for herself."

The Countess, a little confused, said nothing.

At home to no one, there were no visitors that evening. The next day Mme. de Guilleroy spent wholly in shopping, selecting or ordering what she needed. From her youth, almost from her infancy, she had enjoyed those long hours before the mirrors of the great shops. From the very moment of her entrance she rejoiced at the thought of all the details of that minute rehearsal in the wings of Parisian life. She adored the rustle of the sales-women's dresses, hastening forward at her approach, their smiles, their offers, their questions, and the dress-maker, the milliner or the corset-maker, was to her a person of value, whom she treated as an artist when she uttered an opinion, seeking advice. She liked still better to feel herself in the skilful hands of the young girls who undressed and re-dressed her, turning her gently around before her graceful reflection. The shiver that followed the touch of their deft fingers upon her skin, her neck, or in her hair, was one of the sweetest and most valued of the delicate trifles which go to make up the life of an elegant woman.

That day, however, it was with a certain anxiety that she passed, unveiled and bareheaded, before all those truthful mirrors. Her first visit to the milliner reassured her. The three hats which she chose became her charmingly; she could not doubt the fact, and when the tradeswoman had said to her, with a positive air, " Oh, Madame la Comtesse, fair women should never leave off mourning," she went away quite elated, and entered the other shops with restored confidence.

She found at home a note from the Duchess, who had come to see her, stating that she would return during the evening; then she wrote some letters; then she fell a-dreaming for some time, surprised to find that a simple change of surroundings should have put back into a past that seemed already remote the great misfortune that had crushed her. She could not even believe that her return from Roncières dated only from the day before, so altered was the condition of her soul since her return to Paris, as though that little change had healed her wounds.

Bertin, arriving at dinner time, exclaimed when he saw her:

"You are dazzling this evening."

And that infused her with a warm wave of happiness.

As they were leaving the table the Count, who was passionately fond of billiards, suggested to Bertin that they play a game together, and the two women accompanied them into the billiard-room, where the coffee was served.

The men were still playing when the Duchess was announced, and they all returned to the drawing-room. Mme. de Corbelle and her husband appeared at the same moment, their voices full of tears. For a few moments, it seemed from the doleful accents, that everybody was about to weep. But after a proper display of sympathy and the usual questions they glided into a more cheerful vein; the tones at once grew clearer, and they began to talk naturally, as though the shadow of the sorrow which had in an instant fallen on every one present had been suddenly dissipated.

Then Bertin rose, took Annette by the hand, led her under the portrait of her mother beneath the full light of the reflector, and asked:

"Is not that stupefying?"

The Duchess was so surprised that she seemed beside herself, and kept repeating:

"Heavens! is it possible? Heavens! is it

possible? It is one come from the dead. To think I never saw that on entering. Oh! my little Any. How I find you again, I who knew you so well then in your first mourning as a woman; no, your second, for you had already lost your father. Oh! that Annette, in black like that. Why, it is her mother returned to earth! What a miracle! Without that portrait it would not have been noticed. Your daughter resembles you now very much, but she resembles much more that portrait."

Musadieu came in, having heard of Mme. de Guilleroy's return, anxious to be one of the first to offer her the " homage of his sorrowful sympathy."

He interrupted his formalities on perceiving the young girl standing against the frame, enveloped in the same flood of light, and who appeared the living sister of the painting. He exclaimed:

" Ah! I declare, there is one of the most astonishing things I ever saw."

And the Corbelles, whose convictions always followed established opinions, marvelled in their turn with more subdued ardor.

The heart of the Countess seemed to shrink little by little, as if these unanimous exclamations of astonishment contracted and hurt it. Without a word, she gazed at her daughter by the side of her own image. A feeling of complete enervation overcame her. She wanted to cry out: " Do be quiet! I know well enough that she resembles me."

Throughout the evening she was melancholy, losing again the confidence that she had gained the day before.

Bertin was talking with her, when the Marquis of Farandal was announced. The painter on seeing him enter and approach the hostess, rose, slipped behind her armchair, murmuring: " This is fine! there comes that blockhead now." Then, in a circuitous fashion, he reached the door and went away.

The Countess, after the salutations of the new-comer, looked about for Olivier, to resume with him the conversation which had interested her. As she did not find him, she asked:

" What! has the great man gone?"

Her husband answered:

" I believe so, my dear, I just saw him take an English leave."

She was surprised, reflected a moment, then began to chat with the Marquis.

The intimate friends, however, soon withdrew, discriminately, for she had only half opened her door, so soon after her misfortune.

Then, when she found herself stretched upon her couch, all the griefs which had assailed her in the country reappeared; they were stronger; deeper; she felt old!

That evening, for the first time, she had understood that in her own salon—where thus far
she alone had been admired, complimented,
courted, loved—another, her daughter, was taking her place. She had understood that at once,
on feeling the homage drifting toward Annette.
In that realm, the house of a pretty woman, in
that realm where she will suffer no shadow,
whence she turns aside with cautious and steadfast care all perilous comparison, where she permits the entrance of her equals only to turn them
into vassals, she saw clearly that her daughter
was about to become the sovereign. How
strange that oppression of her heart had been
when all eyes turned toward Annette whom Bertin held by the hand, standing by the picture.
She had suddenly felt as if she had vanished,
dispossessed, dethroned. Everybody looked at
Annette; no one had turned to her more. She
was so accustomed to hear compliments and
flattery whenever her portrait was admired; she
was so sure of the eulogistic phrases, which she
had held so lightly, but which pleased her none
the less, that this desertion, this unexpected de-
fection, this admiration instantly and wholly carried toward her daughter, had moved, astonished
and struck her more than if it had been a question of no matter what rivalry under any circumstances whatever.

But as she had one of those natures which,

in all crises, after the first blow, react, struggle and find arguments for consolation, she thought that once her dear little daughter married, when they should cease to live under the same roof, she would no longer be obliged to stand that constant comparison which was beginning to become too painful for her under the eyes of her friends.

Yet the shock had been very great. She was feverish, and slept but little.

Next morning she awoke tired and stiff, and then there rose within her an irresistible longing to be comforted again, to be succored, to ask for help from some one who might cure her of all her pains, of all these moral and physical troubles.

She felt really so ill at ease, so weak, that she thought of consulting a physician. She was perhaps about to fall seriously ill, for it was not natural that she should pass in a few hours through those successive phases of suffering and pacification. She, therefore, summoned him by telegraph, and waited.

He arrived toward eleven o'clock. He was one of those grave, fashionable physicians whose decorations and titles are a guaranty of capacity, whose tact equals, at least, mere knowledge, and who have, above all, when dealing with women, skilful words surer than drugs.

He entered, bowed, looked at his patient, and with a smile:

" Come, this is not serious. With eyes like yours one is never very ill."

She was at once grateful to him for this beginning, and told him of her ailments, her despondency, her melancholy; then, without dwelling on the subject, her alarmingly ill looks. When he had listened to her with an air of attention, refraining from any questions, however, except as to her appetite, as if he knew very well the secret of that feminine malady, he sounded her, examined her, touched the flesh of her shoulder with the end of his finger, lifted her arms, having undoubtedly met her thought, and understood with the shrewdness of a practitioner who lifts all veils, that she had consulted him for her beauty much more than her health. Then he said:

" Yes, we have a little enemy, some nervous difficulty. This is not surprising, since we have suffered great grief. I will give you a little prescription which will rectify all that. But above all, you must take strengthening food, beef-tea, drink no water, only beer. I will name an excellent brand. Do not fatigue yourself by keeping late hours, but walk as much as you can. Sleep much and get a little stouter. It is all the advice I can give you, my fair patient."

She had listened to him with intense interest, endeavoring to guess all that was implied by his words.

She caught at the last word.

"Yes, I have grown thin. I was a little stout at one time, and I have perhaps become a little weaker in consequence of beginning to diet."

"Without the least doubt. There is no harm in remaining thin when one has always been so, but when one grows thin on principle, it is always at the expense of something. Fortunately, that is soon remedied. Good bye, madame."

She already felt better, more alert, and she wanted the beer he had named procured for breakfast, at its headquarters, that it might be the fresher.

She was leaving the table when Bertin was announced.

"It is I again," said he, "always I. I have come to ask a question. Have you anything to do presently?"

"No, nothing, why?"

"And Annette?"

"Nothing, either."

"Then, can you come to me at about four o'clock?"

"Yes, but for what purpose?"

"I am sketching the face of the *Rêverie*, of which I spoke to you when I asked you whether your daughter might pose a few moments for me. She would render me a great service if I had her only for one hour to-day. Will you?"

The Countess hesitated, annoyed, she knew not why. However, she replied:

" It is agreed, my friend. We shall be at your house at four o'clock."

" Thank you; you are kindness itself."

And he went off to prepare the canvas and study his subject, that he might not weary his model too much.

The Countess went out alone, on foot, to complete her purchases. She walked down to the great central thoroughfares, then came up the Boulevard Malesherbes, slowly, for she felt as though her limbs were broken. As she was passing before St. Augustin's she was seized with a desire to enter the church and rest. She pushed the padded door, sighed with satisfaction as she breathed the cool air of the vast nave, took a chair and sat down.

She was religious after the manner of many Parisian women. She believed in God without a doubt, unable to admit the existence of the Universe without the existence of a Creator. But associating, as everybody does, the attributes of Divinity with the nature of created matter within her vision, she almost personified the Almighty in accordance with what she knew of His works, without, for all that, having very clear ideas of what that mysterious Maker might in reality be.

She believed in Him firmly, adored Him

theoretically, feared Him very vaguely, for she ignored, in all fairness, His intentions and His will, having but very limited confidence in priests, whom she regarded generally as peasants' sons seeking refuge from military exactions. Her father, a Parisian of the middle class, having inculcated no principles of devotion, she had gone on heedlessly until her marriage. Then, her new position marking more strictly her apparent obligations to the Church, she had conformed punctiliously to this light servitude.

She was lady patroness to numerous and very well-known infant-asylums, never failed to attend mass at one o'clock on Sundays, gave alms for herself directly, and for the world through the medium of an abbot, vicar of the parish.

She had often prayed from a sense of duty, as a soldier mounts guard at his general's door. Sometimes she had prayed because her heart was sad, especially when she feared Olivier's desertion. Then, without confiding to Heaven the origin of her supplication, treating God with the same naïve hypocrisy that one does a husband, she asked Him to succor her. Formerly, at her father's death, and again, quite recently, at her mother's, she had had violent paroxysms of fervor, had implored, with sudden passionate outbursts, Him who watches over us and consoles us.

And lo! to-day, in the church she had just

entered by chance, she felt a profound need to pray, not for somebody or something, but for herself, herself alone, as the other day already she had prayed on her mother's grave. She must have help from some source, and she called upon God now as she had that very morning called a physician.

She remained long kneeling, in the silence of the church, broken now and then by a noise of footsteps. Then, at once, as if a clock had struck in her heart, she recollected herself, drew out her watch, was startled when she saw that it was nearly four o'clock, and ran away to get her daughter, whom Olivier must be already expecting.

They found the artist in his studio, studying upon his canvas the pose of his *Rêverie.* He wished to reproduce exactly what he had seen in the Park Monceau while walking about with Annette—a poor girl, dreaming, with a book open on her lap. He had long hesitated as to whether he should make her ugly or pretty. Homely, she would have more character, would awaken more thought, more emotion, would contain more philosophy. Pretty, she would be more winning, would diffuse greater charm, would please better.

The desire to make a study after his young friend decided him. The *Rêveuse* should be pretty, and might consequently realize her poetic vision some day or other, while if homely she would remain condemned to an endless and hopeless dream.

As soon as the two women had entered, Olivier said, rubbing his hands:

" Well, Miss Nané, we are going to work together, then ? "

The Countess seemed anxious. She sat in an easy chair and watched Olivier as he placed a garden chair of iron rush in the required light. He then opened his book-case to get a book, and hesitating:

" What does your daughter read ? "

" Mon Dieu! anything you like. Give her a volume of Victor Hugo."

"La Légende des Siècles?"

" Yes, you may."

He resumed:

" Little one, sit down here, and take this volume of poetry. Find page—page 336, where you will see a poem entitled: *les Pauvres Gens.* Absorb it as one would drink the best of wines, very slowly, word by word, and let it intoxicate you, let it move you. Listen to what your heart will say to you. Then close the book, raise your eyes, think and dream. And I will go and prepare my implements."

He went into a corner to prepare his palette, but, while emptying upon the thin little board the lead tubes from which came out slender,

twisted snakes of color, he turned round from
time to time to look at the young girl absorbed
in her reading.

His heart was oppressed, his fingers trembled; he no longer knew what he was doing, and
was mixing the tones as he mixed the little
piles of paste, such an irresistible wave of emotion did he suddenly feel before that apparition,
before that resurrection, in that same place,
after twelve years.

Now, she had finished her reading, and was
looking before her. Coming nearer he discovered in her eyes two bright tears, which fell and
ran down her cheeks. He was startled by one
of those shocks which disarm a man, and he
murmured, turning to the Countess:

" God! how beautiful she is."

But he remained stupefied before the livid
and convulsed face of Mme. de Guilleroy.

She was gazing at them, her daughter and
Olivier, with her great eyes full of a sort of
terror. He came nearer, in much concern asking:

" What is the matter ? "

" I wish to speak with you."

Rising, she said to Annette quickly.

" Wait a minute, my child, I have a word to
say to M. Bertin."

She passed rapidly into the little reception-
room adjoining, where he often made his visit-

ors wait. He followed her, his brain in a whirl, understanding not. As soon as they were alone she seized his hands and stammered:

"Olivier! Olivier! I beg of you, do not make her pose any more."

He murmured, troubled:

"But why?"

She answered, precipitately:

"Why? Why? He asks it? You do not feel it, then? Why? Oh! I should have guessed it sooner myself, but I have just discovered it a moment ago —I can say nothing to you now— nothing. Go and get my daughter. Tell her that I feel ill; call a cab, and come to see how I am in an hour. I will receive you alone."

"But, after all, what is the matter?"

She seemed to be approaching a hysterical condition.

"Leave me. I cannot speak here. Go and get my daughter and call a cab."

He was obliged to obey, and re-entered the studio. Annette, without any suspicion, had resumed her reading, her heart filled with sadness by the lamentable story of the poem. Olivier said to her:

"Your mother is indisposed. She came near fainting as she entered the reception-room. Go to her. I will bring some ether."

He went out, ran to his room for a smelling bottle, and returned.

He found them weeping in each other's arms. Annette, moved by the *Pauvres Gens*, gave vent to her emotion, and the Countess was somewhat relieved by confounding her grief with that sweet sorrow, mingling her tears with those of her daughter.

He waited for some time, not daring to speak, and looking at them, himself oppressed with an incomprehensible melancholy.

Finally, he said:

" Well, are you better ? "

The Countess answered:

" Yes; a little. It is nothing. Did you call a carriage ? "

" Yes, it will be here presently."

" Thanks, my friend, it is nothing. I have had too much sorrow for some time past."

" The carriage waits," a servant announced a moment later.

And Bertin, full of secret anguish, escorted as far as the carriage his pale and still faltering friend, whose heart-beat he felt beneath her dress.

When he was alone he asked himself: " But what is the matter with her? Why this scene ? " And he began to seek, wandering around the truth without resolving to discover it. Finally, he came near it: " Come," said he to himself, " does she believe I am paying court to her daughter? No, that would be too absurd."

And combating with ingenious and loyal arguments that possible conviction, he was indignant
that she should have lent for a moment any appearance of gallantry whatever to this healthy,
almost parental, affection. He became more and
more irritated at the Countess, unwilling to concede that she should dare to suspect him of such
dishonor, of such an unqualifiable infamy, and
resolved not to spare her the expression of his
resentment when he should answer her shortly.

After a little while he went out for the purpose of seeing her, impatient to have an explanation. All along the way he rehearsed with
increasing vexation the arguments that were to
justify him and absolve him from such a suspicion.

He found her upon her lounge, her face
changed by suffering.

"Well," said he, in a dry tone, "my dear
friend, please explain to me the strange scene
of a little while ago."

She answered, in a crushed voice:

"What! you have not yet understood ? "

"No, I confess I have not."

"Come, Olivier, look well into your heart."

"In my heart ? "

"Yes, in the depths of your heart."

"I do not understand. Explain yourself better."

"Look well into the depths of your heart, and

see if you find nothing there that is dangerous for you and for me."

" I repeat that I do not understand you. I guess that there is something in your imagination, but in my conscience I see nothing."

" I am not speaking of your conscience. I am talking of your heart."

" I am not good at conundrums. I pray you to be clearer."

Slowly raising both her hands, she took those of the painter, and kept them; then, as if each word were rending her heart:

" Beware, my friend, or you will fall in love with my daughter."

He abruptly withdrew his hands, and with the energy of innocence under a shameful accusation, with kindling animation and passionate gestures, he defended himself, accusing her in his turn, of having thus suspected him.

She let him speak at length, obstinately incredulous, sure of her position; then she resumed:

" But I am not suspicious of you, my friend. You are unconscious of what is taking place within you, as I was ignorant of it myself until this morning. You treat me as if I accused you of wanting to lead Annette astray. Oh, no! Oh, no! I know how loyal you are, and how worthy of the highest trust and completest confidence. I only pray you, I beseech you, to look into the bottom of your heart, and see whether the affection which, in spite of you, you are beginning to entertain for my daughter is not characterized by something a little different from simple friendship."

He was offended, and growing more and more excited, again began to plead his loyalty, as he had argued with himself through the streets.

She waited for him to finish his protestations; then, without anger, without being shaken in her conviction, but frightfully pale, she said:

" Olivier, I know very well all that you are saying to me, and I think as you do; but I am sure I am not mistaken. Listen; reflect; understand. My daughter resembles me too much; she is too much what I formerly was when you began to love me, that you should not begin to love her also."

" Then," he exclaimed, " you dare to throw such a thing in my face, upon this simple supposition and ridiculous reasoning: ' He loves me; my daughter resembles me—therefore, he will love her.' "

But seeing the growing change in the Countess's face, he continued, in a softer tone:

" Come, my dear Any, why, it is just because I find you once more in her that I so much like that young girl. It is yourself, yourself alone, I love as I look at her."

" Yes, it is precisely that which is beginning
to make me suffer, and of which I am so apprehensive. You do not yet distinguish what you
feel. You will have no doubt concerning it in
a little while."

" Any, I assure you, you are mad."

" Do you want proofs ? "

" Yes."

" You had not come to Roncières for the last
three years, notwithstanding my entreaties. But
this time you simply rushed when it was proposed to you to come after us."

" Ah! indeed. You reproach me for not leaving you alone yonder, knowing you to be ill,
after your mother's death."

" Be it so. I shall not insist. But this: the
need of seeing Annette again is so imperative
with you that you could not pass this day without asking me to take her to your house, under
pretext of posing."

" And you do not suppose it was you I sought
to see ? "

" Now you are arguing against yourself; you
are endeavoring to convince yourself; you do
not deceive me. Listen again. Why did you
leave abruptly night before last, when the Marquis of Farandal entered? Do you know ? "

He hesitated, very much surprised, very anxious, disarmed by this question. Then, slowly:

" Why—I hardly know—I was tired—and, to

be frank with you, that blockhead makes me nervous."

" How long since ? "

" He always did."

' 'I beg your pardon. I have heard you praise him. You liked him once. Be quite sincere, Olivier."

He reflected a few moments, and then, choosing his words:

" Yes, it is possible that the great love I bear you makes me so love all yours as to influence my opinion of that simpleton, whom I might meet now and then with indifference, but whom I should be sorry to see in your house almost daily."

" My daughter's house will not be mine. But enough. I know the uprightness of your heart. I know that you will reflect much upon what I have just said to you. When you have reflected you will understand that I pointed out a great danger to you when it was yet time to escape from it. And you will beware. Let us talk of something else, will you ? "

He did not insist, ill at ease now, no longer knowing what to think, having indeed need for reflection. And he went away after a quarter of an hour's conversation on indifferent subjects.

CHAPTER IV.

WITH slow steps Olivier was returning home, troubled as if he had just discovered some shameful family secret. He endeavored to sound his heart, to see clearly within him, to read those intimate pages of the inner book which seemed glued together, and which sometimes a strange finger alone may turn over by separating them. He certainly did not believe himself in love with Annette. The Countess, whose suspicious jealousy was ever on the alert, had scented the danger from afar, and had signaled it even before it existed. But might that danger exist, to-morrow, the next day, in a month? It was this sincere question that he was trying to answer sincerely. Assuredly, the young girl stirred up his instincts of tenderness; but those instincts are so numerous in men that the formidable ones should not be confounded with those which are inoffensive. Thus for instance, he adored animals, cats especially, and could not see their silky fur without experiencing an irresistible sensuous desire to stroke their soft, undulating backs and kiss their electric hair. The attraction which the young girl had for him resembled somewhat those obscure and innocent desires

which constitute a part of all the unceasing and
unmitigable vibrations of human nerves. The
eye of the artist and the eye of the man were
charmed by her freshness, by that growth of
beautiful clear life, by that essence of youth resplendent in her, and his heart, full of the recollections of his long intimacy with the Countess,
finding in the extraordinary resemblance of Annette to her mother a resurrection of former
emotions, the sleeping emotions of the beginning of his love, had been a little startled, perhaps, by the sensation of an awakening. An
awakening? Yes. Was that it? That idea
enlightened him. He felt that he was awaking
after years of sleep. Had he unconsciously loved
the little one he would have experienced near
her that feeling of rejuvenescence of the entire
being which creates a different man as soon as
the flame of a new desire is kindled within him.
No, that child had only fanned the old fire. It
was indeed the mother he continued to love, but
a little more than before, unquestionably, because of her daughter, that new edition of herself. And he formulated the ascertainment of
this with the tranquillizing sophism: " We love
but once. The heart may be often stirred at the
meeting with another being, for every one exercises upon others attractions or repulsions. All
these influences create friendship, caprice, desire
for possession, intense and fleeting passion, but

not true love. That this love may exist, it is
necessary that two beings should be so truly
born for each other, should be bound to each
other in so many ways, by such similarity of
tastes, such affinities of body, mind, character—
so many ties of all sorts as to form a network of
bonds. What we love, after all, is not so much
Mme. X—— or M. Z——; it is a woman or a
man, a nameless creature, born of Nature, that
great mother, with organs, a form, a heart, a
mind, an aggregation of qualities which, like a
lode-stone, attract our organs, eyes, lips, our
hearts, our minds, all our sensuous and intellectual appetites. We love a type, that is to say,
the union in one single person of all human qualities which separately may charm us in others."
     The Countess of Guilleroy had been this type
for him, and the continuance of their intimacy,
of which he had not wearied, proved it to him
undeniably. Now, physically, Annette so resembled what her mother had been as to deceive
the eye. There was therefore nothing astonishing if the heart of the man had been taken by
surprise, without being led away. He had
adored a woman. Another woman was born of
her, almost like her. He really could not help
bestowing upon the latter a moderate affectionate remnant of the passionate attachment he had
felt for the former. There was no harm, there
was no danger in that. His vision and his mem-

ory only were deluded by this semblance of resurrection; but his instinct was not led astray, for
he had never felt the slightest disturbance of a
desire for the young girl.

Yet the Countess reproached him with being
jealous of the Marquis. Was it true ? He again
examined his conscience severely, and ascer-
tained that in truth he was a little jealous. What
was there astonishing about that, after all? Are
we not at every instant jealous of men who pay
their court to no matter what woman? Do we
not in the street, the restaurant, the theatre, feel
a sort of enmity against the gentleman who is
passing, or enters with a beautiful woman on his
arm ? Every possessor of a woman is a rival.
It is a man who has won, a conqueror, who is
envied by the other men. And then, without
entering into these physiological considerations,
if it was natural that he should have for Annette
a sympathy rendered somewhat too active by his
love for her mother, was it not therefore natural
that he should feel rising within him a little animal hatred of the future husband ? He would
have no difficulty in overcoming this ignoble
feeling.

In his heart, nevertheless, there remained a
sort of acrimonious discontent with himself and
the Countess. Would they not be made uncomfortable in their daily relations by the suspicion
he would constantly feel that she harbored ?

Would he not be obliged to watch with tiresome and scrupulous attention every word, every act, every glance, his most insignificant attitudes toward the young girl; for all he might do, all he might say, would become suspicious to the mother. He returned home out of sorts, and began to smoke cigarettes with the impetuosity of a man who is irritated and uses ten matches to light his tobacco. In vain did he try to work. His hand, his eye, and his mind seemed to have lost the habit of painting, as if they had forgotten it, as if they had never known and practiced that art. He had taken out a little canvas already commenced, which he desired to finish—a street corner and a blind man singing—and he looked at it with unconquerable indifference, with such powerlessness to continue it that he sat before it, palette in hand, and forgot it, although still contemplating it with steadfast and abstracted intentness.

Then, suddenly, his impatience at the tediousness of the waning hour, at the interminable minutes, began to gnaw him with its intolerable fever. Since he could not work, what should he do till the hour of his dinner at the Club? The thought of the street wearied him beforehand, filled him with disgust for the sidewalks, the passers-by, the carriages and shops, and the thought of paying calls that day, to no matter whom, awoke in him an instantaneous hatred for all the people he knew.

So, what should he do ? Should he walk up
and down his studio, looking at every turn towards the clock, at the needle displaced every
few seconds ? Ah ! He knew those journeys
from the door to the cabinet, loaded with trifles.
In the hours of fervor, of impulse, of animation,
of fruitful and facile execution, those goings and
comings across the large room, brightened, in-
vigorated, warmed by work, were delightful rec-
reations; but in the hours of powerlessness and
nausea, in the miserable hours when nothing
seemed worth the trouble of an effort or a motion, it was the odious tramp of the prisoner in
his cell. If only he could have gone to sleep for
but an hour on his divan. But no, he would not
sleep; he would agitate himself until he trembled
with exasperation. Whence came this sudden
access of ill temper? He reflected: " I am becoming horribly nervous to get into such a state
through such an insignificant cause."

Then, he thought he would take a book. The
volume of the *Légende des Siècles* had remained
on the iron chair where Annette had laid it down.
He opened it, read two pages of verse without
comprehending them. He understood them no
more than if they had been written in a foreign
tongue. He was obstinate, and began over again
only to find that the meaning made really no impression upon him. " Come," said he to himself;
" it seems that my wits have left me." But about

two o'clock it flashed through his mind that he
must dally until dinner-time. He had a warm
bath prepared, and stretched himself out in it,
softened, relieved by the tepid water, and remained there till his valet, who was bringing the
linen, awakened him from a doze. He then went
to the Club, where he found his usual compan-
ions, who received him with open arms and exclamations, for they had not seen him for several
days.

" I am just in from the country," said he.

All those men, except the landscape artist,
Maldant, professed a profound scorn for the
fields. Rocdiane and Landa, it is true, went
hunting there, but on the plains or in the woods
they only enjoyed the pleasure of seeing pheas-
ants, quails or partridges falling like bundles of
feathery rags under their shot, or little rabbits
done to death, turning head-over-heels, like
clowns, five or six times in succession, showing
at every caper the white tufted tails. With the
exception of these Autumn and Winter sports,
they thought the country wearisome. Rocdiane
would say, " I prefer fresh women to fresh peas."

The dinner was, as usual, noisy and jovial, enlivened by discussions in which nothing unexpected can arise. Bertin, to divert himself,
talked much. They found him droll, but as soon
as he had taken his coffee and played a sixty
point game of billiards with the banker Liverdy,

he went out, strolled a little while from the Madeleine to the Rue Taitbout, passed three times before the Vaudeville, asking himself whether he should go in, almost hailed a cab to take him to the Hippodrome, changed his mind and went off in the direction of the Nouveau-Cirque, then made an abrupt half turn, without any purpose, object or pretext, walked up the Boulevard Malesherbes, and moderated his pace as he approached the residence of the Countess of Guilleroy. "She may think it strange to see me come back this evening," he thought. But he felt reassured as he reflected that there was nothing surprising in his calling to get news of her a second time.

She was alone with Annette, in the little drawing-room at the back, and still working on the blanket for the poor.

As she saw him enter, she said simply:

"Oh! it is you, my friend?"

"Yes, I felt uneasy; I wanted to see you. How are you?"

"Thank you, quite well."

She waited an instant, then added with marked intention:

"And you?"

He began to laugh with an easy air as he answered:

"Oh, I am very well. There was not the slightest foundation for your fears."

Stopping her knitting, she raised her eyes and rested them slowly upon him—an earnest glance of supplication and doubt.

" Really," said he.

" So much the better," she answered with a somewhat forced smile.

He sat down, and for the first time in that house he was seized with irresistible uneasiness, a sort of mental paralysis yet more complete than that which had possessed him that day before his canvas.

The Countess said to her daughter:

" You may continue, my child; it will not disturb him."

" What was she doing?" he asked.

" She was studying a fantasy."

Annette rose to go to the piano. He followed her with his eyes, unconsciously, as he always did, finding her pretty. Then he felt the eye of the mother upon him, and he quickly turned his head, as though he were looking for something in the dark corner of the room.

The Countess took from her work-table a little gold case which he had given her, opened it, and offering him some cigarettes:

" Smoke, my friend; you know that I like it when we are alone here."

He complied, and they listened to Annette's music. It was the music of a by-gone taste, graceful and light, one of those compositions with which the artist seems to have been inspired on a very soft moonlight evening in the spring-time.

Olivier asked:

" Whose music is that ? "

The Countess replied:

" Schumann's. It is but little known, and it is charming."

A desire to look at Annette was growing stronger, and he did not dare. He would have to make but a slight motion, a slight motion of the neck, for he saw sideways the two flames of the candles lighting the score, but he guessed so well, read so clearly the Countess's watchful at-tention, that he remained motionless, his eyes looking up before him, interested, so it seemed, in the thread of grey tobacco smoke.

Mme. de Guilleroy whispered:

" It is all you have to say to me ? "

He smiled.

" You must not mind. You know that music hypnotizes me; it drinks my thoughts. I shall speak presently."

" By the way," said she, " I had studied some-thing for you before mother's death. I never had you hear it. I will play it for you when the little one shall have finished; you shall see how odd it is."

She had real talent, and a subtle comprehen-sion of the emotion that flows through sound.

It was indeed one of her surest powers over the painter's sensibility.

As soon as Annette had finished the pastoral symphony of Méhul, the Countess rose, took her place, and awakened a strange melody by her fingers, a melody every phrase of which seemed a complaint, manifold complaints, changing, numerous, interrupted by a single note, continually recurring, dropping into the midst of the strains, cutting them, scanning them, shattering them, like a monotonously incessant, persecuting cry, the insatiable call of importunity.

But Olivier was looking at Annette, who had just seated herself before him, and he heard nothing, understood nothing.

He was looking at her, without thinking, feasting upon the sight of her as upon a good and habitual thing of which he had just been deprived, drinking her in wholesomely, as we drink water when we are thirsty.

"Well!" said the Countess, "is it not beautiful?"

Awakened, he cried:

"Admirable, superb; by whom?"

"You do not know?"

"No."

"What! you do not know; you?"

"No indeed."

"By Schubert."

He answered in a tone of profound conviction:

"That does not surprise me. It is superb. You would be charming if you began over again."

She did so, and he, turning his head, again began to gaze at Annette, but listening to the music also, that he might enjoy two luxuries at the same time.

Then when Mme. de Guilleroy had resumed her seat, in simple acquiescence to the natural duplicity of man, he withdrew his eyes from the fair profile of the young girl who was knitting opposite her mother on the other side of the lamp.

But if he did not see her he tasted the sweetness of her presence, as one feels the neighborhood of a warm hearth; and the desire of darting rapid glances at her only to let them fall immediately upon the Countess, was goading him, the desire of the school-boy who climbs to the street window as soon as the master has turned his back.

He went away early, for his tongue shared the paralysis of his mind, and his continued silence might be interpreted.

As soon as he found himself in the street a desire for roaming took possession of him, for whenever he listened to music it continued in him for a long time, led him into musings that seemed the melodies dreamed—a more precise sequel. The strains returned, intermittent and fugitive, bringing isolated measures, weakened, distant as an echo; then were silent, seemed to leave thought to give a meaning to the themes, and to wander after a sort of harmonious and tender ideal. When he reached the outward Boulevard he turned to the left, as he perceived the fairy-like illumination of the Park Monceau, and entered the central avenue rounded under the electric moons. A policeman was sauntering slowly; now and then a belated cab passed; at the foot of a bronze mast bearing the resplendent globe a man was seated on a bench in a bluish bath of electric light, reading a newspaper. Other lights on the lawn among the trees, shed their cold and penetrating beams into the foliage and on the turf, animating this great city garden with a pale light.

Bertin, with his hands behind him, strolled along the sidewalk, and thought of his promenade with Annette in this same park when he had recognized in her the voice of her mother.

He let himself fall upon a bench, and inhaling the cool breath of the watered lawns, he was assailed by all the passionate expectancy which renders the souls of striplings the incoherent canvas of an unfinished romance of love. Formerly he had known such evenings, those evenings of roving fancy, when he let his caprice wander into imaginary adventures and was astonished to feel a return of sensations, which were no longer of his age.

But, like the obstinate note of Schubert's melody, the thought of Annette, the vision of her face bowed under the lamp, and the strange suspicion of the Countess, took possession of him again and again. In spite of himself, he continued to occupy his heart with this question, to sound the impenetrable depths where human sentiments germinate before their birth. This obstinate research excited him ; this constant occupation of his thoughts by the young girl seemed to open a path for his soul to tender reveries. He could no longer dismiss her from his mind ; he bore within him a sort of evocation of her, as formerly, when the Countess left him; he would keep the strange feeling of her presence within the walls of his studio.

Suddenly, impatient at this sway of a memory, he murmured as he rose :

" It was stupid of Any to say that to me. Now she will make me think of the little one."

He returned home, uneasy about himself. When he had gone to bed he felt that sleep would not come, for a fever ran in his veins, and the spirit of revery was fermenting in his heart. Fearing wakefulness, that enervating insomnia induced by agitation of the soul, he thought he would try a book. How many times a short reading had served him as a narcotic ! He rose,

therefore, and stepped into the library, to choose
a profitable and soporific book ; but his mind,
aroused in spite of himself, eager for any emotion whatever, sought on the shelves an author's
name which would respond to his state of exaltation and expectancy. Balzac, whom he adored,
said nothing to him ; he disdained Hugo,
scorned Lamartine who, nevertheless, always left
him moved, and pounced upon Musset, the poet
of youth. He took a volume and carried it away
to bed, to read a few pages at random.

When he returned to bed he began to drink,
with a drunkard's thirst, those flowing verses of
an inspired poet, who, like a bird, sang the
dawn of existence, and having breath only for
the morning, was silent before the glaring light
of day—those verses of a poet who was, above
all, a man intoxicated with life, giving forth rapture in glowing and simple fanfares of love, the
echo of all young hearts bewildered with desires.

Never had Bertin so understood the physical
charm of these poems, which stir the senses and
scarcely move the mind. His eyes upon those
vibrating verses, he felt that his soul was but
twenty, buoyant with hope, and he read almost
the entire volume in a boyish intoxication. The
clock struck three, and he was astounded at his
wakefulness. He rose to close the window
which he had left open and to carry his book to
the table in the middle of the room ; but as the

cold draught of night touched him, a pain, which the seasons at Aix had not fully cured, shot along his back like a signal, like a warning, and he flung the poet aside, impatiently muttering, "What an old fool!" Then he returned to bed and blew out the light.

The next day he did not go to the Countess', and he even took the energetic resolution not to return for two days. But whatever he did, whether he tried to paint or undertook to walk, or dragged his melancholy from house to house, everywhere he was harassed by the persistent presence of those two women.

Having forbidden himself to go and see them, he found comfort in thinking of them, and he let his mind and his heart fill with memories of them. And it often happened that in that sort of hallucination in which he lulled his isolation the two faces approached each other, different, such as he knew them, then passed one before the other, mingled, melted together, forming now but one face, somewhat confused, which was no longer the mother's, not quite the daughter's, but that of a woman worshiped once, now, ever.

Then he felt remorseful for thus giving himself up to the sway of these emotions which he knew to be both powerful and dangerous. To escape them, to force them back, to free himself from this sweet and captivating dream, he

directed his thoughts toward all sorts of fancies
and theories, toward all possible subjects for reflection and meditation. In vain ! All the roads
of distraction which he followed brought him
back to the same point, where he met a fair
young face that seemed to lie in wait for him.
It was something vague and inevitable that was
besetting him, recalling and arresting him, however circuitous the road by which he might
choose to fly.

The confusion of these two beings, which had
so troubled him on the evening of their walk
at Roncières, was reviving again in his memory, when, as ceasing to reflect and reason, he
evoked them and undertook to comprehend
what strange emotion was stirring his being.
He said : " Let us see, do I love Annette more
than I should ? " And searching his heart, he
felt it burning with affection for a woman who
was quite young, who had Annette's features,
but who was not she. And he reassured himself
in a cowardly manner, thinking : " No, I do not
love the little one ; I am the victim of her likeness."

Still, the two days spent at Roncières remained in his soul like a source of warmth, of
happiness, of intoxication ; and their least details came back to him one by one, with precision, more enjoyable even than in reality. All
at once, threading the course of these recollec-

tions, he saw again the road they followed on going out from the cemetery, the young girl gathering flowers, and he suddenly remembered then that he had promised her a corn-flower of sapphires as soon as they returned to Paris.

All his resolutions took flight, and, without further struggle, he took his hat and went out, quite overcome at the thought of the pleasure he would afford her.

The Guilleroys' footman answered him when he presented himself.

"Madame is out, but mademoiselle is at home."

He was delighted.

"Tell her I would like to speak with her."

He slipped into the drawing-room with light steps, as if he had feared detection.

Annette appeared almost immediately.

"Good morning, dear master," said she, with gravity.

He began to laugh, shook hands with her, and sitting down near her :

"Guess why I have come ? "

She thought a few seconds.

"I don't know."

"To take you and your mother to the jeweler's to choose the sapphire corn-flower I promised you at Roncières."

The young girl's face lighted up with pleasure.

"Oh ! " said she, "and mamma has gone out.

But she will return soon. You will wait, will you not ? "

" Yes, if she is not too long."

" Oh! what insolence; too long, with me. You treat me like a little child."

" No," said he, " not as much as you think."

He wanted to please her, to be gallant and witty, as in the most dashing days of his youth, one of those instinctive desires which stimulate all the powers of charming, which cause a peacock to spread its tail and a poet to write verses. Phrases came to his lips, quick, vivacious, and he spoke as he knew how to speak in his best moments. The young girl caught his spirit, and answered him with all the mischief and frolicsome shrewdness that were latent in her.

Suddenly, as he was discussing an opinion, he exclaimed :

" But you have already told me that often, and I answered you . . . . "

She interrupted him with a peal of laughter:

" Well, you no longer say ' tu ' to me. You take me for mamma."

He blushed and was silent, then stammered :

" Well, your mother has already defended that opinion a hundred times with me."

His eloquence was spent ; he no longer knew what to say, and he was afraid now, incomprehensibly afraid, of this little girl.

" Here comes mamma," said she.

She had heard the door open in the first drawing-room, and Olivier, apprehensive as if he had
been discovered in some fault, explained how he
had suddenly remembered his promise and had
come after them both to go to the jeweler's.

" I have a coupé," said he, " I shall sit on the
bracket seat."

They started out, and a few moments later
they went in to Montara's.

Having spent his whole life in the intimacy,
observation, study and affection of women, having always occupied himself about them, having
had to sound and discover their tastes, be acquainted, like them, with questions of dress and
of fashion, all the minute details of their private
life, he had reached a point which enabled him
often to share some of their sensations, and
whenever he entered one of the shops where
the charming and delicate accessories of their
beauty are to be found, he experienced a thrill of
pleasure almost equal to that which animated
them. He was interested as they were in those
coquettish trifles with which they adorn themselves ; the stuffs pleased his eyes ; the laces
attracted his hands ; the most insignificant, elegant gew-gaws riveted his attention. In jewel-
ers' establishments he felt for the show cases a
shade of religious respect, as before the sanc-
tuaries of opulent seduction; and the desk, covered with dark cloth, upon which the supple

fingers of the goldsmith roll the jewels with
their precious reflections, inspired him with a
certain esteem.

When he had placed the Countess and her
daughter before this severe piece of furniture on
which, by an instinctive motion, both placed a
hand, he stated his desire ; and they showed
him models of little flowers.

Then sapphires were spread out before them,
four of which had to be chosen. It took a long
while. The two women turned them over on
the cloth with the tips of their fingers, then took
them cautiously, looked through them, studying
them with learned and passionate attention.
When those which they had selected had been
laid aside they needed three emeralds for the
leaves, then a little bit of a diamond that would
tremble in the centre like a drop of dew.

Then Olivier, who was intoxicated with the
pleasure of giving, said to the Countess :

" Will you do me the favor to choose two
rings ? "

" I ? "

" Yes, one for you, one for Annette. Let me
present you with these little gifts in memory of
the two days spent at Roncières."

She refused. He insisted. A long discussion
followed, a fight of words and arguments, which
ended, not without difficulty, however, in his
triumph.

The rings were brought, the rarest, alone in special cases ; others, grouped by classes, where all the fancifulness of their settings was aligned upon the velvet cloth. The painter was seated between the two women, and began with the same earnest curiosity to pick up the gold rings, one by one, from the narrow slits that held them. He then deposited them before him on the desk-cloth, where they were piled up in two heaps, one containing those which were discarded at first sight, the second those from which they would choose.

Time was passing insensibly and sweetly in this pretty work of selection, more captivating than all the pleasures of the world, distracting and varied as a play, stirring also, almost sensuous, an exquisite enjoyment of woman's heart.

Then they compared, grew animated, and the choice of the three judges settled upon a little golden serpent holding a beautiful ruby between his thin mouth and his twisted tail.

Olivier was beaming. Rising, he said :

" I leave you my carriage. I have some business to attend to; I am going."

But Annette begged her mother to return home on foot in this beautiful weather.

The Countess consented, and, having thanked Bertin, went out into the street with her daughter.

They walked for some time in silence ; in the

sweet enjoyment of accepted gifts ; then they
began to speak of all the jewels they had seen
and handled. Their minds were still filled with a
sort of glittering, a sort of jingling, a sort of
elation. They walked rapidly through the crowd
which at five o'clock follows the sidewalks on
summer evenings. Men turned round to look
at Annette, and whispered indistinct words of
admiration as they passed. It was the first time
since her mourning, since black was adding that
brilliancy to her daughter's beauty, that the
Countess had gone out with her in Paris; and
the sensation of that street success, that roused
attention, those whispered compliments, that little eddy of flattering emotion which the passing
of a pretty woman leaves in a crowd of men, oppressed her heart little by little with the same
painful shrinking she had experienced the other
evening in her drawing-room, when the young
girl was being compared to her own portrait.
In spite of her she was watching for those
glances of which Annette was the attraction; she
felt them coming from afar, glance off her face
without stopping, suddenly arrested by the fair
face at her side. She guessed, she saw in the
eyes the rapid and silent homage to this blooming youth, to the attractive charm of that freshness, and she thought, " I looked as well as she,
if not better." Suddenly the thought of Olivier
shot through her brain, and she was seized, as

she had been at Roncières, with an irresistible desire to run away.

She did not wish to feel herself any longer in this light in this stream of people, seen by all those men who were not looking at her. Those days were far away, yet quite recent, when she sought, provoked, a comparison with her daughter. Who to-day, among those passers-by, thought of comparing them ? One only had, perhaps, thought of it, just now, in that jeweler's shop ? He ? Oh ! What suffering ! Was it possible that his mind was not ceaselessly beset with that comparison ? Surely, he could not see them together without thinking of it, and remembering the time when she used to enter his house, so fresh, so pretty, so sure of being loved.

" I feel ill," said she. "We'll take a cab, my child."

Annette, alarmed, asked :

" What is the matter, mamma ? "

" It is nothing; you know that since the death of your grandmother I have often this faintness."

CHAPTER V.

FIXED ideas have the tenacity of incurable diseases. Once they have entered the soul they consume it, leave it no longer free to think of anything, be interested in anything, to have any taste for the least thing. Whatever she might be doing, at home or elsewhere, alone or surrounded by others, the Countess could no more rid herself of the thought which had seized her as she came back side by side with her daughter: Was it possible that Olivier, seeing them almost daily, was not ceaselessly beset with this temptation to compare them ?

Surely, he must do so in spite of himself, continually, himself haunted by a resemblance that could not be forgotten for a moment, still further accentuated by the imitation of gestures and intonation so lately pursued. Every time that he came in she immediately thought of that comparison; she read it in his glance, guessed it, speculated upon it in her heart and in her mind. Then she was tortured with a desire to hide herself, to disappear, to no longer show herself by the side of her daughter.

She was suffering, furthermore, in every way, feeling no longer at home in her own house.

That wounded sense of dispossession which she had experienced one evening, when all eyes were gazing at Annette under her portrait, was more pronounced, and exasperated her at times. She reproached herself continually for that inward need for deliverance, that unavoidable desire to send her daughter from her like a troublesome and obstinate guest, and she worked at it with unconscious skill, possessed with the urgency of yet struggling to retain, at any cost, the man she loved.

Unable to hasten unduly Annette's marriage, somewhat delayed by their recent mourning, she feared, with a confused and forceful apprehensiveness, any possible termination of that scheme, and she sought, almost against her will, to cultivate some love for the Marquis in her daughter's heart.

All the shrewd diplomacy which she had exercised for so long to keep Olivier was now taking with her a new form, keener, more secret, and exerted itself in attempting to create an affection between the young people and keeping the men apart.

As the painter, who was systematic in his habits of work, seldom breakfasted from home, and usually gave only his evenings to his friends, she often invited the Marquis to breakfast. He would come in, spreading around him the animation of his ride, a sort of matutinal breath of

air. And he talked gaily on all those worldly
subjects which seemed to float every day upon
the autumnal awakening of brilliant horse-fancy-
ing Paris in the Avenues of the Bois. Annette
was interested in listening to him, was acquiring
a taste for those topics of the day which he
thus brought her, quite fresh and varnished with
chic, as it were. A youthful intimacy was being
established between them, an affectionate companionship which a common and passionate
taste for horses naturally cemented. When he
had gone the Countess and the Count would
skilfully sing his praises, saying of him what need
be said in order that the young girl might understand that it wholly depended upon herself to
marry him if she liked him.

She had understood very quickly, however,
and reasoning ingeniously, thought it very natural to take for a husband that fine-looking
fellow, who would give her, besides other satis-
factions, that which she preferred to all others, a
gallop every morning by his side on a thorough-
bred.

Quite naturally one day they were betrothed,
after a handshake and a smile, and their marriage was talked of as a thing decided upon long
ago. Then the Marquis began to bring gifts,
and the Duchess treated Annette like her own
daughter. So all this affair had been brewed by
common accord with a little blaze of intimacy,

during the calm hours of day, and the Marquis having, besides, many other occupations, many connections, obligations and duties, seldom came of an evening.

It was Olivier's turn. He dined regularly every week at his friend's, and also continued to appear unexpectedly for a cup of tea between ten o'clock and midnight.

As soon as he entered the Countess began to watch him, possessed with the desire to know what was taking place in his heart. She immediately interpreted his every glance, his every gesture, and was tormented with the thought: " It is impossible that he should not love her, seeing us near each other."

He also was bringing gifts. No week passed that he did not appear bearing in his hands two little packages, offering one to the mother and one to the daughter; and the Countess, opening the boxes, which often contained articles of value, felt a sinking of the heart. She well understood that desire to give, which as a woman she had never been able to satisfy, that desire to bring something, to afford pleasure, to purchase something, to find in the shops the trifle that will please.

Once before the painter had gone through such a crisis, and she had seen him enter many times with that same smile, that same gesture, a little package in his hand. Then it had abated, and now it was beginning again. For whom ? She had no doubt. It was not for her.

He had a wearied look, thinner. She concluded that he was suffering. She compared his entrances, his manners, his deportment with the attitude of the Marquis, who was also beginning to be moved by Annette's grace. It was not the same thing. M. de Farandal was smitten, Olivier Bertin loved. She believed so at least during her hours of torture; then, during her moments of calm, she still hoped that she might be mistaken.

She was often on the point of questioning him when they were alone, praying, beseeching him to speak to her, to confess all, to conceal nothing. She preferred to know and weep under certainty rather than suffer thus under doubt and to be unable to read that closed heart wherein she felt another love was growing.

The heart that she valued more than her life, that she had watched over, warmed, animated with her love for twelve years past, of which she felt sure, that she had hoped was unalterably won, conquered, submitted, passionately devoted for the rest of their lives. Lo ! that heart was escaping from her by an inconceivable, horrible and monstrous fatality. Yes, it had suddenly closed, burying a secret. She could no longer open its door with a familiar word, roll her affection up in it as in a sure retreat, open to her-

self alone. Of what avail is it to love, to give
one's self unreservedly, if at once he to whom one
has offered one's whole being, one's whole existence, all, everything one had in the world,
escapes, because another face has pleased him,
and becomes then in the lapse of days almost a
stranger.

A stranger ! He ! Olivier ! He spoke to
her as formerly, with the same words, the same
voice, the same tones. And yet there was something between them, something inexplicable, intangible, invincible, almost nothing, that almost
nothing that causes a sail to drift away when
the wind changes.

He was drifting away, indeed; he was drifting
away from her a little more every day, by all the
glances he bestowed on Annette. He himself
did not try to see clearly into his heart. He felt
quite plainly that fermentation of love, that irresistible attraction, but he would not understand;
he trusted to events, to the unforeseen hazards of
life.

He no longer had any other care than that
of his dinners or evenings spent between these
two women, separated by their mourning from
all the fashionable whirl. Meeting at their house
only indifferent faces, such as the Corbelles, and
oftenest that of Musadieu, he thought himself
almost alone in the world with them, and as he
now seldom saw the Duchess and the Marquis,

for whom the morning and the mid-day were reserved, he wished to forget them, suspecting that the marriage had been postponed to some indeterminate period.

Moreover, Annette never spoke of M. de Farandal before him. Was it from instinctive modesty, or, perhaps, one of those secret intuitions of the feminine heart which enables them to foresee what they cannot know?

Weeks followed weeks, bringing no change in this life, and with the Autumn came the re-opening of the Chambers, earlier than usual, on account of the threatening political aspect.

On the day of the re-opening the Count of Guilleroy was to take Mme. de Mortemain, the Marquis and Annette, after breakfasting with him, to the meeting of Parliament. The Countess alone, isolated in her ever increasing sorrow, had announced her intention of remaining at home.

They had left the table and were drinking coffee quite gayly in the large drawing-room. The Count, pleased with the resumption of parliamentary duties, his only pleasure, spoke almost with spirit of the present situation and the difficulties of the Republic; the Marquis, decidedly in love, answered him with animation, looking at Annette, and the Duchess was almost equally gratified by the emotion of her nephew and the distress of the Government. The air of the drawing-room was warm with that first concentrated heat of newly kindled furnace fires, heat of hangings, carpets, walls, in which the perfume of asphyxiated flowers was quickly evaporating. There was an atmosphere of intimacy, of homeliness and satisfaction in this closed room filled with the aroma of the coffee, when the door was opened before Olivier Bertin.

He stopped at the threshold, so surprised that he hesitated about entering, surprised as a deceived husband who is the witness of his wife's crime. In his confused anger and the emotion which almost suffocated him, he recognized his heart worm-eaten with love. All that had been concealed from him, and all that he had concealed from himself, appeared to him as he perceived the Marquis installed in the house, like a betrothed.

Startled and exasperated, he clearly understood all that he would have preferred not to know, and all that they had not dared to tell him. He did not ask himself why all those preparations for marriage had been kept from him. He guessed it, and his eyes, now hard, met those of the Countess, who blushed. They understood each other.

When he was seated there was silence for a few moments, his unexpected entrance having checked their mounting spirits; then the Duchess began to speak with him, and he answered sharply, in a strange, metallic tone.

He looked around him at these people, who were chatting again, and said to himself, " They have made a fool of me. They shall pay for it." He was especially incensed against the Countess and Annette, whose innocent dissembling he suddenly understood.

The Count, looking at the clock, exclaimed: " Oh ! Oh ! It is time to start."

Then, turning toward the painter:

" We were going to the opening of Parliament. My wife only remains at home. Will you accompany us ? I should be very glad."

Olivier answered, in a dry tone:

" No, thanks. Your Chamber is no temptation to me."

Then Annette came toward him, and in a playful manner:

" Oh! come, dear master. I am sure that you will amuse us much more than the deputies."

" No, really. You will be very well amused without me."

Guessing that he was discontented and sad, she insisted, in the wish to show herself kind:

" Yes, do come, *monsieur le peintre.* I assure you, that as for me, I cannot get along without you."

A few words escaped him so impulsively that he was able neither to stop them on his lips nor to modify their tone.

"Bah! you get along without me like everybody else."

Somewhat surprised by his manner, she exclaimed:

"Well, now! If he does not begin again to drop his 'tu' in speaking to me."

His lips shaped themselves into one of those bitter smiles which indicate the suffering of a soul, and with a slight bow:

"I shall have to accustom myself to it, in any case, one of these days."

"Why so?"

"Because you will marry, and your husband, whoever he may be, would have the right to find such familiarity on my part rather out of place."

The Countess hastened to say:

"It will be time enough then to think of it. But I hope that Annette will not marry a man so susceptible as to take exception to such familiarity from so old a friend."

The Count was calling:

"Come, come; let us go; we shall be late."

And those who were to accompany him having risen, followed him out after the usual handshaking and the kisses, which the Duchess, the Countess and her daughter exchanged at every meeting and every parting.

They remained alone, she and he, standing behind the hangings of the closed door.

" Sit down, my friend," said she, softly.

But he answered, almost violently:

" No, thanks; I am going, too."

She murmured, beseechingly:

" Oh ! why ? "

" Because it is not my hour, it seems. I beg your pardon for having come without advising you."

" Olivier, what is the matter with you ? "

" Nothing; I only regret having disturbed a premeditated pleasure party."

She seized his hand:

" What do you mean ? They were about starting out, since they are going to the opening of the session. I was remaining; on the contrary, you were positively inspired to come to-day when I am alone."

He laughed, sneeringly:

" Inspired ! Yes, I was inspired ! "

She seized both his wrists, and, looking deeply into his eyes, she whispered, very low:

" Confess to me that you love her ? "

He freed his hands, unable longer to control his impatience:

" But you are insane with that idea ! "

Again she laid hold of his arms, and her fingers, tightening on his sleeves, beseechingly:

" Olivier ! confess, confess ! I prefer to know. I am certain of it, but I prefer to know. I would rather—Oh ! you do not understand what my life has become."

He shrugged his shoulders.

" How can I help it ? Is it my fault if you lose your head ? "

She held him, drawing him toward the other room at the back, where they would not be heard. She dragged him by his coat, clinging to him, panting for breath. When she had led him as far as the little round divan she compelled him to let himself fall into it, and then she seated herself by his side.

" Olivier, my friend, my only friend. I pray you, tell me that you love her. I know it. I feel it from all that you do. I cannot doubt it. I am dying from it, but I want to know it from your own lips."

As he still struggled, she sank down, kneeling at his feet. Her voice was quivering:

" Oh, my friend, my friend, my only friend; is it true that you love her ? "

He exclaimed, as he endeavored to lift her up:

" Why, no! why, no! I swear to you I do not."

She stretched out her hand toward his mouth, and closed her fingers over it tightly, stammering:

" Oh ! do not lie; I suffer too much."

Then she let her head fall upon this man's knees, sobbing.

He could see only the back of her head, a mass of blonde hair, mixed with many white ones, and he was touched with immense pity, immense grief.

Burying his hands in the heavy hair, he raised her head violently, turning up toward him two bewildered eyes, from which the tears were flowing freely. And then, upon those tearful eyes he pressed his lips again and again, repeating:

" Any ! Any ! my dear, my dear Any ! "

Then she, trying to smile, and speaking in the hesitating voice of a child whom grief is choking:

" Oh ! my friend, only tell me that you love me a little still."

He again embraced her.

" Yes, I love you, my dear Any."

She rose again, seated herself once more by his side, seized his hands again, looked at him, and, speaking tenderly:

" We have loved each other such a long time. It should not end thus."

He asked, as he pressed her to him:

" Why should it end ? "

" Because I am old, and Annette resembles too much what I was when you first knew me."

It was his turn to close that sorrowful mouth with the tips of his fingers, saying:

" Again ! I beg of you speak no more of it. I swear to you that you are mistaken."

" Oh! if you will only love me a little," she repeated.

" Yes, I love you," said he once more.

Then they remained a long time without uttering a word, with hands clasped, very much moved and very sad.

Finally, she broke the silence, and murmured:

" O! the hours that remain for me to live will not be gay."

" I shall endeavor to render them sweet to you."

The shadow of those cloudy skies which precede twilight by two hours was overspreading the drawing-room, gradually burying them under the gray mist of an Autumn evening.

The clock struck the hour.

" We have been here a long while," said she. " You should go, for some one might come, and we are not calm."

He rose, clasped her in his arms, kissing her half opened mouth as he used to do; then they crossed again the two drawing-rooms, arm-in-arm, like newly married people.

" Good bye, my friend."

" Good bye, my friend."

And the portière fell behind him.

He went down the stair, turned toward the Madeleine, began to walk without realizing what he was doing, stunned as if he had received a blow, his legs weak, his heart hot and palpitating, like a burning rag shaken in his breast. For two or three hours, or perhaps longer, he went straight before him in a sort of mental stupor and physical prostration, which left him just sufficient strength to put one foot before the other. Then he returned home to reflect.

So, then, he loved this little girl. He now understood all that he had felt near her since his walk in the Park Monceau, when he found in her mouth the call of a scarcely recognized voice, of the voice that had formerly awakened his heart; then all that slow, irresistible revival of an ill-extinguished love, not yet grown cold, which he was bent upon not recognizing.

What should he do ? But what could he do ? When she was married he would avoid seeing her often, that was all. Meanwhile he would continue to return to the house, that no one should have any suspicion, and he would hide his secret from everybody.

He dined at home, which he was never accustomed to do. Then he had a fire built in the large stove in his studio, for the night promised to be intensely cold. He even ordered the chandeliers to be lighted, as if he feared dark corners, and shut himself in. What strange, profound, physical, frightfully sad emotion had seized him. He felt it in his throat, in his breast, in all his relaxed muscles, as well as in his sinking soul. The walls of the room oppressed him; all his life was held within them, his life as an artist, his life as a man. Every painted study hanging there recalled a success, every piece of furniture held a recollection. But successes and recollections were things of the past. His life ? How short it seemed; empty, yet full. He had made pictures, and pictures, and still more pictures, and loved one woman. He recalled the evenings of exaltation after their meetings in this same studio. He had walked entire nights with his being full of fever. In the joy of happy love, the joy of worldly success, the unique intoxication of glory, he had tasted never-to-be-forgotten hours of inward triumph.

He had loved a woman, and that woman had loved him. Through her he had received that baptism which reveals to man the mysterious world of emotions and of love. She had opened his heart almost by force, and now he might no more close it again. Another love was entering, in spite of himself, through that breach, another, or rather, the same one, rekindled by a new face, the same strengthened by all the force that this need to adore takes as it grows old. So then he loved this little girl. There need be no more struggles, resistance or denials. He loved her with the despair of knowing that he should not even receive a little pity from her, that she would always be ignorant of his excruciating torment, and that another would wed her. At

this constantly recurring thought, impossible to
dismiss, he was possessed with an animal desire
to howl like a chained dog, for, like him, he felt
powerless, enslaved, bound. Growing more and
more nervous, the more he reflected the more he
kept crossing with rapid steps the vast apartment,
lighted up as for a feast. Finally, unable longer
to tolerate the pain of that reopened wound, he
thought he would try to soothe it with the recollection of his former love, to drown it in the
evocation of his first and great passion. From
the press, where he kept it, he took the copy of
the Countess's portrait, which he had formerly
painted for himself, placed it upon his easel, and,
seating himself before it, gazed at it. He tried
to see her again, to find her living again, such
as he had previously loved her. But it was
always Annette that appeared upon the canvas.
The mother had disappeared, had vanished, leaving in her place that other face which resembled
hers so strangely. It was the young girl, with
her hair a little lighter, her smile a little more
roguish, her manner a little more mocking, and
he felt, indeed, that he belonged, body and soul,
to that young being, as he had never belonged
to the other, as a sinking boat belongs to the
billows !

Then he rose, and in order to dismiss the apparition, he turned the painting over; then, filled
with sadness, he went to his room to get and

bring into the studio the drawer of his desk in which were sleeping all the letters of his fond love. They were there as in a bed, one upon the other, forming a thick layer of little thin pieces of paper. He dipped his hands into this, into all these phrases that spoke of them, in this bath of their long intimacy. He gazed on that narrow board coffin in which was lying that mass of piled up envelopes upon which his name, his name alone, was always written. He thought that a love, that the tender attachment of two beings one for the other, that the history of two hearts, were told therein, in that yellowish wave of papers, with spots made by the red seals, and he inhaled as he bent over them an old scent, a melancholy odor of enclosed letters.

He wished to read them again, and searching in the bottom of the drawer, he took a handful of the oldest. As fast as he opened them recollections came out of them, distinct, and they stirred his soul. He recognized many which he had carried about with him entire weeks, and found again all along the small handwriting that told him such sweet things, the forgotten emotions of former days. Suddenly, he felt under his fingers a fine embroidered handkerchief. What was it ? He thought a few moments, and then remembered. One day, at his house, she had wept because she was a little jealous, and he stole her handkerchief, bathed with tears, that he might keep it.

Ah ! What sad things ! What sad things ! Poor woman !

From the depths of this drawer, from the depths of his past, all those reminiscences rose like a vapor; it was nothing more than the impalpable vapor of exhausted reality. Yet he suffered for this, and wept upon those letters, as one weeps over the dead because they are no more.

But the stirring up of the old love caused the kindling of a new and youthful ardor within him, a wave of irresistible tenderness which recalled to his mind the radiant face of Annette. He had loved the mother in a passionate burst of voluntary servitude; he was beginning to love this young girl like a slave, like an old trembling slave, on whom fetters are riveted which he will never break.

That he felt in the depths of his being, and it terrified him.

He tried to comprehend how and why she so possessed him. He knew her so little. She was hardly a woman, but one whose heart and soul were still sleeping with the sleep of youth.

He, now, was almost at the end of life. How was it, then, that this child had captivated him with a few smiles and locks of her hair? Ah! the smiles, the hair of that blonde little girl made him feel like falling upon his knees and bowing his head to the ground.

Do we know, do we ever know, why a woman's face has suddenly the power of a poison upon us? It would seem as though we had been drinking her with our eyes, that she had become our mind and our body. We are intoxicated by her, mad with her; we live of that absorbed image, and we would die of it.

How one suffers sometimes through the ferocious and incomprehensible power of the form of a face upon a man's heart.

Olivier Bertin had resumed his walking; night was advancing, his fire had gone out. Through the window panes the cold from without was entering. Then he sought his bed, where until daylight he continued to muse and suffer.

He was up early, without knowing why, nor what he was about to do, nervously agitated, as irresolute as a revolving weather-vane.

By dint of seeking some distraction for his mind and occupation for his body, he remembered that on that very day some members of his Club were accustomed to meet every week at the Bains Maure, where they breakfasted after the bath. He dressed quickly, therefore, hoping that the hot room and the shower bath would calm his nerves, and he went out.

As soon as he stepped outside he felt the cold, keen air, that first crisp cold of the first frost that kills the last remnants of Summer in a single night.

All along the boulevards there fell a thick rain of large yellow leaves, with a dry, soft sound. They fell, as far as the eye could reach, from one end of the wide avenue to the other, between the house fronts, as if all the stems had been severed from the branches by the sharp edge of a thin blade of ice. The streets and sidewalks were already covered with them, and resembled for some hours the forest paths at the beginning of winter. All this dead foliage crackled under foot, and was occasionally piled up in light waves by puffs of wind.

It was one of those days of transition which constitute the end of one season and the beginning of another, which have a special savor of sadness, the sadness of approaching death or the savor of reviving sap.

As he crossed the threshold of the Bain Turk the thought of the heat that would presently penetrate his flesh, after passing through the frosty air of the streets, brought a thrill of satisfaction to Olivier's sad heart. He undressed, quickly wrapping about his waist the light scarf which the attendant was holding out to him, and disappeared behind the padded door opened before him.

A warm, oppressive breath, which seemed to come from a distant furnace, made him breathe as if he needed air as he traversed a Moorish gallery lighted by two Oriental lanterns. Then a woolly negro, his only apparel a belt, with shining body and muscular limbs, rushed before him to raise a portière at the other end, and Bertin entered the hot-air bath, a round room with high ceiling, silent, almost as mystical as a temple. The light fell from above, from the cupola and through trefoils of colored glass into the immense circular room paved with flagstones, whose walls were covered with decorated pottery, after the Arabic fashion.

Men of all ages, almost naked, were walking slowly, gravely, silently; others were seated upon marble benches with arms crossed; others were chatting in an undertone.

The hot air made one pant even at the entrance. There was something ancient-like and mysterious about the place, this stifling and decorated circus, where human flesh was heated, where black and brown *masseurs*, with copper-colored legs, were circulating.

The first face the painter saw was that of the Count de Landa. He was going around like a Roman wrestler, proud of his enormous chest and his large arms crossed over it. A frequenter of the hot-air baths, he felt there like a favorite actor upon the stage, and he criticised the discussed muscling of the strong men of Paris after the manner of an expert.

" Good morning, Bertin," he said.

They shook hands, then Landa continued:

" Hein ! fine weather for sweating."

" Yes, magnificent."

" Have you seen Rocdiane ? He is down yonder. I called for him as he was getting up. Oh !
just look at that anatomy."

A little gentleman was passing, bow-legged,
with slender arms and thin flanks, who made
these two old models of human vigor smile
scornfully.

They sat down upon a long marble slab and
began to talk as if they were in a drawing-room.
The attendants were circulating, offering drinking water. One could hear the slaps of the
masseurs on the bare flesh and the sudden gush
of the shower bath. A continuous splashing of
water, coming from all corners of the great amphitheatre, filled it also with the light noise of
rain.

At every instant a new comer greeted the
three friends or approached to shake hands.
They were the big Duke of Harrison, little
Prince Epilati, Baron Flach and others.

Suddenly Rocdiane exclaimed:

" Halloo, Farandal ! "

The Marquis entered, his hands on his hips,
walking with that ease of well-built men who
are never embarrassed.

Landa murmured:

" He is a gladiator, that fellow."

Rocdiane resumed, turning toward Bertin:
" Is it true that he is going to marry the daughter of your friends ? "

" I think so," said the painter.

But that question, before that man, at that moment, in that place, made Olivier's heart quake frightfully with despair and rebellion. The horror of all the foreseen realities appeared to him for a second with such acuteness that he struggled for a few moments against a brutal desire to hurl himself upon the Marquis.

Then he rose.

" I am tired," said he.   " I am going at once to the *massage.*"

An Arab was passing.

" Ahmed, are you disengaged ? "

" Yes, Monsieur Bertin."

And he started off hurriedly to avoid shaking hands with Farandal, who was coming along, slowly going around the Hammam.

He remained scarcely a quarter of an hour in the large cooling-room, so calm, which is surrounded by cells containing the beds, around a plot of African plants and a *jet d'eau* falling in drops in the centre.   He had a sense of being pursued, threatened, that the Marquis was about to join him, and that he would be obliged, with outstretched hand, to treat him as a friend, with a desire to kill him.

He soon found himself again on the Boulevard, which was covered with dead leaves. They were falling no more, the last having been shaken down by a long blast. Their red and yellow carpet was shivering, stirring, waving from one pavement to the other, driven by gusts of the rising wind.

Suddenly a sort of roaring sound came over the roofs, that bellowing of the passing blast, and at the same time a furious gust, which seemed to come from la Madeleine, blew hard through the boulevard.

The leaves, all the fallen leaves, that appeared to be waiting for it, rose as it drew near. They ran before it, assembling, whirling and rising spirally to the tops of the houses. It drove them like a flock, a mad flock, that was flying, going, running away toward the gates of Paris, toward the free sky of the suburbs. And when one large cloud of leaves and dust disappeared upon the heights of the *quartier* Malesherbes the streets and sidewalks remained bare, strangely clean and swept.

Bertin was thinking, " What will become of me ? What shall I do ? Where shall I go ? "

And he was returning home, unable to think of anything.

A kiosk caught his eye. He purchased seven or eight newspapers, hoping, perhaps, that he would find something to interest him for an hour or two.

" I will breakfast here," he said as he entered his house, and went up to his studio.

But he realized as he sat down that he would not be able to stay there, for he felt through his whole frame the excitement of a mad beast.

The newspapers which he skimmed could not distract his soul for a moment; the news he read met his eye without reaching his mind. In the middle of an article which he was making no effort to understand, the name of Guilleroy startled him. It was about the meeting of the Chamber, where the Count had spoken a few words.

His attention, awakened by that call, next observed the name of the celebrated tenor Montrosé, who, toward the end of December, was to give a unique performance at the Opera. It was to be a magnificent musical occasion, it went on to say, for the tenor Montrosé, who had been away from Paris six years, had just won unprecedented success throughout Europe and America, and furthermore he would be supported by the famous Swedish singer Hellson, who also had not been heard in Paris for the last five years.

Olivier was at once struck with the idea, which seemed to spring from the bottom of his heart, of affording Annette the pleasure of wit-

nessing this performance.   Then he reflected
that the Countess's mourning would be an obsta-
cle to this plan, and he sought some means of
carrying out his purpose in any event.   One
way only offered itself.   He must take a stage
box where one was almost invisible, and if the
Countess should yet refuse to go, have Annette
accompanied by her father and the Duchess.   In
this case the box should be offered to the Duchess.   But then he would have to invite the Marquis.

He hesitated and reflected long.

Surely, the marriage was decided upon, nay, it
was a settled thing unquestionably.   He guessed
the haste of his friend in having it over with.
He understood that within the shortest possible
time she would give her daughter to Farandal.
He could not help it.   He could neither prevent,
nor modify, nor retard that frightful event.
Since he must endure it, was it not better that
he should try to master his soul, conceal his suffering, appear content, and no longer permit
himself to be carried away by bursts of anger,
as he had just done?

Yes, he would invite the Marquis, thereby
allaying the Countess's suspicions, and keeping
a friendly door for himself in the young household.

As soon as he had breakfasted he went down
to the Opera to secure one of the boxes hidden

behind the curtain. It was promised him. Then he hastened to the Guilleroys.

The Countess appeared almost immediately, and still somewhat moved by their emotion of the previous day:

"How kind of you to have returned to-day," she said.

He stammered:

"I am bringing you something."

"What is it?"

"A box on the stage of the Opera for a unique performance of Hellson and Montrosé."

"Oh! my friend, what a pity! And my mourning?"

"Your mourning dates almost four months back."

"I assure you that I cannot."

"And Annette? Think that she will perhaps never again have such an opportunity."

"With whom could she go?"

"With her father and the Duchess, whom I am about to invite. I intend also to offer the Marquis a seat."

She looked into the depths of his eyes, while a mad desire to embrace him rose to her lips. She repeated, hardly believing her ears:

"To the Marquis?"

"Why, yes."

She subscribed at once to this arrangement. He continued in an indifferent tone:

"Have you fixed the date of their marriage ?"

"Mon Dieu ! yes, nearly so. We have reasons for hurrying it very much, the more so that it was already decided upon before my mother's death. You remember ?"

"Yes, indeed, and when will it take place ?"

"Well, about the beginning of January. I beg your pardon for not telling you before."

Annette came in. He felt his heart leaping in his breast as if it were on springs, and all the tenderness which drew him toward her was suddenly changed to bitterness, and created within him that sort of strange passionate animosity into which love turns when lashed by jealousy.

"I bring you something," said he.

She answered:

"So we have decidedly adopted the 'you.'"

He took on a paternal air.

"Look here, my child, I am acquainted with the event in store for you. I assure you that in a little while it will be indispensable. Better at once than later."

She shrugged her shoulders discontentedly, while the Countess remained silent, looking into the distance, her mind intent.

Annette asked:

"What did you bring me ?"

He told her about the performance and the invitations he expected to give. She was delighted, and throwing her arms about his neck with the impulse of a little child, she kissed him on both cheeks.

He felt like fainting, and understood under the repeated gentle caress of that little mouth with its sweet breath, that he would never recover.

The Countess irritated, said to her daughter: "You know that your father is waiting for you."

"Yes, mamma, I am going."

She ran off, still sending kisses with the tips of her fingers.

As soon as she had gone out, Olivier asked: "Will they travel?"

"Yes, for three months."

And in spite of himself he murmured: "So much the better."

"We shall resume our former life," said the Countess.

He stammered: "Indeed, I hope so."

"Meanwhile, do not neglect me."

"No, my friend."

The impulse he had shown the day before as he saw her weep, and the plan he had just announced of inviting the Marquis to this performance at the Opera, had revived a little hope in the Countess.

It was of short duration. Before a week was over she was again following upon this man's

face, with torturing and jealous attention, every
stage of his suffering. She could ignore nothing,
since she herself endured all the pain she could
guess in him, and Annette's constant presence
reminded her at every moment of the day of the
powerlessness of her efforts.

Everything weighed her down at the same
time—years and her mourning. Her active, intelligent and ingenuous coquetry, which all her
life long had insured her triumph with him, found
itself paralyzed by that black uniform which em-
phasized her paleness and the alteration of her
features, while the adolescence of her child was
by the same means rendered dazzling. The time
was already long past, yet quite recent, of Annette's return to Paris, when she proudly sought
similar toilets which were then favorable to her.
Now she was furiously tempted to tear from her
body those vestments of the dead which made
her look ugly and so tormented her.

Had she felt that all the resources of elegance
were at her service, had she been able to choose
and make use of delicately tinted stuffs, harmon-
izing with her complexion, that would have given
a studied power to her dying charm, as captivating as her daughter's inert grace, she would undoubtedly have known how to remain still the
most attractive.

She knew so well the influence of the fever-
imparting evening toilets, and the soft, sensuous

morning robes, of the disturbing déshabillé worn at breakfast, with intimate friends, and which invests a woman until midday with a sort of savor of her rising, the material and warm impression of the bed she has left and of her perfumed room.

But what could she attempt under that sepulchral dress, under that convict's uniform, which would cover her for a whole year? A year! She would remain for a year imprisoned in that black shell, inactive and vanquished. For a year she would feel herself growing old day by day, hour by hour, minute by minute, under that crape sheath. What would she be in a year if her poor ailing body continued so to alter under the anguish of her soul?

These thoughts haunted her, spoiled everything she might have relished, turned into grief everything that would have given her joy, left her not a pleasure, a contentment or gaiety intact. She was ever trembling with an exasperated need of shaking off this burden of misery that crushed her, for without this distressing importunity she would yet have been so happy, alert and healthy. She felt that her soul was spirited and fresh, her heart ever young, the ardor of a being that is beginning to live, an insatiable appetite for happiness, more ravenous even than heretofore, and a devouring· desire to love.

And lo! all good things, all sweet, delicious

poetic things, which embellish life and render it
enjoyable were withdrawing from her, because
she was growing old. It was all over. Yet she
still found within her the sensibility of the young
girl and the passionate impulse of the young woman. Nothing had grown old but her body, her
miserable skin, that covering of the bones, faded
little by little, moth-eaten like the cloth cover of
a piece of furniture. The curse of this decay had
fastened upon her and become almost a physical
suffering. This fixed idea had created a sensation of the epidermis, the feeling of growing old,
continuous and perceptible, like that of cold or
heat. She believed indeed that she felt a vague
sort of itching, the slow appearance of wrinkles
upon her forehead, the sinking of the tissues of
cheeks and neck, and the multiplication of those
innumerable little strokes which wear out the
wearied skin. Like a being affected by a con-
suming disease, which a constant prurience compels to scratch itself, the perception and terror of
that abominable and imperceptible work of rapid
time imbued her soul with an irresistible need of
ascertaining it in the mirrors. They called her,
attracted her, forced her to come, with staring
eyes to see, look again, to observe continually,
to touch with her finger, as though to make
more sure of it, the indelible wear of years. It
was at first an intermittent thought, recurring
every time that she saw the polished surface of

the dreaded glass at home or elsewhere. She stopped on the sidewalks to look at herself in the shop windows, hanging, as it were, by one hand to all the plates of glass with which the tradesmen adorn their fronts. It became a disease, a mania. She carried in her pocket a pretty little ivory rice powder-box, as large as a walnut, whose inside cover contained an imperceptible glass, and often while walking she held it open in her hand and raised it toward her eyes.

When she sat down to read or write in the drawing-room hung with tapestries, her mind, distracted for a moment by this new employment, would soon return to its obsession. She struggled, tried to divert her attention, to think of something else, to continue her work. All in vain! She was goaded by desire, and soon dropping her book or her pen, her hand would stretch out with an irresistible motion toward the little old silver-handled glass lying on her desk. In this chiselled and oval frame her whole face was enclosed like a face of earlier days, like a portrait of the last century, like a pastel once fresh which the sun had tarnished. Then, after she had long gazed at herself, with a tired motion she rested the little glass upon the desk and tried to resume her work, but before she had read two pages or written twenty lines, she was again possessed with the invincible and tormenting need

of looking at herself; and again she stretched
out her arm to grasp the glass..

She now handled it like an irritating and
familiar plaything which the hand cannot leave,
used it at every instant while receiving her
friends, and became nervous enough to cry out,
hated it as a sentient being while twirling it in
her fingers.

One day, exasperated by this struggle between herself and this bit of glass, she flung it
against the wall, where it split and was shivered
to pieces.

But after awhile her husband, who had it
repaired, handed it to her, clearer than ever, and
she was obliged to take it and thank him, resigned to keep it.

Every evening, and every morning also, shut
up in her room, she began over again, in spite
of herself, that minute and patient examination
of this odious and quiet havoc.

When in bed she could not sleep; she would
relight a candle and lie with her eyes open, thinking how sleeplessness and sorrow irretrievably
hasten the horrible work of fleeting time.   She
listened in the silence of the night to the pendu-
lum of her clock, which, with its regular and
monotonous tick-tack seemed to whisper, " Ça
va, ça va, ça va," and her heart shriveled with
such suffering that, with the sheet between her
teeth, she groaned in despair.

Formerly, like everybody else, she had some notion of the passing years and of the changes they bring. Like every one, she had said to herself every winter, every spring and every summer: "I have changed much since last year." But ever beautiful, with a somewhat varying beauty, she took no thought of it. To-day, all at once, instead of again peaceably realizing the slow changes of seasons, she had just discovered and understood the formidable flight of the moments. She had had a sudden revelation of that slipping away of the hour, of that imperceptible race, maddening when one thinks of it, of that infinite procession of little hurried seconds which nibble at the body and life of man.

After these miserable nights she had long, quieter periods of drowsiness, in the warmth of the bed, when her maid had opened the curtains and lighted the bright morning fire. She remained weary, drowsy, neither awake nor asleep, in the mental torpor which permits the involuntary revival of that instinctive and God-given hope which lights and feeds the hearts and smiles of men to the last hour.

Every morning now, as soon as she had risen, she felt impelled by a powerful desire to pray to God and obtain from Him a little relief and consolation.

Then she knelt before a tall oak crucifix, a gift of Olivier, a rare work by him discovered, and with closed lips imploring with the voice of the soul, the voice with which we speak to ourselves, she offered up a sorrowful supplication to the Divine martyr. Distracted by the want of being heard and succored, simple in her distress, like all the faithful on their knees, she could not doubt that He was listening to her, that He was attentive to her request and perhaps touched by her sorrow. She did not ask Him to do for her what He never did for any one—to leave her charm, her freshness and her grace until her death; she only asked for a little respite and repose. Of course, she must grow old, as she must die. But why so soon? Some women remain beautiful to such an advanced age. Could He not grant that she be one of those? How good He would be. He who had also suffered so much, if He only gave her for two or three years more the remnant of charm she needed in order to please.

She did not say these things to Him, but she sighed them to Him, in the confused complaint of her soul.

Then, having risen, she would sit before her dressing-table, and with a tension of thought as ardent as in her prayer, she would handle her powders, her cosmetics, her pencils, the puffs and brushes, which gave her once more a beauty of plaster—evanescent and fragile.

CHAPTER VI.

Upon the boulevards all tongues were sounding two names: " Emma Hellson" and "Montrosé." The nearer one drew to the Opera, the oftener did he hear those names repeated. Furthermore, immense placards, posted on the Morris columns, held them up conspicuously before the passers-by, and there was in the evening air the excitement of an event.

The heavy monument called " l'Académie nationale de Musique," cowering under the black sky, exhibited to the public gathered in front of it its pompous and whitish façade and the marble colonnade of its gallery, illuminated like a stage scene by invisible electric lights.

Upon the square the mounted Republican Guards directed the traffic, and innumerable carriages arrived from all quarters of Paris, giving glimpses of creamy light stuffs and pale heads behind the lowered windows.

The coupés and landaus followed in a line under the reserved arcades, and stopping for a moment, fashionable and other women would alight, in their evening pelisses, trimmed with furs, feathers and priceless laces—precious bodies, divinely adorned.

295

All the way up the famous stairway there was a fairy-like ascent, an uninterrupted mounting of ladies arrayed like queens, whose throats and ears were ablaze with flashing jewels, and whose long trains swept the steps.

The auditorium was filling early, for no one wished to lose a note of the two illustrious artists; and throughout the vast amphitheatre, under the resplendent electric light falling from the chandelier, the surging crowd were finding their seats amid the loud clamor of voices.

From the stage box, already occupied by the Duchess, Annette, the Count, the Marquis, Bertin and M. de Musadieu, nothing could be seen but the wings, where men were chatting, running or shouting; they were machinists in their blouses, gentlemen in full dress, actors in costume. But behind the lowered drop-curtain one could hear the deep voice of the crowd, feel the presence of a mass of stirring, over-excited beings, whose agitation seemed to penetrate through the curtain, to spread out even to the decorations.

The opera was " Faust."

Musadieu was relating anecdotes connected with the first performances of this work at the Théâtre Lyrique, the partial failure at the time and the brilliant success that followed, about the original cast, and their rendition of every selec-

tion. Annette, partly turned toward him, listened with the youthful and greedy curiosity
with which she encompassed the whole world,
and occasionally she threw upon her betrothed,
who would be her husband in a few days, an
affectionate glance. She loved him, now, as
simple hearts love, that is to say, that she loved
in him all the promises of the morrow. The
intoxication of the first feasts of life and the
ardent wish to be happy made her shiver with
joy and expectation.

And Olivier, who saw everything, who knew
everything, who had gone down all the steps of
secret, helpless and jealous love, down to the
fireplace of human suffering, where the heart
seems to crackle like flesh upon hot coals,
Olivier stood at the back of the box looking at
both with the eyes of a martyr.

The three blows were struck, the quick, sharp
rap of a bow upon the desk of the orchestral
leader stopped abruptly all movement, all cough-
ing and whispers; then, after a short and profound silence, the first measures of the overture
were heard, filling the auditorium with the invisible and irresistible mystery of the music which
penetrates our bodies, fills our nerves and souls
with a poetic and sensuous fever, mingling with
the air we breathe a sonorous wave to which we
listen.

Olivier sat down at the back of the box, pain-fully moved, as if the wounds of his heart had been touched by those sounds.

But with the rising of the curtain he stood up again and saw the Doctor Faust in a meditative attitude, the scene representing the study of an alchemist.

Twenty times had he already heard that opera, which he knew almost by heart, and his attention, immediately leaving the play, turned to the auditorium. He could see but a little section of it behind the frame of the stage which concealed his box, but this section, reaching from the orchestra to the upper gallery, showed him an entire portion of the audience in which he recognized many faces. In the orchestra chairs, men in white cravats, side by side in a row, seemed a museum of familiar faces, worldlings, artists, journalists, representing all classes of those who never fail to be where everybody goes. In the balcony, in the stalls, he mentally designated and called out the names of the women he saw. The Countess of Lochrist, in a proscenium box, looked absolutely charming, while a little farther a bride, the Marchioness of Ebelin, was already raising her opera-glass. "A pretty début," Bertin thought.

People listened with great attention, with evident sympathy, to the tenor Montrosé, who was bewailing life.

Olivier was thinking : " What a huge joke !

There is Faust, the mysterious and sublime Faust, who sings the horrible disgust and nothingness of everything; and the crowd are asking themselves anxiously whether Montrosé's voice has not changed." Then he listened, like the rest, and behind the commonplace words of the libretto, through the music which rouses in the depths of the soul profound perceptions, he had a sort of revelation of Goethe's conception of Faust's heart.

He had formerly read the poem, which he deemed very beautiful, without being moved by it, and lo! he suddenly felt its unfathomable depth, for it seemed to him on that evening that he himself was becoming a Faust.

Leaning over a little on the front of the box, Annette was listening intently; and murmurs of satisfaction were beginning to go up from the audience, for Montrosé's voice was in better tune and broader than formerly.

Bertin had closed his eyes. For a month past all that he saw, all that he felt, all that he encountered in life he immediately made a sort of accessory to his passion. He threw the world and himself as food to this fixed idea. All that he saw which was beautiful, rare, all that he imagined which was charming, he instantly offered mentally to his little friend, and he had no longer a thought which he did not bring back to his love.

Now he listened deep in his heart to the echo of Faust's lamentations; and the desire to die sprang up within him—the desire to have done with all his sorrows, with all the misery of his hopeless love. He gazed at Annette's fine profile and saw the Marquis of Farandal seated. He felt old, done for, lost! Ah! to be waiting for nothing more, to be hoping for nothing more, no longer to have even the right to desire, to feel out of his sphere, retired from life, like a superannuated functionary whose career is finished—what intolerable torture!

There was a burst of applause; Montrosé was already triumphant. And Mephisto (Labarrière) sprang out of the ground.

Olivier, who had never heard him in this character, listened with revived attention. The recollection of Aubin, so dramatic with his bass voice, then of Faure, so charming with his baritone voice, distracted him for a few moments.

But suddenly a phrase sung by Montrosé with irresistible power moved his very heart. Faust was saying to Satan:

> "I would possess a treasure,
> Would enhance them all,
> Fresh youth to enjoy them."

And the tenor appeared in silken doublet, a sword by his side, a plumed cap on his head, elegant, young and handsome, with the affected beauty of the singer.

A murmur went up. He looked very fine, and the women liked him. Olivier, on the contrary, felt a chill of disappointment, for the poignant evocation of Goethe's dramatic poem disappeared in this metamorphosis. He had henceforth before his eyes but a fairy scene full of pretty bits of song, and talented actors whose voices alone he was now listening to. That man in a doublet, that fine-looking fellow with his roulades, who exhibited his thighs and his notes, displeased him. It was not the true, the irresistible and wicked knight Faust, he who was about to win Marguerite.

He sat down again, and the strain he had just heard returned to his mind:

> "I would possess a treasure,
> Would enhance them all,
> Fresh youth to enjoy them."

He whispered it between his teeth, sang it sorrowfully in the depths of his soul, and with his eyes fixed upon Annette's blonde head, which rose in the square opening of the box, he felt all the bitterness of that unattainable desire.

But Montrosé has just finished the first act with such perfection that the enthusiasm burst forth. For several minutes the noise of applause, of the stamping and the bravos, filled the theatre like a storm. At all the boxes the women were seen tapping their gloves one against the other, while the men, standing behind them, shouted as they clapped their hands.

The curtain fell, but it was raised twice before the excitement had subsided. Then when the curtain was lowered for the third time, separating the stage and inside boxes from the audience, the Duchess and Annette still continued to applaud for some seconds, and were specially rewarded with a little discreet bow from the tenor.

" Oh, he saw us," said Annette.

" What an admirable artist ! " exclaimed the Duchess.

And Bertin, who had been leaning forward, looked with a confused feeling of irritation and scorn upon the applauded actor as he disappeared between two side-lights, waddling a little, his leg stiff, his hand on his hip, in the guarded pose of a theatrical hero.

They began to speak of him. His successes aroused as much interest as his talent. He had been in all the capitals, in the rapturous presence of women, who, knowing beforehand that he was irresistible, felt their hearts beat as he came upon the stage. He seemed to care very little, however, it was said, for this sentimental delirium, and was content with musical triumphs. Musadieu was relating in very ambiguous terms, because of Annette, the life of this handsome singer, and the Duchess, carried away, understood and approved all the follies within his power to create—this great musician whom she thought so charming, elegant and *distingué*. And she concluded, laughing:

" Besides, how can one resist such a voice ! "

Olivier was displeased and severe. He did not understand really how any one might care for a strolling actor, for that perpetual representation of human types which he never fulfilled, that delusive personification of imaginary men, that nocturnal and painted manikin who plays characters at so much per night.

" You are jealous of them," said the Duchess. " You men of the world and artists are all envious of actors because they are more successful than you."

Then turning toward Annette:

" Come, little one, you who are entering into life and look at it with healthy eyes, what do you think of this tenor ? "

Annette answered with conviction:

" Why, I think he is very fine."

The three strokes were sounding for the second act, and the curtain rose on the Kirmess.

Hellson's passage was superb. She also seemed to have more voice than formerly and to handle it with more complete certainty. She had truly become the great, excellent, exquisite singer whose reputation in the world equalled that of Bismarck or Lesseps.

When Faust rushed toward her, when he addressed to her with his bewitching voice the words so full of charm:

> "Ne permettrez-vous pas, ma belle demoiselle,
> Qu'on vous offre le bras, pour faire le chemin !"

And when Marguerite answered him:

> "Non, monsieur, je ne suis demoiselle ni belle,
> Et je n'ai pas besoin qu'on me donne la main,
> Qu'on m'offre le bras, pour faire le chemin !"

the whole house was thrilled with the deep impulse of pleasure.

The applause as the curtain fell was deafening, and Annette applauded so long that Bertin was tempted to take hold of her hands to stop her. His heart was wrung by a new torment. He did not speak between the acts, for he was pursuing in the wings, with his fixed thought now full of hatred, following to his box, where he saw him replacing the powder on his cheeks, the odious singer who was so over-exciting this child.

Then the curtain rose on the "Garden" scene.

At once a sort of fever of love overspread the house, for never had that music which seems but a breathing of kisses found two such interpreters. It was no longer two illustrious actors, Montrosé and Hellson, but two beings from the ideal world, hardly two beings, but two voices: the eternal voice of man who loves, the eternal voice

of woman who yields; and they sighed together
all the poetry of human tenderness.

When Faust sang

"Laisse-moi, laisse-moi contempler ton visage,"

there was in the notes that soared from his
mouth such an accent of adoration, of rapture
and supplication, that really for a moment all
hearts were stirred with a desire to love.

Olivier remembered that he himself had murmured this strain, under the castle windows, in
the park at Roncières. Till then he had thought
it rather commonplace, now it came to his lips
like a last passionate cry, a last prayer, the last
hope and the last favor he might expect in this
life.

Then he listened to nothing more, heard
nothing more. A sharp paroxysm of jealousy
attacked him, for he had just seen Annette putting her handkerchief up to her eyes.

She wept! Therefore her heart was awakening, becoming animated, excited, her little
woman's heart which knew nothing yet. There,
quite near him, without her dreaming of him, she
had a revelation of the manner in which love
may overthrow a human being, and that revelation, that initiation had come to her from that
miserable strolling singer.

Ah! he had but little spite against the Marquis
of Farandal, that simpleton who saw nothing,

20

who did not know, who did not understand!
But how he hated that man in tights, who was
illuminating that young girl's soul!

He was tempted to rush up to her as one
rushes toward a person in danger of being
trampled under foot by an unmanageable horse,
seize her by the arm, lead her, hurry her away
and say to her: " Let us go, let us go. I beg
of you ! "

How she listened, how her heart throbbed !
and how he suffered! He had suffered thus
before, but not so cruelly! He remembered,
because the pangs of jealousy revive like reopened wounds. It was at Roncières first, on
returning from the cemetery, when he felt for
the first time that she was escaping from him,
that he had no power over her, over that little
girl as independent as a young animal. But
yonder, when she had vexed him by leaving him
to gather flowers, he felt a sort of brutal desire
to check her impulses, to retain her presence
near him; to-day it was her very soul that was
fleeting, intangible. Ah! that gnawing irritation
he had just recognized, how often had he not
still felt it through all the little inexpressible con-
tusions by which fond hearts are continually
bruised. He recalled all the painful impressions
of petty jealousy falling upon him, by little blows.
day by day. Every time she had noticed, admired,
liked, desired something, he had been jealous of

it; jealous of everything in an imperceptible and continuous fashion, of everything that absorbed the time, glances, attention, gaiety, astonishment, affection of Annette, for all that took a little of her from him. He had been jealous of all that she did without him, of all he did not know, of her outings, her readings, of all that seemed to afford her pleasure, jealous of an heroic officer wounded in Africa and who was the talk of Paris for about a week, of the author of a highly praised novel, of a young unknown poet she had not seen, but whose verses Musadieu recited, finally of all men praised before her, even in an indifferent sort of way, for, when one loves a woman one cannot tolerate without anguish that she should even think of any other with an appearance of interest. One feels at heart the imperious need of being the only one in the world in her eyes. One wishes her to see, to know, to appreciate no one else. As soon as she manifests a desire to turn round to look at or recognize anybody, one throws himself before her vision, and, if unsuccessful in turning it aside or absorbing it entirely, suffers to the bottom of his soul.

Thus did Olivier suffer before this singer, who seemed to scatter and gather love in that opera house; and he had a spite against everybody on account of the tenor's success, against the overexcited women in the boxes, the men, those fools who were giving an apotheosis to this coxcomb.

An artist ! They called him an artist, a great artist ! And he had successes, this hireling, this paltry interpreter of a foreign thought such as no creator had ever known! Ah! that was like the justice and intelligence of people of fashion, those ignorant and pretentious amateurs for whom the masters of human art work unto death. He gazed at them as they applauded, shouted, went into ecstasies; and that early hostility that had always been dormant in the bottom of the proud and haughty heart of a parvenu became exasperated, a furious rage against those imbeciles, all powerful by virtue of rank and wealth alone.

He remained silent, a prey to his thoughts, till the end of the performance. Then, when the final storm of enthusiasm had subsided, he offered his arm to the Duchess, while the Marquis offered his to Annette. They again descended the grand staircase, floating down in a stream of men and women, in a sort of magnificent and slow cascade of bare shoulders, sumptuous dresses and black coats. Then the Duchess, the young girl, her father and the Marquis stepped into the same landau, and Olivier Bertin remained alone with Musadieu upon the Place de l'Opera.

Suddenly he experienced an impulse of affection for this man, or rather that natural attraction we feel for a fellow countryman whom we meet in a distant land, for he felt now lost in that strange, indifferent, tumultuous crowd, while with Musadieu he might still speak of her.

He therefore took his arm.

" You are not going home immediately," said he. " The weather is fine; let us take a walk."

" Willingly."

They went down toward the Madeleine, mixed with the crowd of night-strollers in that short and violent midnight excitement which shakes the boulevards as people come out of the theatres.

Musadieu had a thousand things in his mind, all his subjects for conversation from the instant that Bertin should name his " bill of fare," and he let his loquacity flow upon the two or three themes which interested him most. The painter let him go on without listening to him, holding him by the arm, sure to lead him presently to speak of her, and he walked without seeing anything around him, imprisoned in his love. He walked, exhausted by that paroxysm of jealousy which had bruised him like a fall, crushed by the conviction that he had nothing more to do in the world.

He would suffer thus, more and more, without expecting anything. He would go through empty days, one after the other, looking on from

afar to see her living, happy, loved, loving. A
lover! She would have a lover perhaps, as her
mother had had one. He felt in himself such
numerous sources of suffering, so different and
complicated, such an afflux of misfortunes, so
many inevitable torments, he felt so completely
lost, so far launched, from this very moment,
into an unimaginable agony, that he could not
suppose any one had ever suffered like him.

And he thought at once of the puerility of
poets who have invented the useless labor of
Sisyphus, the material thirst of Tantalus, the
devoured heart of Prometheus ! Oh ! had they
foreseen, had they proved the distracted love of
an aged man for a young girl, how would they
have expressed the frightful and secret striving
of a being who can no longer inspire love, the
torments of fruitless desire, and, worse than a
vulture's beak, a little blonde face tearing an old
heart to pieces.

Musadieu continued to talk and Bertin interrupted him, murmuring almost in spite of himself, under the power of his fixed idea:

" Annette was charming this evening."

" Yes, delightful."

To prevent Musadieu from resuming the
broken thread of his thoughts, the painter added:

" She is prettier than her mother ever was."

His companion assented absent-mindedly, repeating several times in succession: " Yes—yes

—yes—" without his mind having yet embraced this new idea.

Olivier endeavored to keep him there, and in order to anchor him with one of Musadieu's favorite preoccupations, he cunningly continued:

" She will have one of the first salons in Paris after her marriage."

That was sufficient, and the inspector of fine arts, the satisfied man of the world, began learnedly to formulate an opinion of the position which the Marchioness of Farandal would occupy in French society.

Bertin listened to him, and he imagined Annette in a large drawing-room brilliantly lighted, surrounded by women and men. This vision again made him jealous. They were going up the Boulevard Malesherbes now. When they passed before the Guilleroy mansion the painter looked up. Lights seemed to be shining at the windows, through the opening in the curtains. He had a suspicion that the Duchess and her nephew had perhaps been invited to come and take a cup of tea. And he was seized with a rage that caused him horrible suffering.

He was still clinging to Musadieu's arm, and now and then he revived, by a contradiction, his views on the future Marchioness. .That commonplace voice speaking of her caused her image to flit about them in the night.

When they reached the painter's door, Avenue de Villiers, Bertin asked:

" Are you coming in ? "

" No, thanks. It is late. I am going to bed."

" Come, come up for half an hour; we'll chat a little while longer."

" No, really; it is too late ! "

" Do come up. I wish you to choose a study I have been wanting to offer you this long while."

His companion, knowing that painters are not always in a giving mood, grasped at the opportunity. In his capacity of Inspector des Beaux-Arts he owned a gallery which had been collected with skill.

" I follow you," said he.

They entered.

The valet being aroused brought them some rum, and the conversation dragged along upon painting for a while. Bertin was showing some studies, begging Musadieu to choose the one he liked best; and Musadieu hesitated, confused by the gas-light, which deceived him in the matter of tones. Finally he chose a group of little girls jumping the rope on a sidewalk; and almost immediately afterward he was ready to take his leave and carry away his gift.

" I shall have it taken to your house," said the painter.

" No, I prefer to have it this very evening to admire it before I go to bed."

Nothing could detain him, and once more Olivier Bertin found himself alone in his house, that prison of his recollections and painful agitation.

The next morning when the servant entered, bringing tea and the newspapers, he found his master sitting up in bed, so pale that he was frightened.

" Is Monsieur ill ? " said he.

" It is nothing but a little headache."

" Does not Monsieur wish me to fetch something ? "

" No. How is the weather ? "

" It rains, sir."

" Very well. That is all."

The man, placing the tea-tray and the news-papers upon the customary little table, withdrew.

Olivier took up the *Figaro* and opened it. The leading article was entitled " Modern Painting." It was a dithyrambic panegyric of four or five young painters who, gifted with real abilities as colorists, exaggerated them for effect in the pretension of being revolutionists and renovators of genius.

Like all the elder ones, Bertin was vexed with these new comers, was irritated at their ostracism, disputed their doctrines. He began therefore to read this article with the rising anger

which readily thrills a nervous heart, then glancing further along, he perceived his own name;
and those few words at the end of a sen-
tence struck him like a blow of the fist full
in the breast : " Olivier Bertin's antiquated
art."

He had always been sensitive to criticism and
sensitive to praise, but way down in his consciousness, notwithstanding his legitimate vanity, his pain under criticism was greater than
his pleasure under praise, a consequence of the
uneasiness concerning himself which his hesita-
tions had always fed. Formerly, however, in the
days of his triumphs, the waving of incense was
so frequent that it made him forget the pin-
strokes. To-day, before the ceaseless growth of
new artists and new admirers, congratulations
were more rare and disparagement more emphatic. He felt that he was enrolled in the bat-
talion of old painters of talent whom the younger
do not treat as masters ; and since he was as intelligent as he was perspicacious, he now suffered
from the slightest insinuations as much as from
direct attacks.

Yet never had a wound to his artistic pride
proved so painful. He remained gasping, and
read the article over in order to understand its
slightest shades. A few colleagues and himself
were swept aside with outrageous unconcern ;
and he rose murmuring these words that re-

mained on his lips: " Olivier Bertin's antiquated art. . . . "

Never had such sadness, such discouragement, such sense of the end of everything, of the end of his physical and his thinking being, thrown him into such desperate distress of soul. He sat in his arm-chair till two o'clock, before the chimney, his legs stretched out toward the fire, having no strength to move, to do anything. Then the need of being consoled rose within him, the need of clasping devoted hands, of seeing faithful eyes, of being pitied, succored, caressed with friendly words.

He went therefore, as usual, to the Countess.

When he entered, Annette was alone in the drawing-room, standing with her back to the door, hurriedly writing an address. On the table, by her side, the *Figaro* was spread out. Bertin saw the newspaper at the same time that he saw the young girl, and he was bewildered, not daring to step forward. Oh! if she had read it! She turned, and in a preoccupied, hurried way, her mind busy with feminine cares, she said to him:

"Ah! good morning, *monsieur le peintre*. You will excuse me if I leave you. My dressmaker is upstairs waiting for me. You understand that the dressmaker at the time of a wedding is an important person. I will lend you mamma, who is discussing and arguing with my artist. If I need her I will recall her for a few minutes."

And she hurried away, running a little to show her haste.

This sudden departure without a word of affection, without a soft glance for him who loved her so much—so much—upset him quite. His glance fell again on the *Figaro*, and he thought: " She has read it ! They make game of me, they deny me. She no longer believes in me. I am nothing to her any more."

He took a couple of steps toward the newspaper as one walks up to a man to slap him in the face. Then he thought: " Perhaps she has not read it, after all. She is so busy to-day. But they will speak of it before her this evening at dinner, undoubtedly, and they will give her the notion of reading it ! "

With a spontaneous, almost unthinking motion, he seized the journal, closed it, folded it, and slipped it into his pocket with the rapidity of a thief.

The Countess entered. As soon as she saw Olivier's pale and convulsed countenance she guessed that he was reaching the limits of his suffering.

She was impelled toward him with an impulse of all her poor soul so torn, also, of all her poor body that was itself so bruised. Throwing her hands upon his shoulders and her glance in the depth of his eyes, she said to him:

"Oh ! how unhappy you are !"

This time he did not deny it, and his throat quivering spasmodically, he stammered out:

" Yes—yes—yes !"

She felt that he was on the verge of tears, and led him into the darkest corner of the drawing-room, toward two easy-chairs hidden by a little screen of antique silk. They sat down behind this thin embroidered wall, veiled also by the grey light of a rainy day.

She resumed, ever pitying him, distressed by such grief:

" My poor Olivier, how you suffer ! "

He leaned his white head upon his friend's shoulder.

" More than you believe ! " said he.

She murmured, so sadly:

"Oh ! I knew it. I have felt it all. I saw it spring up and grow ! "

He replied as though she had accused him:

" It is not my fault, Any."

" I know that—I am not reproaching you for anything—"

And softly, turning a little, she placed her lips upon one of Olivier's eyes, where she found a bitter tear.

She was startled, as if she had drunk a drop of despair, and repeated several times:

" Ah ! my poor friend—poor friend—poor
friend !" Then after a moment of silence, she
added :

" It is the fault of our hearts that have not
grown old. I feel mine so full of life ! "

He tried to speak, and could not, for now sobs
were choking him. She listened to the stifling in
his breast as he leaned against her. Then, seized
again by the selfish anguish of love, which had
been gnawing at her so long, she said in the
heart-rending tone in which one realizes a horrible misfortune :

" My God ! how you love her ! "

Once more he confessed :

"Ah ! yes, I love her !"

She thought a few moments, and resumed :

" You never loved *me* so ?"

He did not deny it, for it was one of those
hours where one speaks the whole truth, and
murmured :

" No, I was too young then ! "

She was surprised.

" Too young? Why ? "

" Because life was too sweet. It is only at our
age that one loves desperately."

She asked :

" Does what you feel when near her resemble
what you used to feel when near me ? "

" Yes and no . . . and yet it is almost the
same thing. I have loved you as much as any

one may love a woman. I love her like yourself, since she is yourself; but that love has
become something irresistible, destructive,
stronger than death. I belong to it as a burning
building belongs to the flames."

She felt her compassion wither under the
breath of jealousy, and assuming a consoling
tone:

" My poor friend! In a few days she will be
married and will go away. Seeing her no more,
you will surely get over it."

He shook his head.

" Oh! I am quite lost, lost ! "

" Why, no, no! You will not see her for three
months. That will be enough. Three months
were indeed sufficient for you to love her more
than you love me, whom you knew for more
than twelve years."

Then he implored her in his infinite distress:

" Any, you will not desert me ? "

" What can I do, my friend ? "

" Do not leave me alone."

" I shall go and see you as much as you like."

" No. Keep me here, as much as you can."

" You would be near her."

" And near you."

" You must not see her again before her marriage."

" Oh! Any ! "

" Or, at least, very seldom."

" May I stay here, this evening ? "

" No, not in the condition in which you are. You must amuse yourself, go to the Club, to the theatre, anywhere, but do not remain here."

" I beg of you."

" No, Olivier, it is impossible. And then I have some people at dinner whose presence would disturb you again."

" The Duchess? and—him——?"

" Yes."

" But I spent last evening with them."

" You speak of it ! You are in a fine condition to-day."

" I promise you to be calm."

" No, it is impossible."

" Then I am going."

" Why are you in such a hurry ? "

" I need to walk."

" That's right, walk much, walk till night, kill yourself with fatigue and then go to bed ! "

He had risen.

" Good-bye, Any."

" Good-bye, dear friend. I shall go and see you to-morrow morning. Would you like me to be very imprudent, as formerly, make believe that I am breakfasting here at noon, and go and breakfast with you at a quarter past one ? "

" Yes, I would. You are kind ! "

" It is because I love you."

" So do I love you."

" Oh! speak no more of that."

" Good-bye, Any."

" Good-bye, dear friend.   Till to-morrow."

" Good-bye."

He was kissing her hands over and over again,
then he kissed her temples, then the corner of
the lips.   His eyes were now dry, his air reso-
lute.   When he was about to go out he seized
her, wound his arms entirely around her, and,
pressing his lips to her forehead, he seemed to
drink, to inhale from her, all the love she had
for him.

Then he went away very quickly, without
turning round.

When she was alone she let herself fall upon
a seat, sobbing.   She would have remained there
till night if Annette had not unexpectedly come
for her.

The Countess, to gain time to dry her red eyes,
answered:

" I have a few words to write, my child.   Go
up again, and I will follow you in a few
seconds."

Till evening she had to busy herself about
the engrossing question of the trousseau.

The Duchess and her nephew were dining at
the Guilleroys, a family affair.

They had just taken their seats at the table
and were still speaking of the play of the pre-

ceding night, when the butler entered, bearing three enormous bouquets.

Mme. de Mortemain was astonished.

" Heavens; what is that ? "

Annette exclaimed:

"Oh ! how beautiful they are !   Who can possibly have sent them ? "

Her mother answered:

" Olivier Bertin, of course."

Since his departure she was thinking of him. He had appeared so gloomy to her, so tragic, she saw so clearly his hopeless misfortune, she felt so cruelly the counter-stroke of that grief, she loved him so much, so tenderly, so completely, that her heart was crushed under mournful presentiments.

In the three bouquets were found, indeed, three cards of the painter.   He had written upon each, with pencil, the names of the Countess, the Duchess and Annette.

Mme. de Mortemain asked:

" Is your friend Bertin ill ?   I thought he looked quite badly yesterday."

And Mme. de Guilleroy replied:

" Yes; he worries me a little, although he does not complain."

Her husband added:

" Oh! he is doing as we do; he is growing old. In fact, he is growing old quite rapidly just now. I believe, however, that bachelors usually break

down all at once. They succumb more suddenly
than others. He has changed very much indeed."

The Countess sighed:

" Oh! yes ! "

Farandal suddenly stopped whispering to Annette to say:

" The *Figaro* contained a very disagreeable
article for him this morning."

Any attack, criticism or allusion unfavorable
to her friend's talent threw the Countess into a
rage.

" Oh ! " said she, "men of Bertin's worth do
not need to mind such rudeness."

Guilleroy was surprised:

" What! a disagreeable article for Olivier; but
I have not read it.   On what page ? "

The Marquis informed him.

"First page, at the top, with the title: ' Modern Painting.' "

And the Deputy ceased to be surprised.

" Yes, yes.   I did not read it, because it was
about painting."

They smiled, every one knowing that outside
of politics and agriculture, M. de Guilleroy was
not interested in much of anything.

Then the conversation drifted to other subjects till they withdrew to the drawing-room
for coffee.   The Countess was not listening,
hardly answered, worried by the thought of

what Olivier might be doing. Where was he? Where had he dined? Where was he dragging his incurable heart at this moment? She now felt a burning regret to have let him go, not to have detained him; she imagined him roaming the streets, so sad, wandering, lonely, fleeing under his sorrowful burden.

Till the time when the Duchess and her nephew took their leave she hardly spoke, lashed by vague and superstitious fears; then she went to bed, and remained there, her eyes open in the dark, thinking of him!

A very long time had elapsed when she thought she heard the bell ring. She was startled and sat up and listened. For the second time the sharp tinkling sound was heard in the night. She bounded out of bed, and with all her strength pressed the electric button that was to awaken her maid. Then, candle in hand, she ran to the hall.

Through the door she asked:

"Who is there?"

An unknown voice answered:

" It is a letter."

" A letter, from whom?"

" From a physician."

" What physician?"

" I do not know; it is about an accident."

Hesitating no longer, she opened the door and found herself face to face with a cab driver with his oil-skin cap. He held a paper in his hand and presented it. She read: "Very urgent— Monsieur le Comte de Guilleroy."

The writing was unknown.

" Come in, my friend," said she; "sit down and wait for me."

When before her husband's door her heart began to beat so loudly that she could not call him. She rapped on the wood with the metal part of her candle-stick. The Count was sleeping and did not hear her.

Then impatient, excited, she kicked the door and heard a sleepy voice asking:

" Who is there? What time is it ?"

She answered:

" It is I. I have an urgent letter for you, brought by a coachman. It is about an accident."

He stammered from behind the bed curtains:

" Wait; I'll get up. I am coming."

And in a moment he appeared in his dressing gown. At the same time two servants, awakened by the ringing of the bells, came hurrying up. They looked bewildered, flurried, having discovered a stranger sitting on a chair in the dining-room.

The Count had taken the letter and turned it over in his fingers, murmuring:

" What is that? I do not understand."

She said feverishly:

"Why! read it!"

He tore open the envelope, unfolded the paper, uttered an exclamation of astonishment, then looked at his wife in a bewildered manner.

"Heavens! What is it?" said she.

He was stammering, hardly able to speak, so profoundly moved was he.

"Ah! A great misfortune! A great misfortune! Bertin has fallen under a carriage."

She cried:

"Dead!"

"No, no," said he; "read for yourself."

She snatched from his hands the letter he was holding out, and read:

"SIR:

"A great misfortune has just happened. Your friend, the eminent artist M. Olivier Bertin, has been thrown down by an omnibus, the wheels of which passed over his body. I cannot yet speak positively about the probable consequences of this accident, which may not be serious, while it may also have an immediate and fatal issue. M. Bertin begs you earnestly and beseeches Mme. la Comtesse de Guilleroy to come to him at once. I hope, sir, that the Countess and yourself will be disposed to grant the desire of our mutual friend, whose life may have passed away before daylight.

.   "DR. DE RIVIL."

The Countess was gazing at her husband with staring eyes, set, frightened. Then she experienced, like an electric shock, an awakening of that courage that women sometimes have and which makes them in trying hours the most courageous of beings.

Turning to her maid:

" Quick, I want to dress."

The servant asked:

" What will Madame put on ?"

" No matter what; anything you like."

" James," she then said, " be ready in five minutes."

Returning toward her apartment, her soul in dismay, she noticed the coachman, who was still waiting, and said to him:

" You have your carriage ? "

" Yes, Madame."

" Very well; we shall take it."

Then she ran to her room.

Madly, with hasty motions, she threw upon herself, hooked, clasped, tied, fastened her clothing at hap-hazard; then, before her glass, she turned up and twisted her hair carelessly, looking unconsciously, this time, at her pale face and haggard eyes in the mirror.

When her cloak was on her shoulders she rushed toward her husband's apartment, who was not yet ready. She led him along.

"Come," said she; "remember that he may die."

The bewildered Count followed her, stumb-
ling along, feeling for the dark stairway with his
feet, trying to distinguish the steps, not to fall.

The drive was short and silent. The Countess
was trembling so that her teeth chattered, and
through the window she saw the gas jets, veiled
by the rain, flying past. The sidewalks were
shining, the boulevards were deserted; the night
was inauspicious. They found, on arriving, that
the painter's door had been left open and the
concierge's lodge lighted and empty.

At the head of the stairs the physician, Dr.
de Rivil, a little, gray man, short, round, very
carefully dressed, very polite, advanced to meet
them. He bowed very low to the Countess, and
then held out his hand to the Count.

She asked him, panting as if the ascent of the
stairs had put her completely out of breath:

" Well, doctor ?"

" Well, Madame, I hope that it will be less
serious than I at first anticipated."

She exclaimed: ·

" He will not die ? "

" No; at least, I do not think so."

" Do you guarantee that ?"

" No; I only say that I hope I have only to
deal with a simple abdominal contusion without
internal lesions."

" What do you call lesions ? "

" Lacerations."

" How do you know there are none ? "

" I suppose so."

" And if there were ? "

" Ah! then it would be serious."

" Might he die of them ? "

" Yes."

" Very soon ? "

" Very soon.   In a few moments, or even in a few seconds.   But take courage, Madame.   I am convinced that he will have recovered in a fort-night."

She had listened with profound attention, to know all, to understand all.

She continued:

" What laceration might there be ? "

" A laceration of the liver, for instance."

" Would that be very dangerous ? "

" Yes; but I should be surprised to meet with a complication now.   Let us go in to him. It will do him good, for he expects you with great impatience."

What she first saw on entering the room was a pale face on a white pillow. A few candles and the fire of the hearth threw their light upon it, brought out the profile, deepened the shadows; and in that livid face the Countess saw two eyes that watched her coming.

All her courage, all her energy, all her resolution failed her, so much did those hollow and dis-torted features resemble those of a dying person.

He whom she had seen only a little while ago had become that thing, that spectre! She murmured between her lips: "Oh! my God!" and walked toward him, palpitating with horror.

He tried to smile, to encourage her, and the grimace which followed that attempt was frightful.

When she was quite near the bed she laid both her hands gently upon that of Olivier, stretched out alongside the body, and stammered:

"Oh! my poor friend."

"It is nothing," he said, in a low voice, without moving his head.

She was now gazing upon him, distracted with this change. He was so pale that he seemed no longer to have a drop of blood under the skin. His hollow cheeks seemed to be drawn in from the inside of the face, and his eyes also were sunken as if pulled by an inward string.

He plainly saw the terror of his friend and sighed:

"Here I am in a fine condition."

She said to him, ever looking at him fixedly:

"How did it happen?"

He was making great efforts to speak, and his whole face at times was convulsed with nervous shocks.

"I was not looking about me . . . I was thinking of something else . . . something quite different . . . oh! yes . . . an omnibus knocked me down and passed over me . . . "

As she listened she could see the accident, and she said, carried away by fright:

" Did you bleed ?"

" No. I am only a little bruised . . . somewhat crushed."

She asked:

" Where did it take place ? "

He answered very low:

" I hardly know. It was quite far."

The physician was rolling up an easy-chair, into which the Countess sank. The Count remained standing at the foot of the bed, repeating between his teeth:

" Oh! my poor friend . . . my poor friend . . what a frightful misfortune !"

And he felt, indeed, very great sorrow, for he really loved Olivier.

The Countess said again:

" But, where did it take place ? "

The physician answered:

" I hardly know anything about it myself, or rather I don't understand it at all. It was at the Gobelins, almost outside of Paris. At least the cab driver, who brought him back, stated to me that he took him up at a pharmacy of that quarter, where he had been carried, at nine o'clock in the evening !"

Then leaning toward Olivier:

" Is it true that the accident happened near the Gobelins ? "

Bertin closed his eyes as though to remember, then murmured:

" I do not know."

" But where were you going ? "

" I do not remember. I was walking straight before me ! "

A groan she could not suppress came from the Countess's lips; then, stifled and breathless for a few seconds, she took her handkerchief from her pocket and covered her eyes, weeping bitterly.

She knew; she guessed ! Something intolerable, overwhelming, had just fallen on her heart; remorse for not keeping Olivier at her house, for driving him out, throwing him into the street, where, staggering with grief, he had rolled under that carriage.

He said to her in that expressionless tone he now had:

" Do not weep. It distresses me."

With a supreme effort of the will she ceased sobbing, uncovered her face and looked at him with eyes wide open, without a contraction of her features, though tears continued to flow slowly.

They gazed at each other, both motionless, their hands clasped under the bed cover. They gazed at each other, no longer knowing that any

one else was in the room, and their glances carried a superhuman emotion from one heart to
the other.

It was between them the rapid, silent and ter-
rible evocation of all their recollections, of all
their love, crushed also; of all they had felt together, of all they had united and blended in
their lives, in that impulse that made them give
themselves to each other.

They gazed at each other, and the need of
talking to one another, of hearing those thousand intimate things, so sad, which they still had
to speak arose to their lips irresistibly. She felt
that she must at any price get rid of the two
men behind her, that she must find some means,
a subterfuge, an inspiration, she, the woman
fruitful in resources. And she began to reflect,
her eyes always fixed on Olivier.

Her husband and the physician were talking
in low tones. They were discussing the care to
be given.

Turning her head, she said to the physician:

" Did you bring a nurse ? "

" No. I prefer to send a house surgeon, who
will be better able to watch the situation."

" Send both. We can never be too careful.
Can you obtain them to-night yet, for I do not
suppose you will remain till morning ? "

" Indeed, I was about to return home. I have
been here four hours already."

" But, as you return you will send us the nurse and the house surgeon ? "

" It is rather difficult in the middle of the night. However, I shall try."

" You must! "

" They may promise, but will they come ?"

" My husband will accompany you and bring them back, whether they will or not."

" But you, Madame, cannot remain here alone."

" I !" . . . she said with a sort of cry, of defiance, of indignant protest against any resistance to her will. Then she explained, in that authoritative way which leaves no room for a reply, the necessities of the situation. It was necessary that, to avoid all accidents, the house surgeon and the nurse should be procured inside of an hour. To do so some one must get them out of bed and bring them. Her husband alone could do that. During this time she would remain near the sick, she whose duty and right it was. She was simply fulfilling her rôle of friend, of woman. In any case, she wished it so, and no one could dissuade her from it.

Her argument was sensible. They could but grant that, and they decided to act accordingly.

She had risen, filled with the thought of their going, in haste to feel them away and herself left alone. Now, in order that she might be guilty of no clumsiness during their absence, she listened, trying to comprehend clearly, to remember everything, to forget nothing of the physician's recommendations. The painter's valet, standing near her, was listening also, and behind him, his wife, the cook, who had assisted during the first dressings, indicated by signs of the head that she also understood. When the Countess had recited all these instructions, like a lesson, she hurried the two men away, repeating to her husband:

" Come back quickly, of all things; return quickly."

" I shall take you in my coupé," said the physician to the Count. " It will bring you back earlier. You will be here in an hour."

Before starting, the doctor again examined the patient at length, in order to make sure that his condition was satisfactory.

Guilleroy was still hesitating. He said:

" You do not think we are acting imprudently ? "

" No; there is no danger. He only needs rest and calm. Madame de Guilleroy will please not let him speak and speak to him as little as possible."

The Countess was dumfounded and replied:

" Then he must not be spoken to ? "

"Oh ! no, Madame. Take an arm-chair and sit near him. He will not feel alone, and it will be good for him; but no fatigue, no fatigue of

words or even of thought. I shall be here at
about nine o'clock in the morning. Good-bye,
Madame. I am your faithful servant."

He went off, bowing very low, followed by
the Count, who kept repeating:

" Be of good heart, my dear. I shall be back
in less than an hour, and you will be able to return home."

When they were gone she listened to the noise
of the door below being closed, then the rumbling off of the coupé in the street.

The servant and the cook had remained in the
room waiting for orders. The Countess dis-
missed them.

" You may retire," said she. " I shall ring if
I need anything."

They also went off, and she remained alone
near him.

She had come back quite close to the bed, and
laying her hands upon the two edges of the pillow, on both sides of that beloved head, she bent
down to gaze upon it. Then she asked, her face
so near his that she seemed to breathe her words
upon his skin:

" Did you throw yourself under that carriage ? "

He answered, still trying to smile:

" No; it was the carriage that threw itself on
me."

" It is not true; it *is* you."

" No ; I assure you it was *it.*"

After a few moments of silence, moments in which their souls seemed to be entwined in glances, she murmured :

"Oh! my dear, dear Olivier! to think that I let you go and did not detain you!"

He answered with an air of conviction :

"It would have happened to me, just the same, some day or other."

They still gazed on one another, trying to perceive their most secret thoughts. He went on :

"I do not think I shall recover. I suffer too much."

She whispered :

"Are you suffering much ?"

"Oh! yes."

Bending a little more, she grazed his forehead, then his eyes, then his cheeks with slow kisses, light, delicate as cares. She touched him with the tip of her lips, with that little breathing noise that children make when they embrace. And that lasted a long, long time. He let that shower of sweet little caresses fall on him, and it seemed to soothe, to refresh him, for his contracted face quivered less than before.

Then he said :

"Any ?"

She ceased kissing to hear him.

" What, my friend ? "

" You must make me a promise."

" I will promise you all you like."

" If I am not dead before morning, swear to me that you will bring Annette to me, once, only once! I so wish not to die without having seen her again . . . Only think that . . . to-morrow . . . at this hour . . . I shall perhaps . . . I shall surely have closed my eyes for the last time . . . and that I shall never see you again . . . I . . . neither you . . . nor her . . ."

She stopped him, her heart breaking:

" Oh! hush! . . . hush! . . . yes, I promise you to bring her."

" Will you swear it ? "

" I swear it, my friend . . . But be silent, speak no more. You pain me horribly . . . hush! "

A rapid convulsion passed over all his features; then when it was over, he said:

" If we have but a few moments more to spend together, let us not waste them; let us take advantage of them to speak our farewell. I have loved you so . . ."

She sighed:

" And I . . . how I still love you! "

Again he said:

" I have known happiness only through you. The last days only have been hard . . . It is not your fault. Ah! my poor Any . . . how life seems sad at times . . . and how difficult it is to die!"

"Hush, Olivier. I beg of you . . ."

He continued without listening:

"I would have been such a happy man had you not had your daughter . . ."

"Hush! . . . my God! . . Do be silent . ."

He seemed to dream rather than speak.

"Ah! he who invented this existence and made men was very blind or very wicked . . . "

"Olivier, I beseech you . . . if you ever loved me, be silent . . . do not speak thus any more."

He gazed at her bending toward him, herself so livid that she also looked as if she were dying, and he was silent.

Then she sat in the arm-chair, quite close to his couch, and again took the hand stretched under the cover.

"Now I forbid you to speak," said she. "Do not stir and think of me as I think of you."

Once more they gazed at each other, motionless, joined together by the burning clasp of their hands. She pressed, with gentle motions, the feverish hand she was holding, and he responded to these calls by tightening his fingers a little. Every one of those pressures said something to him, evoked some portion of their finished past, stirring up in their memory the stagnant recollections of their love. Each one of them was a silent question, each one of them a mysterious answer, sad questions and sad replies, " do you remember," of an old love.

Their minds in this agonizing meeting, which might perhaps be the last, followed back through the years the whole history of their passion, and in the room nothing but the crackling of the fire was heard.

Suddenly, as if coming out of a dream, he said, with a start of terror:

" Your letters ! "

She asked:

" What about my letters ? "

" I might have died without destroying them."

She exclaimed:

" Eh ! what matters it to me ? As if that were of any importance now. Let them find and read them; what do I care ?"

He answered:

"I do not wish it. Rise, Any. Open the lower drawer of my desk, the larger one ; they are all there, every one. You must take them and throw them into the fire."

She did not stir and remained crouching, as if he had asked her to do a cowardly act.

He continued:

"Any, I beseech you. If you do not, you will torment me, excite me and drive me mad. Reflect that they might fall into the hands of any one, a notary, a servant . . . or even your husband . . . I do not wish . . ."

She rose, still hesitating, and repeating:

"No; it is too hard, it is too cruel. I feel as though you would make me burn both our hearts."

He was pleading, his face contracted by anguish.

Seeing him suffer thus, she resigned herself and walked toward the desk. As she opened the drawer she found it filled to the top with a thick layer of letters, piled one on top of the other, and she recognized upon all the envelopes the two lines of the address she had written so often. She knew those two lines—a man's name, the name of a street—as well as her own name, as well as one may know the few words which during life have represented all hope and all happiness.

She looked at that, those little square things which contained all that she had known how to say of her love, all that she had been able to take out of herself, to give it to him, with a little ink upon white paper.

He had tried to turn his head upon the pillow to look at her, and he said once more:

"Burn them up, quickly."

Then she took two handfuls and kept them a few moments in her hands. They seemed heavy to her, painful, living, yet dead, so many different things were contained therein, at this moment so many things that were ended, so sweet, felt, dreamed. It was the soul of her soul, the heart of her heart, the essence of her loving being that she was holding there; and she recalled with what rapture she had dashed off. some of them, with what exaltation, what intoxication of living, of adoring some one and expressing it.

Olivier repeated:

" Burn them, burn them, Any."

With a similar motion of both hands she threw into the fireplace the two packages of papers which settled as they fell upon the wood. Then she took others from the desk and threw them on top, then more still, with rapid movements, stooping and rising again hastily to finish the distressing task quickly.

When the chimney was full and the drawer empty she remained standing, waiting, looking at the almost smothered flame as it climbed up from all points on that mountain of envelopes. It attacked them on the sides, gnawed the corners, ran along the edge of the paper, went out, revived again and spread out. Presently all around that white pyramid there was a bright circle of clear fire which filled the chimney with light; and this light, illuminating that woman standing erect and that man lying prostrate, was their burning love, their love turned to ashes.

The Countess turned round, and in the brill-

iant glare of that fire she perceived her friend
leaning with a haggard face on the edge of the
bed.

He was asking: "Are they all there ?"

"Yes; everything."

But before she went back to him she threw a
last glance on that destruction, and on the pile
of papers already half consumed, which were
twisting and turning black, she saw something
red flowing. One would have thought it drops
of blood. It seemed to come out of the very
heart of the letters, of each letter, as out of a
wound, and flowed slowly toward the flame,
leaving a purple train.

The Countess felt in her soul the shock of
supernatural fear, and stepped back as if she had
been witnessing the assassination of a person;
then she understood, she suddenly understood
that she had simply seen the melting of the wax
seals.

Then she returned toward the wounded man,
and raising his head gently, replaced it with caution in the centre of the pillow. But he had
stirred, and the pains increased. He was panting now, his face contorted by frightful suffering, and he seemed no longer to know that she
was there.

She waited for him to be a little more calm, to
lift up his eyes, which he kept obstinately closed,
to be able to say still a word to her.

Finally she asked:

" Are you suffering much ? "

He did not answer.

And she stooped down toward him and placed a finger on his forehead to force him to look at her.

He did indeed open his eyes, bewildered, mad.

She repeated, terrified:

" Are you suffering? . . . Olivier. Answer me. Shall I call . . . make an effort; say something to me."

She thought she heard him mutter:

" Bring her . . . you have sworn it to me . . . "

Then he stirred about under the clothes, his body twisted, his face convulsed.

She repeated:

" Olivier! my God! Olivier, what is the matter ? Shall I call . . . "

He heard her this time, for he answered:

" No . . . it is nothing."

He seemed indeed to grow quieter, to suffer less, to fall all at once into a sort of drowsy stupor. Hoping that he would fall asleep, she sat down again near the bed, took his hand once more, and waited. He no longer moved, his chin on his breast, his mouth half opened by his short breathing, which seemed to rasp his throat as it passed. His fingers alone unconsciously stirred now and then with light shocks' which

the Countess felt to the root of her hair, so pain-
fully that she could almost cry out. They were
no longer the little voluntary pressures which,
instead of the tired lips, told all the sadness of
their hearts; they were involuntary spasms
which only spoke of the torture of the body.

Now, she was afraid, frightfully afraid, and
possessed with a wild desire to go away, to ring,
to call, but she dared not stir, lest she might
trouble his repose.

The far-off noise of carriages in the streets
came in through the walls; and she listened to
detect whether the rumbling of the wheels did
not stop before the door, whether her husband
was not coming to liberate her, to tear her away
at last from this sinister tête-à-tête.

As she tried to disengage her hand from that
of Olivier, he pressed it, uttering a long sigh.
Then she resigned herself to wait, not to disturb
him.

The fire was dying out on the hearth, under
the black ashes of the letters; two candles went
out; a piece of furniture cracked.

In the house all was silent, everything seemed
dead, except the tall Flemish clock in the hall,
which chimed out regularly the hour, half hour
and quarter, singing the march of Time in the
night, modulating it on its different tones.

The Countess, motionless, felt an intolerable
terror growing in her soul; she was assailed by

nightmares; frightful thoughts filled her mind, and she fancied she noticed that Olivier's fingers were growing cold in hers. Was it true ? No, surely. Yet whence had that sensation of an inexpressible and frozen contact come ? She raised herself up, distracted with terror, to look at his face. It had relaxed; it was impassive, inanimate, indifferent to all misery, suddenly calmed by Eternal Oblivion.

THE END.